DON'T SAY HIS NAME

DON'T SAY HIS NAME

RACHEL GIVNEY

ultimo press

Published in 2025 by Ultimo Press,
an imprint of Hardie Grant Publishing

Ultimo Press
Gadigal Country
7, 45 Jones Street
Ultimo, NSW 2007
ultimopress.com.au

ultimopress

NATIONAL LIBRARY OF AUSTRALIA

A catalogue record for this book is available from the National Library of Australia

Don't Say His Name
ISBN 978 1 76115 434 8 (paperback)

Cover design Design by Committee
Cover images Background by TuneLife / Shutterstock; Hand by Ink Drop / Alamy Stock Photo
Text design Simon Paterson, Bookhouse
Typesetting Bookhouse, Sydney | 11.2/17.4 pt Sabon LT Pro
Copyeditor Ali Lavau
Proofreader Rebecca Hamilton

10 9 8 7 6 5 4 3 2 1

Printed in China by RR Donnelley.

MIX
Paper | Supporting responsible forestry
FSC® C144853
FSC www.fsc.org

The paper this book is printed on is from FSC® certified forests and other controlled sources. FSC® promotes environmentally responsible, socially beneficial and economically viable management of the world's forests.

Ultimo Press acknowledges the Traditional Owners of the Country on which we work, the Gadigal People of the Eora Nation and the Wurundjeri People of the Kulin Nation, and recognises their continuing connection to the land, waters and culture. We pay our respects to their Elders past and present.

PROLOGUE

He had four chances to stop her, and he didn't take them.

He could have stopped her as she waited by the podium, swaying. While the other students in the auditorium were picking their nails, kicking the seats in front. Thumbing contraband phones stashed secretly in pockets, willing, begging for the assembly to be over. Actually swaying she was, with a giddy, dog-in-playground energy. No one else had noticed, only him. He could have stopped her then, and none of this would have happened.

He could have stopped her when she gave him that weird look. The moment their eyes met, as the principal was telling the students the importance of wearing their hats and blazers on public transport, even in the last week of school. Mr Catton had looked at the girl, Angelica O'Brien (though no one called her that, she went by Angel), and she had returned his gaze, irises glistening like she was drunk, and he knew she was thinking something, and it wasn't good. He could have stopped her then.

He could have stopped her when that seagull flew into the assembly hall, escaping the baking heat outside, and the students looked up from their seats, roused from their stupors. He could have stopped her as the vice principal tried to shoo the bird with a broom, causing laughter from the students, as it refused to move.

Or when the groundskeeper finally stepped in and captured the bird, circling his large hands around its dirty plumage, silken and grey, holding it gently, everyone looking on in astonishment and admiration. Mr Catton could have strolled over to Angel then, taken her arm softly, and told her, *I don't know what you have planned, but don't do it, whatever it is. This is not the time, nor the place.*

He could have stopped her a full hour earlier, when they were rehearsing the prayer she would be saying. She had stared at him blankly, then given a bared-teeth smile, and he'd almost stumbled backward.

Four chances he'd had. He'd taken none of them.

He might have had a thousand opportunities and still done nothing. Because that's who he was, a coward. That hesitating player, the one who drops the easy catch, who shanks the simple kick. Only this wouldn't mean losing a footy game. This would bring death to Thoorgala. Maybe, also, he didn't want to stop her. He wanted to see what would happen next.

The principal announced, 'Now one of our year eleven students, Angelica, will lead us in a prayer for a safe and happy summer holidays.'

Daniel Catton, PE teacher at Thoorgala Grammar, which charged $42,000 per annum for day tuition, moved towards the podium, but it was too late. He shouted 'no', but all he got was weird looks from colleagues, keen to end the assembly, which had already dragged on too long. The girl called Angelica O'Brien, who everyone called Angel, wasn't saying the prayer as rehearsed. She was saying something different. Grim satisfaction gripped Mr Catton, that he'd been right, as the words tumbled from her mouth to the confused crowd:

'Don't say his name
Don't say it thrice
What happens next
It won't be nice
Tall Harry
Tall Harry
Tall Harry.'

24 DECEMBER

8.32 AM

Detective Sergeant Matthias Stayer took a squad car out to Cundra, leaving it in the deserted car park near the dunes. He exited the car into the baking heat, and continued his journey on foot over the sand, following the coordinates he'd entered into his phone's GPS. He walked for what seemed like hours over long, mildly undulating expanses of sand, under a searing sun, with sand in his shoes. Stayer hated sand.

He had just about decided he was truly lost, and might die out there, when the famous hills of Cundra finally appeared before him, the giant and majestic dunes which littered a thousand social media posts. They ascended to the sky, like they did on the internet, impressing with their scale, but they were grubbier in real life, with more food wrappers and dog turds and broken bottles dotting the swathe of sand, like a polluted waterway.

He arrived at the base of one yellow hill and found that it matched the coordinates that the receptionist at his new station had given him and sighed, realising he would be required to walk up it. The hill soared upwards like a curling tidal wave, ready to break. For every step up he sunk halfway down again, both shoes taking on yet more sand. He finally crested the sandhill and, puffing, saw a body lying on the flat top of the dune. A uniformed policewoman was stringing tape around it. Stayer's exhaustion and annoyance melted away, and he felt refreshed and reinvigorated as the detective in him once again took over: it was a human body, a woman, late twenties maybe. He moved towards her, his mind filling with questions: how had she died, when had she died, what was she doing all the way out here.

The hard flesh struck him first, that pallor you couldn't mistake as anything but dead. The sight of skin without animation still shocked him—not so much the idea that the spirit had departed, but more the magic that made it move in the first place.

The victim lay on her back in a relaxed pose. A briny smell lurked, like from a dried-out rock pool. She wore a black silk dress, like for a cocktail party, and a clump of seaweed covered her face. In her hand, she held a sea squirt.

'Detective Stayer? I'm Sergeant Nichols. Welcome to Thoorgala.'

The uniformed policewoman who had been taping the perimeter strode towards him, offering her hand. Sergeant Nichols wore her hair in a tight, slicked-back bun. A sharply pressed uniform covered her lean frame, and a sports watch, like a triathlete might wear, circled her wrist.

'Nice to meet you,' Stayer said, shaking her hand. Her grip was strong.

She returned her gaze to the dead body. 'That cunjevoi's a long way from home.'

'The which?' Stayer said.

'Cunjevoi, boss,' Sergeant Nichols said, pointing to the furry, knobbly mound in the victim's hand. She'd meant the sea squirt. *Cunjevoi*: Stayer saw it now, on a library poster. A local's word, he'd never used it himself, as if worried he'd pronounce it wrong, like a childhood stammer re-emerging.

'She shouldn't have removed it from the rocks,' Sergeant Nichols continued. 'Damages the ecosystem. I wonder how she did. You need a big knife. I've been staring at her for half an hour and I can't work it out.'

'What's that?'

'How she died.'

Wheezing sounded behind them and Stayer turned. A forensic pathologist appeared over the summit of the sandhill. He carried a stretcher, and the straps of multiple boxes hung across his shoulders. Sweat drenched his white hazmat suit. Stayer and Sergeant Nichols moved to him, arms outstretched, and he passed them items with a grateful glance.

Stayer introduced himself as the pathologist shook his hand.

'Dane Dixon. Welcome to Thoorgala, detective. A murder on your first day. You must be pleased. Maybe not pleased,' he added, 'you know what I mean. We don't get many murders here.' His face was red and damp, and he wore a pair of wraparound sunglasses with mirrored lenses, like a road cyclist.

Stayer motioned to the victim, lying in the sand. 'Your initial impression, doctor?'

The pathologist stepped closer. Ocean waves dumped faintly in the distance, crashing into the sand. This soft, relentless rhythm had drifted into the tiny spare bedroom of his sister's house the night before, keeping Stayer awake.

'The seaweed on her face. Someone's put it there. Wrongful death,' the pathologist said.

Detective Stayer stared at the seaweed. The slick brownish tendrils spread apart in one place, revealing the corner of the victim's mouth.

'The bruises on her wrists indicate a struggle,' Dr Dixon added. 'Someone's grabbed her arms.'

'Could she have died from heat exhaustion?' Sergeant Nichols offered. 'She looks like she was out here most of the night. The bushfires are keeping the temperature up.' She motioned to a column of smoke behind them which rose into the sky in the distance. It had burned for days. A grey haze hung in the air.

'Would it have been hot enough?' Stayer said, looking at the pathologist.

'It's possible,' Dr Dixon said. 'The temperature only got down to thirty degrees last night.'

Stayer had lain awake in a terrible sweat in that tiny room. He'd gone creeping around the steaming fibro house in desperation, finally locating a pedestal fan in the corner of Ruby's bedroom. He'd felt guilty about taking it, depriving his sister of its life-giving breeze, until he realised Ruby wasn't even there. Her bed lay empty.

Dr Dixon looked up. The sun made a fireball in the lens of his sunglasses. 'We need to get her out of here. The three of us can do it.'

'Can't we cover her until more help arrives?' Stayer said.

'I left the tent in the van,' Dr Dixon said. 'I can get it, but we'd lose time. The temperature has already passed forty. Protein starts cooking at thirty-nine. If we don't get her down in the next fifteen minutes, we'll lose evidence. Waste the chance to establish cause of death. The perpetrator has put her up here on purpose, to make it hard for us.'

So that was how they arrived there. A dead body on the summit of a sandhill. Detective Stayer recalled the steepness of the dune; it had felt like climbing a ladder. Now they were going to bring a body down that same incline, with minimal equipment, no vehicle, and no help, and they needed to do it quickly.

'I'll bag up that seaweed first,' the pathologist said.

He fetched an evidence bag the size of a pillowcase, flicked it open, and, with a pair of tweezers the size of tongs, lifted the mop of seaweed from the woman's face.

Dr Dixon, who had been moving quickly, grew still. A hush descended, the hurtling waves becoming the only sound once more.

'Everything alright, doc?' Stayer asked.

The pathologist was staring at the dead woman's face. 'I know her.'

9.05 AM

The pathologist had taken photos of the body on the sand, the immediate vicinity, and bagged up every cigarette butt, bottle cap, and piece of suspicious-looking debris in the area. Stayer and Sergeant Nichols had then helped him lay out the body bag and positioned themselves around the remains, preparing to lift. This had taken eight minutes; according to the pathologist's calculations, they now had seven left before they lost cause of death.

'So who is she?' Stayer asked the pathologist.

'Her surname's Glasson.' The pathologist's face was grey. 'First name Phoebe.'

'How did you know her?'

'Didn't, really,' Dr Dixon said. 'I went to the same school as her. Thoorgala Grammar. I was in year twelve when she was in year eight, I think. Five years apart is like a solar system when you're a teenager.' His brow furrowed. 'You might find priors. Don't know what she's been up to lately, but she was sort of a naughty kid.'

Stayer looked down again at the body. The head moved a little, shifting left in the sand.

Sergeant Nichols whimpered. 'She moved.' She looked spooked.

'Sometimes the gases from the digestive tract come back up the oesophagus and exit the mouth. Makes it look like they're breathing,'

Stayer said, trying to sound kind, not sure how much he needed to explain to another police officer. 'Isn't that right, doc?'

'That's right,' Dr Dixon said. 'Just gases. She didn't move, Nichols—she's dead. Let's get her down.'

They lifted her carefully into the bag then onto the stretcher. The stiffness of a lifeless body never failed to amaze Stayer, even after almost ten years as a cop. It felt like picking up a door.

'Don't zip it up,' the pathologist said to Sergeant Nichols, who had gone to close the body bag. 'She'll start sweating in this heat. Give her as much air as you can.'

'People still sweat after they're dead?' Sergeant Nichols asked.

'Any flesh covered with plastic and left near a heat source will sweat,' the pathologist said. 'Ever left a meat platter out in the sun?'

The sergeant left the zip undone.

'Are you alright, sergeant?' Stayer asked, eyeing her bilious demeanour.

'Yes, sir,' the policewoman said. 'My first dead body.'

'Let's move, people,' the pathologist said. 'We've got five minutes.'

Detective Stayer took the handles at the woman's head, while Sergeant Nichols took the ones at her legs. Dr Dixon slung the black cases and evidence bags from his shoulders. He gave them instructions on how to manoeuvre the stretcher, and then they set off as fast as they could. Stayer stood significantly taller than the sergeant so had to crouch down to keep the stretcher level, his calves and thighs burning. They moved with such speed that the victim's head rocked softly. They arrived at the steepest part of the hill and Dr Dixon reiterated his instruction to keep the stretcher level. Heavy breaths and soft grunts were the only sounds. The heat radiating from the sand burned Stayer's hands as he gripped the handles. They had less than four minutes now and had only descended less than a third of the sand dune. Stayer felt the incline grow steeper underneath them and the body tip upwards. He couldn't see how they were going to manage this.

Then a shriek rang out and the stretcher shook, and Stayer looked ahead of him. Sergeant Nichols had made the sound.

A crab that must have burrowed into the victim's hair had escaped from the open bag. It now crawled onto Sergeant Nichols' arm, scuttling sideways towards her elbow. She shook her arm and, in doing so, lost her grip on the stretcher.

'No!' Stayer yelled, but it was too late. The body slid from the unzipped bag like a surfboard.

Dr Dixon moved down the sand with admirable speed, considering his Santa-like physique, and caught the body with his shin. A moment passed quietly, in horror.

Stayer stared at the body half-escaped from the bag, the pathologist's leg nestled between the woman's head and shoulder.

As they sprang to action to collect and reposition the body, aware of the seconds evaporating, Stayer found himself crouching. He pointed to the woman's right hand, which had been holding the sea squirt. In all the excitement, the cunjevoi had shaken itself free, rolling down the dune. They'd tried to ensure the woman's hand maintained its grip on the creature, so as not to destroy potential evidence. But now Stayer saw the fortune in the squirt's removal, for it revealed something that made the entire group stop breathing.

Someone had carved a symbol into the woman's hand.

Stayer, still in his crouch, squinted at it. The symbol consisted of a number two overlapping a number four. It looked like a number twenty-four you might see on a birthday cake candle, where the numbers were moulded together for stability.

'God almighty,' Dr Dixon said.

'In the sand—look,' Sergeant Nichols said, voice sounding dazed and hoarse. She was sitting on the incline of the dune, looking devastated. Stayer's earlier impression of her had eroded, the appearance of competence conjured by the starched uniform, the hi-tech watch, the tidy hair had vanished, replaced by something more unruly and anxious. She had seemed so capable.

Stayer looked to where the policewoman was pointing. Dr Dixon silently offered him a new pair of gloves. Stayer peeled off the ones he'd been wearing and donned the new pair. He picked up a small scroll of paper, about the width of a matchbox. He unfurled it.

'It fell out with the cunjevoi,' Sergeant Nichols said, eyes wide. 'It was in her hand.'

It was text, printed from a computer. It read:

They shall confess. Or four more.

TH

•

//Thoorgala. A sandy corner of the internet to discuss all things God's country

HaroldBishop • 10.32 am
Anyone hear about the db on Cundra sandhills?

Snookus52 • 10.32 am
As I am not deaf, yes.

JeepRinger • 10.33 am
Not me. What occurred?

HaroldBishop • 10.33 am
Dead chick found on the sandhills. Her hand had something carved into it.

JeepRinger • 10.33 am
Wtf

Snookus52 • 10.33 am
Yessir indeed

JeepRinger • 10.34 am
Searched, couldn't find anything about this

Snookus52 • 10.34 am
Cops staying quiet for now for sure. Wouldn't want this getting out. Carvings in hands, etc.

JeepRinger • 10.34 am
Yerp what does it mean?

Snookus52 • 10.35 am
Dunno.

HaroldBishop • 10.36 am
Maybe it means . . . Harry's back.

TallHarry • 11.02 am
Yes it does.

11.37 AM

Stayer pulled up at his sister's house, a beach shack at the end of a cul-de-sac which looked out onto the hunter green water of Port Joseph Bay. He would be living there for the immediate future. Every other house in the street had been renovated or knocked down and rebuilt into duplexes which rented out for $1200 per week. But this little house remained: a cement-sheeting kit home, built in the 60s.

Sand covered him like glitter, and he stank like salt and dead body. He walked around the house to the only shower, located in the beach-heather filled backyard, attached to the laundry. It was one of those showers you'd use to wash the sand off after taking a swim before entering the house.

He undressed and jumped in the frigid water. A few spaced-out slats of greying timber arranged horizontally were the only thing shielding his private parts from boats cruising past. As he scrubbed the sand and the smell of the dead body off, his phone rang. He fumbled for it in his trouser pocket with a soapy hand. He answered.

'Hello, detective. This is Joan Wilson, the receptionist at Thoorgala station. Could you come in as soon as possible? A woman wants to report a murder.'

Soap ran down Stayer's neck. 'The murder on the sandhills?'

'The only murder I know of. Could you hurry? She's threatening to leave.'

'Don't let her. I'm on my way.'

He flicked off the shower, lassoed a towel around himself and ran inside the little house. He fished out the first shirt and trousers he could find and darted through the living area, hair dripping into his collar. The sight of his sister halted him.

'Ruby. Hello. Didn't know you were home,' he said awkwardly. His little sister was decorating a Christmas tree.

Several things about this gave him pause. Firstly, the tree was dead. The pine needles that once might have shone in rough green had browned. Second, the tree was inverted, tip down, like a funnel, suspended from the ceiling with a wire. Third, for decoration his sister had folded hundreds of little flames from orange paper with gold leaf, so that the tree appeared on fire.

Stayer stole a glance at the polite, cement-rendered duplexes across the street. A Christmas tree stood in each window: pine, green, decorated with gold and silver baubles, minimal tinsel. Ruby's tree was the psychotic cousin of these tasteful ornaments: confronting, contrary, devilish.

'I'm worried about what this tree is saying to the neighbours,' Stayer joked.

'Don't start worrying what they will think,' she said.

'I have to go back into the station,' he told her.

'Fine,' Ruby said carelessly. Her hair was oily and matted, and dirt smeared her feet.

'How do I look?' Stayer asked.

'Like a cop,' Ruby said, without turning around.

'Just the look I was going for.'

She forced another branch into an absurd angle, fixing it with wire. He was convinced it would snap, cracking and straining, but the branch remained where her hands had placed it, dexterous as a surgeon's.

'This isn't just for Christmas—it belongs in a gallery,' he said. 'All your artworks do.' He motioned to a series of clay pots with an aquamarine glaze, a triptych of sketches of human bodies in charcoal. The quality of the work shocked him. At first he had not believed they had been made by his sister, the sight of her signature in the corners astounded him.

'Those are demonstration pieces I made for the kids to show them a technique. They're not for public consumption.'

'They're good enough, though.' He coughed. 'Do you ever paint the view here? The coastline, or the waves?'

She flinched, or at least he though she did. 'I don't paint water,' she said, her voice stern. She continued adding flames to the dusty brown foliage, looking intense and determined. A mad scientist in a singlet top.

Stayer remembered the woman waiting for him at the station. 'Ruby, I have to go. Not sure what time I'll be home, sorry.'

'Doesn't matter. I won't be here,' she said. 'I'm staying at Aunt Carol's tonight. I agreed to help her get the house ready.'

'Of course,' he said. 'Great. Bye.' He located his keys on the peeling laminate kitchen bench and headed to the squad car.

He drove along the streets of Thoorgala, the coastal paradise he now called home. Palm trees lined the main street leading down to the beach. Their long thin trunks stretched skyward, fronds perched at the top like wigs. He turned a corner, and a line of art deco apartments greeted him, grand, stylish, regal, painted in mint greens, pastel blues and cream. The next street held an old wooden boatshed. Muscular men launched a catamaran from its bowels onto the sand, bathed in yellow sunlight. A place of improbable, laughable, stupid beauty. He turned another corner, and a bushfire appeared out the window. It had begun last week and had raged ever since, chewing through the desiccated scrub and oily eucalypts of the nearby bushland. A chimney of smoke chugged from the horizon into a hazy blue sky, past a glowing red sun. The smoke oozed into the car through the air vents, making Stayer cough. The flames and the smell tried valiantly to ruin the vibe. But even this hellish column looked beautiful in Thoorgala, surrounded by palm trees.

Eventually nothing, not the shimmering surf, the regal buildings, not even the chimney of fire could trump thoughts of his sister, and how, for the past fifteen years, they had barely communicated with each other, sometimes going months, even years, without speaking. A lead detective role had come up in Thoorgala, and when he'd mentioned it in passing, in the rare times they texted, Ruby had surprised him by encouraging him to take the job. She'd even offered to put him up while he found his feet.

On the surface, he called the move a sea change. A desire for a quieter life. But secretly, deep down, he saw a chance to patch things up with his sister. He was beginning to worry this might be a farcical hope, that the things which had broken between them could never be repaired. He feared that in moving to Thoorgala, he'd made a huge mistake.

12.22 PM

Stayer entered the police station. A woman in her sixties wearing a police uniform seized him as he walked in. Reading glasses hung from a chain around her neck.

'Detective Stayer? Joan Wilson. Nice to meet you in person.' They shook hands hurriedly.

'Joan. Sorry about the delay.'

'All good.' She led him through a door behind the reception area. She seemed irritated.

An open-plan squad room greeted him: desks arranged in little islands, with dual-screen set-ups, phones, in-trays, trinkets, filing cabinets. The building itself boasted cornices, ceiling roses, thick walls. In Thoorgala, even the police station was pretty.

Joan walked briskly towards a door. 'I'll give you the tour later, but for now, she's in interview one. The woman reporting the murder. Her name is Barbara Lacey.'

The interview room resembled a concrete bunker, the only source of natural light a tiny window high on the east-facing wall. There was a peculiar, ripe smell whose origins he couldn't identify. If a brochure for interview rooms existed, this would have made the 'Dungeon' section.

Barbara Lacey sat on one side of a desk, biting her nails.

Stayer took the seat opposite and gave a nod of thanks to Joan. She loitered in the door for a moment, eyeing the woman, before leaving and shutting the door behind her.

'Ms Lacey? I'm Detective Matthias Stayer. You wish to report a murder?'

Barbara Lacey looked shell-shocked. 'It's Mrs.'

'Apologies, Mrs Lacey.'

'Don't you have air conditioning?'

Stayer noticed what he had been too distracted to earlier: that this was no ordinary warm day; it felt like standing in front of an open oven door. He stood.

'Joan?' he called down the hallway.

The receptionist appeared quickly, looking intrigued. 'What is it, detective?'

'Could we please turn on the air conditioning?'

'Oh,' she answered, face falling. 'It's busted. The repairman has put us to the top of the list. He'll be here in three weeks.'

'Okay. Any fans?'

'I'll see what I can do.' Joan lingered at the door for a moment, then finally left.

Stayer returned to Mrs Lacey, who was fanning herself with her hand. He opened his notebook.

'We'll cool this room down one way or the other, Mrs Lacey. In the meantime, please tell me what you know about the murder.'

Mrs Lacey looked around the room, as if to check that they were alone. Then she leaned forward. 'I didn't want to give details over the phone—who knows who might have been listening? I wanted to tell you in person, detective.'

Stayer held his pen poised. He pictured the woman they had encountered on the sandhills: the seaweed on her face, the symbol carved into her hand, the note left with the body. He nodded eagerly. 'Please go on.'

'The victim's name is Pericles Lacey.'

Stayer kept his pen poised. 'I'm sorry?' The victim on the sandhills was named Phoebe Glasson. He had been expecting this name to leave the woman's mouth.

Mrs Lacey nodded tearfully. 'My cat.'

Stayer looked properly at the woman sitting opposite him in interview room one. Mrs Lacey wore black eyeliner and hoop earrings. Her clothes seemed comprised mainly of layers of some diaphanous fabric. She'd tied her greying hair back with a silk scarf. She spoke with the rasp of someone who'd started smoking at fourteen and never quit, who'd also dabbled in the harder stuff back in the day and probably still now when she was feeling blue.

Mrs Lacey shifted in her seat, fingering some sort of crystal pendant she wore on a chain around her neck—the kind people wore to bring calm. When Stayer had crept into his sister's bedroom to take her fan last night, he'd noticed one hanging on her dresser.

'To confirm. You're reporting the death of a cat?' Stayer said.

She straightened and gave him a look. 'Not death—murder.'

'Under the Crimes Act, the term "murder" only applies to humans. This would be animal cruelty. A crime, but it's not murder.'

'You think because you were a swimming star you're too good for this?'

'I wasn't a star, Mrs Lacey.' He shifted in his seat uneasily, feeling embarrassed. 'I wonder where Joan is with the fan.'

He had, in fact, been a star. He saw then: this was the reason she'd wanted to speak only to him. She'd wanted a private interview with Matthias Stayer, owner of one Olympic gold medal in the 100 metre freestyle and one reconstructed shoulder. Who, for some reason no sport-coated journalist could quite work out, had quit the sacred sport at twenty-four when his other shoulder had blown, even though he'd been assured a second reconstruction would give him another five years and a second Olympic gold, and instead became a policeman.

He still bore the gloss of that earlier career, still shone like a magazine cover for certain people, like the woman facing him now, even though the clean-cut Stayer, the lightning bolt in the pool with the college-boy smile, had long exited the water. They thought he was still there, and they wanted a piece of him.

'I have a suspect,' she said.

'That's helpful.' Stayer felt himself deflating, wanting nothing more than to leave the stuffy room and get back to looking into the body found on the sandhills with the symbol carved into it.

'Janine Fort. My next-door neighbour. I heard her swear at Perry once. She hates him. Hated,' she said, wiping a tear.

'Tell me exactly what happened.' Stayer kept his expression blank.

Mrs Lacey launched into a description of the cat, covering its age, weight, height, medical history, food preferences, favourite toys. Stayer dutifully wrote everything down.

'I came home about five pm yesterday. I'd been on a cruise which had finished early, everyone had caught gastro. Janine had been feeding the cats while I was away. Begrudgingly. I tapped Perry's food bowl, but he never came. He usually slinks around my leg at the sound. I found him lying in some bushes around the side of the house—he likes to lie in the evening sun there sometimes. But when I called him, he didn't move. I saw that he'd vomited, so I rushed him to the vet, but there was nothing they could do. I howled.' She adjusted a layer of fabric. 'We had our differences, but of all my felines, I liked him the best.'

'How many cats do have, Mrs Lacey?'

'Seventeen.' She looked proud, defiant, as though challenging him to tell her there was something wrong with this. 'I've watched many cats pass from this world to the next, but Pericles was the only one to do so eyes open. When you put a feline down, their eyes close, or partially close. But Perry's were wide open, his gaze fixed on mine. I watched his pupils grow huge. I knew he was telling me something.'

'What was he telling you?'

'*Don't let her get away with this.* The vet offered to take his body to dispose of him, but I refused. I said the police needed to know, so I brought him here.'

Stayer stopped twirling his pen.

12.48 PM

Only two types of people exist in this world. Forget upbringing, gender, what flag you sing an anthem to. None of that makes a difference. Two types, that's it. The first group comprises the people who think everything is their fault. The second comprises those who think fault always lies with someone else. The people Detective Stayer put in prison invariably came from the second group. And as he sat there in the stifling interview room, he decided the woman across the desk from him belonged to that group too.

He'd held off as long as he could, but the time had come to open that little window. Stayer stood on his tiptoes and prised the window open, and a hot breath rushed in. A haze came next, making their eyes sting and filling the room with an acrid smell. But the smell of the smoke was preferable to the smell which already lurked. Stayer could finally put a name to the meaty pong in the interview room. He pointed to the shopping bag which rested at Mrs Lacey's feet. 'The cat is in there, Mrs Lacey?'

She nodded. 'I want you to perform an autopsy.'

Stayer felt his stomach heave. 'We don't normally order autopsies on cats. A vet can conduct one and send us the report.'

'I don't want the vet to do it. I want a criminal investigation. Someone who will treat the case with the seriousness it deserves.'

'I don't think the morgue in Solihull takes non-human bodies. I can check . . .' He stood up to leave.

'Sit down, detective,' she said, her voice sharp. 'I'm not finished. I want to make a complaint.' She gave him a wounded look. 'The service I've received here has been terrible.'

'This isn't a service, Mrs Lacey. We're the police, not a car wash.'

'I pay your salary now. Don't forget it.'

'I won't,' he said. 'If you wish to make a complaint, you can go to the website.' He motioned to a poster behind him. *How are we doing?* it asked, with a logo for the New South Wales police, a smile emoji, a frown emoji, and details of a hotline.

The woman rested her head in her hands and made no sound.

'Are you alright, Mrs Lacey?'

She threw her head back, as though straining for air. 'I will get an autopsy. And I'll send you the results.' She retrieved a piece of balled-up tissue from inside her sleeve and wiped an eye with it. 'You think I'm a silly old woman.'

'I don't think that at all, Mrs Lacey.'

'My cat was murdered. I'll prove it.' She stood abruptly and walked out, the cat-filled shopping bag bumping on her thigh.

Stayer was standing in the hallway when Joan approached. 'I'm so sorry, detective. She looked so disturbed. I truly thought she had intel about the murder on the sandhills.'

'Joan. Are you aware that the bag she's holding has a dead cat in it?'

Joan polished her glasses with the bottom of her shirt then put them back on her face. 'Sounds about right. Her husband fell to his death at the Thoorgala blowhole. Barbie never got over it; replaced him with a shitload of cats. You can smell the piss for miles. It's types like her that give Thoorgala its colourful reputation. Smoke?' Joan pulled two rolled cigarettes from her breast pocket and offered one to Stayer.

Stayer shook his head. 'Don't you worry about cancer?'

Joan laughed. 'Mum smoked. She lived to ninety-four.'

'Don't the bushfires affect your breathing, though?'

'I actually think smoking has helped,' Joan replied. 'Toughened my lungs up.'

Turning to face the office, Stayer gestured to the empty desks, the bare office chairs, the screens switched off. 'Where is everyone? I thought there was a staff of fourteen here.'

'Everyone's out working the bushfire. Trying to catch the firebugs that lit up Rexley North and the national park. For the moment it's you, Sergeant Nichols, Constable Walsh and me. I haven't cuffed a perp in thirty years, but I still have a badge. Let's call me half a cop.'

'So I've got three and a half cops at my disposal. Including myself.'

'Correct.' Joan handed him a piece of paper. 'Almost forgot. Evacuation plan.' The note was headed: *What to do in the event of bushfire.*

'So if a bushfire hits Thoorgala, everyone is to congregate on the beach. Bring water and snacks.'

'You've summarised it nicely.'

'That's it? Just head to the beach. Not much of plan.'

'It's a perfect plan. The fire isn't going to burn water.'

A phone rang at an un-manned desk. Joan pressed a button and answered. 'Thoorgala station.'

She listened. Her face fell. 'It's Constable Walsh,' she said to Stayer. 'He needs your help. He's made an arrest in the sandhills case. The victim's mother.'

1.30 PM

Stayer pulled up to the residence of Cassandra Glasson, mother of Phoebe. He exited the car, the engine ticking furiously as it cooled. The sight of the property hit him like a foul wind. Everywhere he looked was something ugly: a fraying couch squatted in the un-mowed lawn; a car missing its wheels, rusted on bricks in the driveway. This was the other side of Thoorgala, which didn't make it on to the lifestyle blogs. Where the porters and maintenance men lived, the invisible people who cleaned the waterfront houses, who made the protein bliss balls, who dry-cleaned the suits.

An officer stepped off the rotting front porch and introduced himself as Constable Robert Walsh. His height rose above six feet, and muscles strained the fabric of his uniform. Comparisons to Arnold Schwarzenegger would not have gone astray. He seemed younger than Stayer but only by a few years; around thirty perhaps. He wore a wide-brimmed navy police hat and his shirtsleeves were creased where he'd rolled them down to deliver the news to the victim's next of kin. A slash of white stretched across the constable's neck, and Stayer stared at it distractedly until he realised it was sunscreen the policeman must have missed rubbing in. Stayer took in Walsh's massive frame and wondered to himself guiltily how he would have preferred to have this giant out on the sand dunes, carrying the stretcher with him. Maybe then they wouldn't have dropped the body.

'The victim's mother is in the backyard,' Constable Walsh told Stayer.

'You had to arrest her?'

'Afraid so. She hit me with a fry pan.'

'Are you alright?'

'I'll live.'

'Why did she hit you?'

'I told her about her daughter. She wasn't even really listening. She jumped up and grabbed something from the kitchen, ran outside and threw it over the fence into the yard next door.'

'What did she throw over there?'

'No idea. I asked her when she came back inside. That's when she grabbed the fry pan. Didn't want to cuff her, but I thought she might knock me out with the next hit. I'll take you to her.'

Stayer followed Constable Walsh into the house and down a water-stained plasterboard hallway, passing a cramped bathroom with a cracked toilet and a grey-ringed tub. The place had a musty, salty odour, like they lived over a mangrove swamp. Stayer had passed an oil refinery on the drive over, its ugly cream vats resembling oversized pots, boiling on some imaginary stove. He'd noticed the road sloping gently downhill. This is the kind of place he would have lived as kid, among the chemicals and swamps.

At the end of the hallway, Constable Walsh pushed open a door with a torn flyscreen. Stayer stepped onto a back verandah which looked over a small rectangle of grass, patchy and brown. Sitting on an outdoor chair on the verandah was Cassandra Glasson.

'I might wait out the front,' Constable Walsh said. 'I think the sight of me makes her angry.' He disappeared back inside the house.

Cassandra wore all black—ebony skirt, inky silk shirt with the top three buttons undone. She sat on the chair with her slim legs crossed. Multiple piercings in each ear glinted gold and silver in the sunlight, and her face was powdered with heavy make-up. She could not have been more than fifty. One wrist lay handcuffed to the chair arm, the metal flashing in the sunlight.

'Hello, Mrs Glasson. I'm so sorry for your loss. I believe my colleague Constable Walsh has given you the details we know so far. May I ask you some questions about Phoebe?' He crouched down in front of the woman so they were at eye level. She didn't look at him.

He made no mention of the handcuffs, of hitting the constable. He didn't ask her what she'd thrown over the fence. This seemed to intrigue her, but she didn't speak.

'Could you tell me the last time you saw or spoke to Phoebe? Perhaps you could check your phone?'

Again, she gave no answer.

A tiny lizard wriggled across the deck, a string of silver.

'Mrs Glasson, I know how difficult this must be.'

'Call me Mrs Glasson again and I'll slap you,' she said, still not looking at him. 'It's Cassie.' Her voice was low and gravelly, like that of a lounge singer. 'I know what you're thinking. A girl from a shithole like this had it coming.'

'I wasn't thinking that at all, Cassie.'

'Doesn't matter. It's not true anyway. Phoebe was the unicorn who got out of this place. I had some things going for me once too. Then I met a pot-smoking surfer with great hair.' She smiled darkly, revealing a black gap where her left incisor should have been. 'My dad punched me in the face when he found out I was pregnant. Mick, Phoebe's father, bolted. I paid for her clothes, bottles, nappies. People might say all sorts about her, but they would never say she wasn't smart. Phoebe sat the exam for Thoorgala Grammar and won a full academic scholarship. Beat out all those kids with fountain pens and private tutors.'

'Sounds like you raised an impressive young woman,' Stayer said. 'Do you know if Phoebe had any enemies? Ex-boyfriends, perhaps, or current ones? Someone she argued with at work? Anyone who might have wanted to hurt Phoebe?'

Cassie pulled out a packet from her shirt pocket and rolled a mixture of tobacco and marijuana into a small white paper with her uncuffed hand, a feat which would have required skill and experience. The little brown fibres, like saffron strands, folded into the greener ones. 'Gonna charge me for this too?'

'I'm not going to charge you,' he said. 'And I'm sure Constable Walsh won't either.' He reached over and unlocked the handcuff gently, releasing her wrist into her lap.

She made a gruff, approving sound. She pointed to a weather-beaten chair and motioned for him to sit. Stayer took the seat gratefully, his knees feeling like they were about to explode from the crouching. Nobody warns ex-elite athletes about that. He was only thirty-three but had the joints of a ninety-year-old.

'There are some brownies in the kitchen, if you'd like to try some. I just baked a tray. Laced with enough THC to stone a horse.'

'I'll pass for now, thanks.'

'Suit yourself.' She continued rolling her joint. 'Phoebe had some issues with her ex, Jackson. Bad break-up.'

'Jackson's last name?'

'Millwall. He's a wellness bro.' She said *wellness bro* with such disdain that Stayer had to repress a smile. He wrote the name down.

Cassie lit the rolled joint. A sweet, smoky fragrance entered the air. The sound of dogs growling rose up, a deep rumbling vibration. He shot a glance over to the neighbour's yard.

'Was Phoebe ever involved in any religious groups? Or cults?'

Cassie's expression was incredulous. 'Doesn't sound like Phoebe. She wasn't baptised. Never been inside a church. Why?'

'This is sensitive, and I don't want to upset you.'

'Nothing's gonna upset me at this point, mate. My daughter is dead.'

Stayer nodded respectfully. 'Phoebe's body had a symbol carved into it.'

For the first time, Cassie met his eye. Her irises were a piercing blue, like spring water. 'I don't understand.'

'Someone—your daughter's killer, I believe—used a knife or some other sharp implement to carve a small symbol into Phoebe's skin.'

'Where?'

'Into her skin.'

'No, I mean where on her body?'

'On her hand. Her right hand.'

'Jesus Christ.' She seemed to crumple into the chair. She placed her head in one hand and wrapped the other arm around her middle. 'You silly bitch. It's finally caught up with you.'

1.55 PM

Sounds of the desperate suburb surrounded them—dogs growled next door, cars with clogged mufflers chugged down the potholed road. A couple of children fought in the dirt a few houses away, their voices shrill. He wondered how many despairing nights the victim had spent here.

Stayer sat forward. 'What do you mean, Mrs Glasson—Cassie? What finally caught up with your daughter?'

The woman smoked her joint, holding it like a whistle.

'Cassie? Please. This could help. What did you mean when you said that?'

'It could be anything. Phoebe was a wild girl, always involved in schemes. She flew too close to the sun. Burned this time.'

'Cassie. From what you said, it sounded like you were referring to a specific incident or event that has finally caught up with your daughter. Something from Phoebe's past?'

'Didn't sound like that to me, mate. I'm stoned; I wouldn't take anything I say seriously.'

Stayer tried to remain cool, reminding himself that this woman had just lost her daughter. 'There was something else,' Stayer said. 'Someone left a note by your daughter's body.'

'What did it say?'

'It said, *They shall confess. Or four more*. It was signed *TH*. Does that mean anything to you?'

'About Phoebe confessing? Confessing to what?'

'I don't know,' Stayer said. 'Do you?'

Their eyes met again. Stayer had checked Phoebe Glasson's record before he came. The woman they'd found on the sandhills had a prior conviction for drug possession with intent to sell, and an affray charge.

Cassie calmly rolled another joint and smoked it, never breaking her eye contact with him. The marijuana wafted into Stayer's nose and burned his eyes, and he was starting to feel a little stoned himself.

'What did you throw over the fence?'

'Bugger off.'

'What will I find if I go over there?'

'I wouldn't. Those dogs were supposed to have been put down. They mauled some kid last year. Have a taste for human blood now. The owners skipped town last week. Dogs haven't been fed for days. You'll be disembowelled.'

Stayer jumped off the verandah into the yard. Constable Walsh joined him. Cassie took her chance and darted back inside, long black skirt floating behind her, disappearing back down the stained hallway and out the front door.

'Should I go after her, boss?' Walsh said.

'Leave her. She won't be hard to track down if we need to find her. What we really want is what she threw over the fence.'

'Okay.' Constable Walsh removed his hat and wiped sweat from his brow, revealing a shock of black hair. It had a strange sheen, a uniform shininess which didn't look natural. Stayer peered closer and noticed a hint of reddish orange at the constable's hairline. He had dyed his red hair to black.

They both peered over the fence into the neighbouring yard. As if sensing their gazes, two Rottweilers leaped upwards, teeth pointed and gleaming, breaths heinous. They banged into the fence, scratching furiously. One dog jumped again with brutal energy and almost made it over. Stayer stumbled backward, retracting limbs. Constable Walsh cowered next to him.

'We can't go over there, boss. They'll maul us. Maybe call animal welfare?'

'They'll all be at the bushfires, rescuing koalas. A callout might take hours.'

Stayer walked back towards the house.

'Where are you going?' Walsh asked as Stayer reached the back door and went inside. He returned with a tray of brownies. Before the constable could ask, Stayer threw them over the fence. The sound of the dogs pouncing on the tray followed. Then snarling, chewing, swallowing.

'They're eating it,' Walsh said.

'Good,' Stayer replied.

They sat on the verandah in the baking heat. Less than ten minutes passed before a thud rang out, then another. Stayer peered gingerly over the fence. Constable Walsh joined him. 'They're asleep!' he said. Stayer smiled.

'What was in those brownies?'

'A bunch of marijuana.' Stayer began climbing the fence.

'Careful, boss,' Constable Walsh said, looking horrified. 'What if they wake up?'

'Let's hope they don't.'

Stayer moved over the sagging, grey palings and jumped down into the neighbouring yard. The long brown grass was interspersed with broken bottles, rusted car parts, a broken Hills hoist. The smell of canine was horrendous, like hot faeces. The two dogs snored heavily in the dirt, black heads tilted and sagging, brown jowls laden with white foamy drool. Stayer looked around frantically for the object Cassie had thrown over there. He searched from corner to corner, over broken glass, faded food packets, headless dolls and other broken toys, glancing every few seconds back at the dogs, checking they were still asleep. Just when he began to despair, he saw it.

A glint of silver. Under the paw of one of the Rottweilers.

Stayer moved slowly towards the dog. He lifted the heavy, meaty paw, the claws long and sharp. He pulled the object out and dropped the dog's foot to the ground. It stiffened. Stayer looked up.

A pair of black eyes stared at him.

Stayer leaped to the fence and scrambled upwards, willing his legs to carry him to safety. He could hear the dog behind him, ferocious, strong, its fleshy breath at his heels. The dog snapped its jaws at Stayer's leg. It missed and fell back down onto the grass. It jumped again, but Stayer hauled himself over the fence, tumbling back into Cassie's backyard. Constable Walsh rushed to him. 'Are you alright, boss?'

He nodded, breathing wildly. He waited for his breath to slow, then held up the silver object he'd fetched from the yard. It was a mobile phone in a silver case, with a small card holder on the back. Inside were a driver's licence and a couple of credit cards, all in the name of Phoebe Glasson.

2.16 PM

Ruby stepped back and surveyed her Christmas tree. The monstrous sculpture loomed over her. The gold leaf glinted. She felt exhausted, spent, and something approaching satisfaction. Not happiness as such, more a glad oblivion. Her hands were full of cuts that stung as the sweat dripped into them.

She would have to patch things up with her brother. When she'd invited him to stay, she'd never thought he'd do it. She'd felt light beams when he'd showed up on her doorstep. But things had been weird between them since.

Her phone rang. She raised it to her ear, still studying the tree. 'Aunt Carol.'

'Great news! Jaime had a cancellation. I've got you in for a colour, cut and blow dry this afternoon. Merry Christmas.' Ruby listened to Aunt Carol, who wasn't really her aunt, sip coffee down the phone line. She would be sitting on her front verandah, listening to the rosellas. 'Ruby, are you there?'

'Why?' Ruby asked, picking a loose fleck of gold from a brown pine needle.

'Don't you want a freshen up before Christmas lunch?'

Ruby balled the bottom of her singlet top into her fist and squeezed. More sweat dripped into her palm, stinging her cuts.

She stank too. She couldn't remember if she'd last showered yesterday or the day before. 'It will just be you, me and Matt for lunch,' she said. 'None of whom cares what my hair looks like.'

'And Julie and Greg, Maryanne and Ron, Peter and Stephanie, Vanessa and her new partner—I forget his name, doubt he will show . . .' Carol's voice was aiming for breezy, but Ruby could hear a note of panic in there too; she picked up speed as she ran through the names, as though she was trying to get them all out before Ruby could stop her.

'Oh god, no,' Ruby said.

'They're our closest friends,' her aunt cried down the phone line.

'Your friends. Not mine.'

'They're excited to see you.'

'No, Carol. I don't want a circus Christmas lunch.' She could hear the pain in her own voice.

'Okay, okay,' Carol said quickly, sounding equally alarmed. 'Just get your hair done, darling—you might as well, as it's already paid for. Don't stress about the lunch. We'll sort something out.'

Her aunt began speaking about what hair style and colour she might like, and the latest trends in layers and highlights. Ruby gazed out the window and let her talk. A postman's motorcycle buzzed down the footpath and paused at her letterbox. Ruby waited for him to move on before walking out front.

She retrieved the letters, mainly addressed to other people, former residents of the property in which she now lived, in this grand and curious experiment to move back to Thoorgala, the place that had been the source of the blackness from the start. The regret of what she'd done came to her in the early hours of the morning, and at twilight, but also at unexpected times, like when a man held the door open for her in the corner shop down the road and the anonymous kindness of it made her burst into tears. She felt like screaming at him, *Don't you know who I am? Don't you know what I did?* but instead smiled and moved past, the faint smell of his aftershave hitting her like a slap.

A final postcard remained in the letterbox, and it was addressed to her. There was no message.

She wondered if it had been sent by an old friend or acquaintance, a colleague who had her new address. She had told a few people when she'd left her old job where she was going, only under duress, from their kind prods. She turned the postcard over to the picture, then watched as it tumbled to the ground.

The postcard rested in the grass, blades of green stabbing the edges. She looked around furtively, glancing down the street to check if the postcard's sender might be lurking in the hedges, behind the bus stop, under a power line. There was no one there.

'Ruby, are you listening to me?' Aunt Carol's voice came back to her, ringing in her ears, and she realised that she was still holding the phone to her ear. Carol was still talking about haircuts.

She said nothing into the phone, just stared at the postcard. The image on the front was a painting of a young woman lying among waves. Ruby hadn't seen this painting in many years, and never reproduced like this, as a postcard, in the daylight. She was surprised it hadn't burned a hole in the grass where it lay. She snatched it up with the other letters and carried them inside the house.

'Ruby? Hello? Can you hear me?' Aunt Carol said down the phone line.

Ruby had been silent way too long. 'I think I want highlights,' she said.

'What I've been saying the whole time.' Carol sounded exasperated and excited. 'You would look beautiful with highlights! Honey-coloured, to bring out the gold in your eyes.'

She continued, speaking about tones, brassiness, warms and cools, as Ruby walked into the kitchen, dropping the letters on the peeling counter and taking the postcard to the sink. She found a barbecue lighter in the pantry and flicked the flame on with the clicker, then moved it to the postcard. The image of the woman lying in the waves caught alight, the paper crinkling, the smoky aroma biting the air.

'Warm highlights, yes,' Ruby said, watching the image curl and disintegrate, the fire devouring the woman's figure. The flames reached her finger and thumb, and she let them lick her for several terrible, exquisite moments, as the pain of the burn took over. Finally, when her skin began blistering, she dropped the postcard into the sink and the flames consumed it.

Her phone remained tucked between ear and shoulder. 'Carol, I need to shower.'

'Fine. But you'll come to the hairdresser?'

'I'll meet you there at four.'

'And you'll stay at our place tonight?' her faux aunt asked. 'Help me set up for tomorrow?'

'Wouldn't miss it.' Ruby hung up and exited the kitchen, leaving her phone on the counter.

2.25 PM

Stayer stopped at a petrol station on his way back from Cassie's house to fill up the squad car. Phoebe Glasson's mobile phone rested in an evidence bag on the passenger seat. Its black screen stared up at the squad car's roof, dull and scratched. Stayer stood at the bowser and inhaled the fumes. He hadn't eaten anything yet, so once inside he selected a pie from the self-serve warmer and tomato sauce in a squeeze pack. As he contemplated how long the pie had been there, a woman appeared and touched his arm.

'Hello,' she said, smiling eagerly.

'Hello?' Stayer said, searching her face for some hint of recognition.

'I'm Nadia Traurig. I own the florist on Beach Lane. I went to school with Ruby. We were best friends.' She paused, as though hoping Stayer would finally twig, and maybe embrace her.

Stayer turned to her. 'Oh. Nice to meet you, Nadia,' searching her face. It wasn't the first time someone had recognised him without him having the faintest clue who they were.

She reached up and kissed his cheek, as though they were old pals. 'I heard you moved in. It's the talk of the town.'

Stayer groaned softly. 'It is? People don't have better things to talk about than a washed-up swimmer moving to their suburb?'

She laughed. 'Not really. And you don't seem washed-up to me.'

Nadia looked him up and down. Stayer shifted his feet awkwardly, and thumbed the tomato sauce packet.

'How do you like Thoorgala so far?'

'What's not to like? It's paradise.'

Nadia smiled broadly. 'Where are you living?'

'I'm staying with Ruby for now. On Sunrise Avenue.'

'In Mad Ned's shack?'

'I'm sorry?'

'Mad Ned. The man who owns that house. He killed his whole family and buried them in the backyard. That's the rumour, anyway. I can't believe you're living there.' She looked shocked and concerned, but kind of excited also, like this was juicy news. 'Dear Ruby. I'm surprised she came back here. After everything.'

Stayer moved closer to Nadia so that an elderly man could get by them to the register. 'Everything? What happened?'

Nadia waved her hands furiously like she'd said too much. 'Nothing. If Ruby hasn't mentioned it.'

'She hasn't mentioned anything.'

Nadia had an innocent expression as she stepped up to the register.

Stayer followed her. 'Wait. What happened?' he said.

She paid for her fuel, thanked the attendant, a bored-looking teenager whose name badge read *Angel*. 'You should ask Ruby,' Nadia said. She touched his forearm again, then walked away.

'Wait,' Stayer called, tapping his card on the reader quickly. He darted outside into the vicious white daylight. He scanned the bowsers and the cars parked beside them, but couldn't see her.

Stayer's breath was coarse, like he'd just run for a bus and missed it.

3.02 PM

Stayer entered the police station from the back car park, carrying Phoebe Glasson's smartphone. After making several wrong turns around the unfamiliar station, he finally found Joan in some sort of kitchenette, with art deco countertops, a kettle, and a vending machine selling protein bars. 'Got a cable to charge this?'

Joan took the evidence bag and tipped the phone sideways, peering into the little port at its base. The dull screen caught the overhead light, flashing under the plastic. 'Might do. We've got a draw of crap I can check. By the way, couple of tip-offs on your desk.' She motioned towards his new office, a box with glass walls on the side of the open-plan room.

Stayer entered. A mountain of yellow sticky notes covered his new keyboard. Each contained a name and a phone number and either 're: sandhills', 're: Tall Harry', or a combination of both.

Stayer moved to the glass door. 'Joan?' he called to the receptionist. 'Is this your handwriting?'

Joan joined him in his office. 'It is,' she said. She wore a satisfied expression. 'They're tip-offs about the murder of Phoebe Glasson.'

'Must be a hundred messages here,' Stayer said, trying to order the notes, shuffling them like a card dealer.

'Ninety-seven actually,' Joan replied. 'My hand aches from writing them all.'

Stayer pointed to the first note. 'Who's Tall Harry?'

The receptionist shrugged. 'Maybe call the numbers and find out. Also, there's a man out front called Daniel Catton. He wants to speak to you. Only you, he says.'

'Did someone murder his cat too?'

'Don't think so. He says it's important.'

'Well, if it's important,' Stayer said, and walked out to reception to meet the waiting man.

'G'day, detective,' the man said, taking off a cap and offering his hand, which Stayer shook. 'Daniel Catton. Merry Christmas for tomorrow.' He was a schoolteacher, he said. He shifted the baseball cap in his hands. The insignia for Thoorgala Grammar was embroidered across the front in gold thread. 'That body that was found on the sandhills,' he said. 'I know who killed her.'

•

Stayer showed the teacher into his new office and offered him a seat, moving a pile of case files left by the person he'd replaced to the side of his desk.

'You're busy,' Mr Catton said. 'I won't take up much of your time.' The man looked down at his cap and laughed ruefully. 'You're going to think I'm crazy,' he said.

'How about we let me be the judge of what's crazy and not,' Stayer said kindly.

'It's okay if you think I'm crazy, because I know I'm not.'

Stayer considered the man in front of him. He was mid-forties and mostly bald. The hair that remained was clipped neatly on top, and shaved to a number one on the sides of his head. He sat with shoulders slightly sloped. 'Who do you think killed Phoebe, Mr Catton?'

Mr Catton turned to the window in Stayer's office and made the mistake of staring at the searing ring of sun. He averted his gaze quickly, like he'd caught sight of something terrifying. 'I was at a school assembly last week, the final one for the year at Thoorgala Grammar. A student came on the stage. Her name is Angelica O'Brien. Goes by Angel. Angel was supposed to say a closing prayer, to end the assembly. She didn't say a prayer. Instead, she said a rhyme. I've written down the words.' The teacher retrieved a piece of paper from his pocket and handed it to Stayer. His hand shook.

Stayer unfolded the note and began reading aloud. '*Don't say his name, don't say it thrice, what happens next, it won't be nice. Tall Harry. Tall—*' Before he could read any more, Mr Catton snatched the paper from him.

'Sorry,' Mr Catton said, 'don't say that name aloud. Just read it to yourself. The damage is already done. Still makes me jump to hear it.'

'Damage?' Stayer said, feeling baffled.

'The student set him loose. By saying his name three times in a row.' He lowered his voice to a whisper. '*Tall Harry.*'

Stayer opened his notebook. 'Okay. Who is Tall Harry?'

The teacher inhaled deeply, as though what he was about to say required extra breath. 'Tall Harry is a monster. He lives in the sandhills. Some say he's the ghost of a convict from the first fleet. I should have come to you the moment the student said his name three times. Now someone's dead. And more will follow . . .' His voice was shaking.

Stayer said nothing for a moment. 'Oh. You're serious.'

'Phoebe Glasson had a symbol carved into her, didn't she?'

'I can't say,' Stayer replied, as Catton wiped his brow. 'Let me get you a drink.' He poured the teacher some water from a cooler into a styrofoam cup. Mr Catton trembled as he sipped the water. A sight drew Stayer's attention: the man only had half an index finger on his right hand. It disarmed Stayer, the unusually smooth and rounded mound of skin at the end of this man's finger: no fingernail, no second or third knuckle.

'How did you lose the end of your finger?' Stayer said. 'If you don't mind me asking.'

Mr Catton flexed his hand so the pink nub pointed to the ceiling, like a cocktail frankfurt. 'Don't mind you asking. A shark bit it off.'

Stayer felt his eyes widen. 'Truly?'

'I was fourteen. Surfing. Had my fingers curled around my board, waiting for a wave. Felt a tugging. Then a snap. Looked down: no finger. The shark probably thought I was a seal.'

Stayer was incredulous, intrigued. 'What kind of shark? Great white?'

Mr Catton chuckled. 'If a great white had bitten me, the tip of my finger would have been the only thing left. Reef shark.'

'Did you ever surf again?'

'Every chance I get. They can be mean, though. The surfers.'

'About your finger?'

'No. About a townie dropping in on "their" waves.' His voice sounded bitter. 'Stupid thing is, I grew up here. Can't afford to buy a house, though. So I'm an outsider. You're one, too. You didn't grow up here, did you?'

'No.'

'They'll never accept you, then. Olympian or not.' Stayer grimaced. This was the third person who had mentioned his being an Olympian. He'd stupidly imagined some kind of anonymity in this place. He now realised how foolish that was.

'Not until you've lived here generations. These people won't help you. But you need to help them. You need to stop him before he kills anyone else.'

Catton downed the last of his water and placed his empty cup on the desk. He'd chewed the rim, making half-moons of teeth marks in the styrofoam.

'I'm sorry, Mr Catton. You're saying the murder on the sandhills was committed by what, an urban legend?'

'Exactly.' Stayer watched as Daniel Catton's face contorted and grew red; he wondered if the man needed a psychiatric referral, he could ask Joan for the number. 'I have a lead.' Mr Catton fetched his phone and navigated with his thumbs. The smooth nub of the missing finger rested on the side of the phone, shiny and pink. He found what he wanted and handed the phone to Stayer. 'Read that.'

The metal felt slim and cool in Stayer's hot hand. Mr Catton had opened a web browser to some sort of forum.

> //Thoorgala. A sandy corner of the internet to discuss all things God's country
>
> HaroldBishop • 4.28 pm
> Catching up those who have recently joined. Woman's body found on the sandhills. Symbol carved into her hand. May be the work of Tall Harry.
> Read about him here:
> Myths and Legends of the Cundra Valley by Catherine Kelley

'This is dismaying to read, Mr Catton,' Stayer said, turning the screen around. The teacher's face glowed blue in its reflection. 'I'm far from happy to see people talking about the crime online. How do they know about the symbol? This information is police only.'

Mr Catton shrugged. 'You can't keep a secret in Thoorgala. The sand has ears. The waves watch everything.' He wore a portentous look. 'That's not the important bit, anyway.'

'What is the important bit?'

'The book. *Myths and Legends of the Cundra Valley*. It has a chapter on Tall Harry. I'd read it if I were you.'

'Thanks,' Stayer replied. 'You've been very helpful.' It was a struggle to sound sincere.

Mr Catton stood and walked to the door, then paused in the doorway. He turned, his eyes falling on the cup on Stayer's desk. His teeth marks glinted in the light. The teacher hesitated, then he snatched up the cup and walked out the door.

6.01 PM

Stayer sat back in his chair and groaned. His fingers were exhausted. His eyes were exhausted. His ears hurt. He had spent the best part of three hours calling the numbers on the ninety-seven tips Joan had placed on his keyboard. If he'd ever had a desire to attend a gathering of conspiracy theorists, he didn't need to bother now—he had already met every one of them within a ten kilometre radius. He could scarcely believe it. Each person—every single one—had told him that Tall Harry had killed the woman on the sandhills. He'd spoken to a local real estate agent, the woman who owned the 7-Eleven, the manager of the local dog kennel. Each told him about their own brushes with Tall Harry; of reading about him on toilet doors as teenagers, of kids slumber parties where he'd supposedly shown up. A dentist had told him about a sighting of Tall Harry he'd had last year, while running in the sandhills. A dentist! In possession of a university degree, who drilled into people's gums for a living. Several mentioned that the sandhills were haunted. He'd made it through just over half when he observed he'd lost all feeling in his butt cheeks from clenching them in frustration.

As he left his desk to stretch his legs, he spotted Mr Catton's baseball cap left behind on the chair he'd been sitting on.

American college style, maroon-coloured fabric, gold letters. The school colours. *Thoorgala Grammar*: the name conjured up BMWs with P-plates in the student car park, families who spent Christmas in Aspen, a tanned and slim student body who would one day either sit on the boards of banks, marry well, or become prime minister in a leadership spill. It was the wealthiest school in the region, with grounds set on five acres of land overlooking Port Joseph Bay. Rowing facilities, a 800-seater basketball stadium, a performing arts centre.

It was the school his sister had attended as a boarder on a seven-year, fully funded art scholarship, and the same school she taught at now. He'd always harboured a secret jealousy that Ruby had gone there while he'd attended Canberra High, with its state-school appropriate excursions to the science museum and walks around Lake Burley Griffin.

He'd considered asking Mr Catton if he knew Ruby, as they were colleagues, but decided against it. He hadn't felt like revealing parts of his personal life to a man who appeared less than rational. Stayer placed the cap on his own head. The fabric felt heavy and soft, the peak curved nicely.

He sat back down at his desk, opened his laptop and found the forum //Thoorgala. Mr Catton was correct about one thing: many people were commenting on the body found on the sandhills. New comments had even been posted since Stayer had been talking with the teacher. He felt disbelief. People were discussing the symbol, the carvings, the location of the body, but most of all they were talking about Tall Harry, the local bogeyman who had allegedly committed the crime.

> Snookus52 • 4.45 pm
>
> Catherine Kelley you're the expert. Can you help? Do you believe Tall Harry is responsible?

Catherine Kelley • 4.46 pm
God bless the victim. May she rest in peace. Happy to help wherever I can. A Tall Harry association may exist. But I would need more about the symbol to be sure. Has anyone seen it?

Snookus52 • 4.47 pm
The symbol? On the dead body?

Catherine Kelley • 4.47 pm
Yes. It would be tremendously helpful to see it.

Snookus52 • 4.48 pm
Woah. You mean like crime scene photos. Okay. Start your engines people. Forensic pics. First one to put them up wins my eternal respect.

Catherine Kelley • 4.48 pm
Please don't make them public. Send to me privately.

Snookus52 • 4.48 pm
Quicker if someone just posts them. Hang tight.

Stayer's blood reached a rolling boil. He accessed the police database, and found a phone number for Catherine Kelley. He dialled. It went to voicemail. He shouted. 'Joan?'

She appeared in the doorway.

'Do you know this woman, Catherine Kelley? She wrote the book *Myths and Legends of the Cundra Valley*.' He motioned to his computer screen.

Joan walked around and read the database entry over his shoulder. 'Vaguely. That book was in the shops a few years back. A hit with the locals. They liked seeing themselves in print.'

'She's asking people online for crime scene photos.'

Stayer watched Joan's eyes moving across the screen. The light reflected in the lenses of her glasses. 'Okay. Not ideal.'

He dialled the number again. Hung up. 'Voicemail. I need to stop this woman before someone puts a photo up.'

'Database says she lives in Garribee,' Joan said. 'Half an hour's drive west. Go to her house.'

Stayer laughed. 'I'm not going over there. I've got better things to do.'

'Like what? I assume you are waiting for the autopsy results and the initial tox, and following up on the ninety-seven tip-offs I handed you, which you don't seem all that confident in. I'd hurry, or soon there will be a photo of a dead body on the internet, with that terrible thing carved into her skin.'

Stayer snatched the car keys off the desk.

6.48 PM

Stayer approached the outskirts of Garribee. He passed an abattoir, an abandoned strip mall, with overgrown weeds poking out of broken windows, and rusty industrial estates. He felt more at home in this neck of the woods than in the glossy streets of Thoorgala.

He arrived at the place listed as Catherine Kelley's address and had to double-check the number was correct. It was a seventies block of units, two storeys, brown-brick veneer. It looked like a motor inn.

Stayer climbed the stairs to the first floor and rang the doorbell. There was a grease spot on the circular pad, the ghosts of a thousand fingers. He waited several moments and received no answer. He considered leaving, but finally, the door swung open.

A woman dressed in a nun's habit stood there. A black veil covered her hair, a black dress covered her body. Stayer stepped back at the sight. He checked the address a third time.

'Can I help you?' the nun said.

'I'm looking for Catherine Kelley.'

'You have found her.' Soft, clear-skinned cheeks sat under a pair of green eyes that moved slowly but purposefully across his face. Her hands were the only flesh visible under her black habit, and the oval of her face poked through the black shroud of her veil, like the head of a caterpillar. She could not have been more than thirty-five.

'May I have your name?' she said. Her voice was quick but had an old-fashioned quality to it, like something you might hear on AM radio.

'Detective Matthias Stayer.'

'Detective?' Her eyes flashed. 'Are you here about the murder in the sandhills?'

'Yes. I've come to stop you asking for crime scene photos online.'

Her face fell. 'That would be very bad idea. They may help solve the case. Won't you come in? I have things to show you.' She stepped aside, holding the door open, as if to usher him into the apartment. Stayer didn't move.

'Absolutely not. You need to stop posting about the murder online. It's not helpful. It's dangerous for the case. It's jeopardising the investigation. It's irresponsible.'

'In what way?' she looked at him innocently.

'For starters, you're speculating about a character from a fairy-tale. This isn't a legitimate line of inquiry. This case will be solved through blood found at the scene, hair samples, eyewitnesses, *not* an urban legend.'

'With respect, detective, I disagree. This urban legend may be exactly how you solve this case. Please come in, you've come all this way. You would like to stop this individual before more women are killed?'

'Of course.' He paused. 'What makes you think more women will be killed?'

'This murder was not random. I guarantee I can help solve this case, or at the very least try to stop this individual before they strike again.'

A dog barked somewhere inside another apartment. A hoarse, weak noise, sounding hot and tired. Stayer groaned. 'Fine. Make it quick.'

She held the door open wide. 'Welcome.'

He stepped inside. A cluttered and depressing bedsit greeted him with threadbare carpet and laminate counters. It smelled like tinned soup and bleach. But all he could focus on was the books. Hundreds, maybe thousands of them. Bookshelves lined every wall, floor-to-ceiling. More books rested on windowsills and bench tops. Piles of them dotted the floor, like islands. He had never seen so many books in one small place. He glanced at the titles on the shelf nearest him. A jumble of subject, author, and genre. Medical textbooks, tomes on philosophy and history. Books about Nazis, ancient Greeks, organic chemistry. Dusty textbooks with cracked leather spines, including an entire set of *Encyclopaedia Britannica*.

'What do you think of my library, detective?'

'Quite the collection,' Stayer replied. 'You're interested in all these things? In Nazis, philosophy, the tribes of Papua New Guinea?'

'I am interested in everything, detective. "The more I know, the more I realise I know nothing," Socrates said.'

'Don't you take a vow of poverty? How do you afford all these books?'

'Parishioners donate some to me. I use my allowance to buy others from charity shops, market stalls. The rest I steal.'

He stared at her in surprise and saw she was smiling.

'Tea, detective?' She moved to the kitchen to fill a plastic kettle.

Stayer checked his watch. The nun smiled expectantly. He sighed. 'Sure.'

She poured the boiled water into a cup, once white but now on its way to beige, then dunked the teabag a few times and disposed of it. She placed the mug in front of him. 'Milk, sugar?'

'White, thanks,' he said.

She added long-life milk. He sipped. It tasted like brown water.

'You still wear the get-up?' he asked, gesturing to her veil and dress.

'Your powers of perception are disarming, detective.'

'I thought nuns didn't bother with it these days.'

'Depends on the order,' she replied. 'Some wear civilian clothes. Others have kept the habit, as it were. My order likes to preserve the distinction between nuns and congregants. But you did not come here to discuss my holy orders; you're here to investigate a murder. May I see the body? Some pictures will do. I don't need to see the actual cadaver.'

Stayer leaned back. The vinyl chair felt like melted cheese against his spine. He exhaled loudly. 'This is why you wanted me to come inside. I already told you. You're not getting pictures of the dead body.'

'You don't have any?'

'I didn't say that.'

'It's illegal to show me?'

He shook his head. 'Not illegal. Unethical. You're a civilian.'

'I'm not actually. I'm a nun.'

'But you're not law enforcement. It would be violating the victim's privacy.'

'I would never show anyone. I told the people online not to post the photos. I would never dream of invading a person's privacy.'

He shook his head. 'Answer's still no.'

'I understand your concern, detective. But I might be able to help. You wish to know what the symbol means, don't you?'

'I do.'

'Then show me a photo. I assume you have them on your phone, yes? I will take a brief glance only, then hand it back to you. You have my word, as a nun.'

Stayer offered a long sigh and took another sip of the terrible tea. 'I'm going against my better judgement here.' He removed the phone from his pocket. 'I'll show you a photo of her hand only—that's where the symbol is.'

'That's all I need.'

'Are you sure you want to see this? It's confronting.'

'I have seen dead bodies before, detective, maybe more than you. We both tend to deal with people on the way out.'

He handed his phone to the nun. He watched her eyes fall on the image of Phoebe Glasson's hand, with the symbol carved into it.

'That poor woman,' she said. 'She would have felt alone and terrified in her final moments.' She made the Christian sign of the cross, her small fingers dusting her shoulders and forehead.

Stayer reached to take the phone back from her, but she moved it closer to herself. She spoke in a cool voice. 'It's a pagan symbol. The number two crossed over the number four: that represents Jupiter. Jupiter was the god of the sky, or lightning and thunder. Parallel to the Greek god Zeus. Jupiter was the king of all gods and the most important of the gods and goddesses in ancient Rome. The Jupiter symbol has been used for millennia to signify different things. It is also the symbol of Tall Harry.'

Sister Catherine Kelley rose and walked to a bookshelf. From between a *Guinness World Records* and a book about circus freaks, she pulled a small leather tome. Its spine cracked as she opened it. She stopped on a page with an illustration of the Jupiter symbol and showed it to Stayer. It matched the one carved into the skin of the woman murdered in the sandhills, down to the thickness of the lines, the dimensions, the point at which the number four intersected with the number two. It could not have matched closer if someone had traced it.

A bus halted at the stop outside of the apartment building. The sound of hydraulic brakes hissing echoed through the open window.

'This symbol represents Tall Harry,' Sister Catherine said, pointing to the page eagerly. She continued to flick through the book, landing on another page. 'That's him,' she said.

Stayer studied the page. It was yellowed and creased, as though it had been handled many times, for many years, and shown to many people. If he'd had a mouthful of tea in that moment, he might have spat it out.

The page contained a hand-drawn cartoon, Victorian-looking. A ghoulish figure in a crow's mask with talons for hands leaped over a yellow sand dune. Underneath a black cape, it was dressed for the seaside, wearing a striped shirt and sailor's trousers. The figure had long limbs, double the length of human arms, which flailed above its head in a berserk wave. Its mask grinned maniacally, exposing a mouth containing teeth sharpened into points. Though the picture was professionally sketched, the image, a kind of steampunk Freddy Krueger, spoke to Stayer of ghost stories during sleepovers, of kids giggling under blankets, daring each other to say 'Bloody Mary' three times in a mirror.

'*Tall Harry is a monstrous, demonic masked figure over ten feet tall who can leap over tidal waves*,' Stayer read aloud in a leaden voice. '*He breathes blue flames. First sighted in London in the 1820s, where he assaulted a series of women on Clapham Common, he made his way to Australia by convict ship and settled in the Cundra Valley*.'

Sister Catherine handed the book to Stayer, and he flipped through the pages. He saw further illustrations of the creature: baring its claws at a woman wearing a bustle and lace gloves in a park; grabbing a woman from behind in a laneway; flashing a group of girls in old-fashioned school uniforms, with blazers and straw hats. The girls looking shocked and red-cheeked, the demon spreading its cape wide, pictured from the back, supposedly naked underneath, exposing himself.

Stayer employed vast amounts of energy to suppress his laughter. He closed the book, revealing the cover. Its title: *Myths and Legends of the Cundra Valley* by Catherine Kelley.

'When someone dies at the hands of Tall Harry, the death is never explained,' Sister Catherine said evenly. 'There might be signs of violence on the flesh—scratches, bite marks, bruises—but no injuries capable of killing. Their death remains a mystery because he's killed them by sucking their souls out. If Tall Harry has killed this poor woman you found in the sandhills, her death will be unexplained, too. And they're not victims,' she said. 'They're wrongdoers.'

'I'm sorry?'

'The women he attacks, assaults, kills, aren't victims. In his eyes, they have committed some crime, for which he's now dispensing justice.' Stayer could feel himself smiling. The nun looked annoyed. Perhaps also a little amused. 'What is it, detective? Why are you smiling?'

'Next thing you will be offering to show me God.'

'Catholics don't evangelise like that. But I will show you God if you'd like. I'd be very happy to do that.'

Stayer drained the last of his tea. 'I checked you out before I came here,' he said. 'You're a folklore expert.'

The nun peered at him warily. 'Yes. I lecture at a university.'

'You teach a third-year unit called Myths and Legends.'

'A very good course. Thorough.'

'One of the texts you set in that course is the Bible.'

'You seem anxious to make a point, detective.'

'My point? You're calling the Bible a fairytale.'

'Am I? If you say so.'

'Surely you don't sleep well at night knowing you're teaching university students that the text you live your life by is nothing but a myth or legend?'

'I sleep very well, thank you. The secret to good sleep is not to force it. Worrying too much about getting eight hours will make you even more anxious.' She offered him a cool smile. 'I'm sorry to have upset you so.'

'You haven't upset me.' He smiled kindly. 'I've wasted time here, which I could've spent following up legitimate lines of inquiry. Thank you sister, for your time. I must go.'

As Sister Catherine walked him to the door, he heard her muttering under her breath.

Stayer turned to face her. 'What's that?'

'I'm praying,' she replied. 'Saying the rosary for the victims.'

'Victims, plural?'

'Indeed. The present victim, and the future ones. There will be more. Unless he's stopped.'

As he stepped out of the apartment and walked down the stairs, he could just make out the words. *Hail Mary, full of grace, the Lord is with thee . . .*

•

Kicking himself for the time he'd wasted, Stayer drove back to the station. He passed a shopping centre with cars rammed into the surrounding car park. All the disabled spaces were taken, and people had slotted vehicles into 'no parking' zones and even up on the median strip. At first he thought people were stockpiling for the approaching bushfire, buying up water and protein bars. Then a middle-aged man walked back to his SUV, arms laden not with non-perishables but with gift bags, and Stayer realised the true reason, far more mundane and depressing: people were last-minute Christmas shopping.

He was stopped at a red light when his phone buzzed. Dr Dixon. Stayer stabbed the screen to accept the call. 'Doc. What's up?'

'Hello, detective. There's a problem with the cause of death.' His voice was shaky on the speaker phone.

The light went green. The car in front did not move; the driver's head was down. Stayer smacked the horn and steered the squad car into the other lane. 'With the cause of death? What problem?'

'There isn't one.'

8.18 PM

The body had been sent to Solihull, the municipal headquarters of Cundra Valley shire, located inland, away from the beaches and surf clubs. An administrative centre, a bus shelter, and a train station with express services running into the city. Hardworking people of the lower middle class lived here, children who would grow up to be solicitors for insurance companies, sales reps for pharmaceutical companies.

Stayer found Dr Dixon in the examination room. Phoebe Glasson's body lay on the slab, a stainless-steel tray that sloped downwards in the middle. Dr Dixon was resting his back on a counter next to her, staring into space, like a commuter listening to music.

'What's going on, doc? No cause of death?'

The pathologist finally looked. 'I've measured and weighed every organ. The liver, spleen, kidneys, heart, lungs—all normal size, no swelling, no infection. No sign of natural causes, internal causes, like cancer, diabetes.'

'What about trauma?'

Dr Dixon pointed to the face. 'She has bruising around her right eye, consistent with being punched. She also has ligature marks on her wrists and ankles. Scratches on her hands. Bruises on her back. None of these could have killed her.'

'What about the carving on the hand? That's trauma.' Stayer motioned to the Jupiter symbol carved on the inside of the victim's palm.

The pathologist turned his eyes away. 'Again, a surface wound, barely reaching the sub-dermis. Not enough to kill someone elderly, let alone a thirty-year-old in good health.'

'Did we leave her out there too long? Did evidence evaporate in the heat?'

'Possibly. But decent evidence remains. Fluid levels, stomach contents, for example. Both still exist. I don't believe the heat destroyed any conclusive evidence.'

'Exposure then? Dehydration? Like Sergeant Nichols suggested?'

'No. There's a decent fluid balance still present, even for someone who hadn't had much to drink in a day. She didn't die from hyperthermia, either. Hyperthermia disrupts the body's blood balance—it sends blood away from the extremities, causing everything to swell. I would have seen swelling in the outer blood vessels . . .' He was starting to ramble.

'Okay, okay,' Stayer said. 'Could she have been drugged? Or poisoned?'

'Most poisoning marks the organs. The liver and spleen enlarge. The heart swells. But every organ in this case is normal size. The basic toxicology results are already back. Tested for about a hundred compounds, all the usual party drugs, alcohol, pharmaceuticals. She had MDMA, alcohol, and marijuana in her system. No levels high enough to kill. Other drugs like opioids, benzos, the standard drugs you would use to kill someone? Negative. We can order a detailed tox next, but those results can take weeks to arrive. Like I said, though, with the organs the normal size, and no internal signs of poisoning, I must conclude that no earthly cause did this.'

The only sound was a leaf blower outside, the buzz-rumble moving through the walls.

Stayer laughed. 'You're not serious.'

Dr Dixon wiped his brow with a white towel. Cool air pumped from a silver vent in the ceiling but was reaching them only in wisps.

'Okay,' Stayer said. 'Backtrack. You said detailed tox is still to come but could take weeks.'

'Correct.'

'Surely that's the answer. The killer has used an exotic poison, and we'll find out in time.'

'But poisoning marks the organs, there's an inflammatory response—'

'You said *some* poisons mark the organs, right? Others don't? I'm guessing some poisons leave the body quicker than others, and the inflammatory response would have reduced by the time the person died? Would that be fair to say?'

'I suppose.'

'Okay. Wonderful. So, we're agreed: it was probably poison, not the regulars but something spicy, that killed the victim. There will be a cause of death, we just wait.'

'Mmm-hmm,' was all the pathologist could say. He'd resumed staring into space. 'What should I ask them to test for?'

'I'm sorry?'

'For the detailed toxicology. If we order one, we must ask them what to test for. Which poison?'

'Can't you just ask for a detailed tox? Test for everything.'

'No. A detailed toxicology means manual testing using assays, titration, to try and isolate a certain compound in the blood. If the tests were simple, the lab would have performed them the first time. It's trial and error, and it's time consuming. It can take numerous attempts over several days or weeks to isolate a certain poison, and even then, the poison might look like something else. You might be barking up the wrong tree entirely. So you must ask them exactly what "spicy" poison to test for. Any suggestions?'

The air conditioner ticked overhead, like something had caught in the vent.

'What exotic poisons are there?' Stayer said. 'Anthrax? Cyanide?'

Dr Dixon shook his head. 'Those are easy to test for. I already performed them in the simple tox screen. Negative on both counts.'

'How about the poison which killed that Russian spy?'

'Polonium 220?' the pathologist laughed. 'Sure. I'll tell them to get the Geiger counter out. It's not Polonium. If this body were radioactive, we'd all be sick by now. Any other suggestions?'

'I'm sorry. I really couldn't tell you. You're looking a little spooked, doc. You okay?'

'Fine,' Dr Dixon said, straightening himself. 'It's just because I know her.'

'Shall we move on for now?' Stayer asked. 'We can come back to the cause of death. How about time of death?'

'Between two and four o'clock this morning. Something else. See these wounds?' He lifted the victim's hand, the one without the symbol carved into it. He gently turned the wrist, so the palm faced the ceiling of the autopsy room. Small scratches and scabs lined the hand, wrist and fingers, like lines of red ink, looking almost purple against the blue-alabaster skin. 'Developers had marked off the area she was found in, preparing to build ten townhouses there. A barbed wire fence surrounded it on three sides. The wounds on her hands are consistent with the victim climbing that fence.'

'She *climbed* the fence?'

He nodded. 'Yes, and then she walked into the sandhills herself, to the place where she died. And see this . . .' Dr Dixon removed a photo from a folder, which had been resting on the side bench, and handed it to Stayer.

It showed an image taken at the crime scene. Footprints dotted the sand going up and down the hill, like pock marks. 'I counted more than eight hundred individual shoe prints in the vicinity. There's a running club that uses that stretch of sand. Then, see here. A set of footprints running perpendicular to all the others. Those are the victim's footprints going across the top of the sandhill. She walked to the place where she would die.'

Stayer looked closer at the shadowy oval pools running across the sand. 'There are two sets of footprints, doc. Going across the top of the hill. At right angles to all the others. Not one set. Two.'

'Let me see that,' the pathologist said, taking the photo. He held a magnifying glass to the image. He smiled. 'Bugger me. The lighter footprints in front must be those of Phoebe Glasson. The heavier ones behind her—'

'Must belong to the killer.'

Dr Dixon took the photo from Stayer's hands and returned it to the folder. He turned back to Stayer and tossed him a pair of gloves. 'Put these on and help me turn the body. I'm going to grab the shoulder and hip and turn her towards me. Then you hold her steady.'

'Alright,' Stayer said as he put on the gloves. The pathologist did what he said he would, easing one side of the body gently off the steel table. Stayer accepted the body and held it.

'Look at her back,' Dr Dixon said.

Stayer moved around the other side of the table to see. 'Bruises?'

'Yes. Small haematomas around the lower and upper spine. Made by a hand or a stick or pole. I wasn't sure why they were there, now I wonder if she was prodded.'

'The killer made her climb the fence, then pushed her out onto the sandhills.'

They eased the body back onto the tray. A black-framed clock moved its second hand on the wall behind them. 'Why did he make her walk out there?' Stayer said.

Dr Dixon smiled. 'I believe that's your job, detective.'

'This is great work, doc. Don't stress. We'll work out what killed her—together. Could I borrow the victim's face?' he held up Phoebe Glasson's mobile phone.

'Sure,' Dr Dixon replied. 'Face ID?'

'Yep.' Stayer pointed the phone at Phoebe Glasson's face. The phone unlocked, and he was taken to the home screen. He changed the passcode before it locked again.

'I'm going for a diet coke,' the pathologist said. 'Want one?'

'No thanks,' Stayer said. 'I'll go home. Thanks, doc. It will be alright.'

'I love how you say that without a hint of irony,' Dr Dixon said.

A technician entered and nodded politely to Stayer, then drew the sheet back over Phoebe Glasson's body. Light from the window made white squares on the blue cotton, and the victim's knees and nose made small mounds under the sheet. Stayer farewelled the pathologist and hurried home.

•

Night had completely fallen by the time Stayer arrived back at his sister's house. He entered briskly, calling Ruby's name, then remembered she was staying at Aunt Carol's. He allowed himself a moment to stare at her hurricane Christmas tree: dead, stark, and impressive. Then he moved to the kitchen table, pulled out Phoebe Glasson's phone, and opened it.

He went first to her search history. News sites, social media, a few alternative sites. Protest sites. Some angry girl music on her playlist. Fiona Apple. Alanis Morrisette. The kind of music girls had listened to when he was a teenager. The victim had good taste. She seemed intelligent, alternative, unconventional. He halted for a moment when he realised that she seemed like someone who wouldn't fit easily in Thoorgala. Thoorgala was beach, status, looking good in a bikini. These didn't seem like things that interested this woman. He switched to her messaging app and opened the messages between Phoebe and her mother. He quickly worked out why Cassie may have thrown the phone over the fence.

Mother and daughter seemed involved in some sort of online marijuana sales ring, where people accessed the product through the dark web and paid using bitcoin. If he wanted to write Cassie up for drug dealing, he could have formed a solid case.

He closed the messages between the victim and her mother and scrolled down. He paused on another exchange: between Phoebe Glasson and Jackson Millwall. His eyes focused, he recognised the name as Phoebe's ex, the one her mother had mentioned. He opened the conversation and wondered why he had spent so much time on her internet history, and why he hadn't gone directly to this.

> Jackson • 11.32 pm
>
> Stop now or you'll get what's coming to you.
>
> Nasty bitch.

25 DECEMBER

9 AM

'Care to explain?' Stayer said. He held the phone in front of Jackson Millwall.

Jackson had entered the police station wearing a faded fisherman's jumper, torn grey tracksuit pants, and no shoes. His lack of footwear was not a result of poverty or drunkenness; Jackson worked for his father, a bookmaker who had a tote at Randwick Racecourse. Nor was it a fuck you to the police, like, *I'm so disdainful of this process I won't cover my feet.* Rather, it was a branding exercise, advertising him as a local.

Since arriving in Thoorgala a few days ago, Stayer had seen people walking around without shoes on. They would duck from their cars in the main street in tracksuit pants, a t-shirt, and no shoes to purchase bread or withdraw cash from the ATM. It was as if they had collectively resolved not to bother with footwear for local tasks. The dress code was an advertisement: *Paradise is my living room.*

Earlier that morning, Stayer had tailed Jackson as he'd driven to the beach (two minutes from his house) to check the morning surf. He'd gone straight to Jackson's house the previous night, but he wasn't home, and repeated calls to him had gone to voicemail.

He'd returned that morning to find him trudging from the house a little after eight-thirty, looking spectacularly hungover.

Apparently finding the swell too choppy for his liking, Jackson slumped back in the car and drove to the main street, where he'd been about to collect a loaf of gluten-free sourdough from the artisanal bakery—which had opened for a few hours on Christmas Day to dispense pre-orders—when Stayer had invited him down to the station for a chat, the nature of which would match his footwear choice: informal.

The young man had accompanied Stayer freely, if somewhat begrudgingly, asking only that he be allowed to collect his bread from the bakery first. Stayer had agreed, and the loaf now sat on the desk of the interview room. Jackson rested a hand on it, like it was a cat. He'd refused to leave it in his car in case the car grew too hot; humidity would compromise the bread's structure, he explained.

The interview had proceeded with great courtesy on both sides, Stayer apologising for holding Jackson up on Christmas Day and Jackson telling the detective not to worry about it, that he wasn't expected at his parents' house until midday. Jackson had spoken at length about the benefits of a gluten-free diet, and after some gentle probing about his eating and sleeping habits, he diagnosed Stayer with gut permeability. Stayer had listened politely and then, once he was sure the young man was comfortable, he read out the last text Jackson had sent his now-deceased ex-girlfriend Phoebe Glasson.

Jackson stared at him.

'*Stop now or you'll get what's coming to you. Nasty bitch.* You sent this text to your ex-girlfriend,' Stayer said. 'What was coming to her exactly?' Stayer held up Phoebe Glasson's mobile phone again. The screen showed an exchange of furious messages.

'That was banter,' he said. 'We had a tumultuous relationship.'

'So tumultuous that you would hurt her.'

Jackson rolled his eyes. 'You think you're a genius. The ex did it, right. You're like Sherlock Holmes. No you're more like Columbo, with your cheap shoes.'

'At least I'm wearing shoes. And I don't mind being compared to Columbo; he always got his man. You sent abusive texts to your ex-girlfriend—'

'Abusive? That was banter!'

Stayer opened the door to the interview room and called down the hall. 'Constable Walsh?'

After a few seconds, the policeman appeared in the door. 'Detective?'

'There's a book sitting on my desk. Could you bring it in?'

The younger man gave a regimented nod. 'Certainly.'

He exited. Stayer offered Jackson a tight smile.

Walsh returned a few moments later with the book. 'Here you go, detective.'

Constable Walsh remained expressionless as he handed Stayer the book. Stayer had only met him the once, briefly, at Cassie's house, but his calm demeanour spoke of a competent police officer, and Joan had told Stayer he was an excellent cop. Still, Stayer had not seen any evidence of this firsthand, so he couldn't be sure it was the right choice to call him in. But he'd set the ball rolling now, so he proceeded. 'Thanks, Constable Walsh. What's the book's title?'

Constable Walsh looked confused but read the title aloud: '*A People's History of Australian Prisons: Part Two*.'

'Interesting. Do you need to have read part one to get what's happening in part two?' Stayer asked.

'Not really,' Constable Walsh replied, without smiling.

'Open it to the bookmark, please, and read from the top of the page,' Stayer said.

Constable Walsh found the page. '*Silverwater Correctional Complex, otherwise known as Silverwater prison, is one of Australia's most notorious prison facilities. Many of Australia's most violent and infamous murderers, rapists and paedophiles have lived and died within its electrified fences.*'

Stayer held up his hand. 'Thanks, Constable Walsh. Illuminating.' He turned to the shoeless man. 'Do you know what a tariff is, Mr Millwall? In the legal sense?'

'Tariff? What are you talking about?'

'Tariff is the legal term for penalty. The tariff for murder is a custodial sentence. Minimum twenty-five years—automatic. You are thirty-two now, meaning you'll be fifty-seven when you get out. *If* you get out. You'll be going to Silverwater, you see. It's notorious for prisoners killing other prisoners. Can't seem to stop them. No gluten-free bread, either. Your gut will leak everywhere.'

Jackson jumped from his seat. 'I didn't do it! I know how those texts look, but I swear I didn't do it.'

'So why did you send threatening text messages to the victim?'

He sighed loudly. 'I posted some bone broth recipes for paleo babies. Phoebe made a disparaging comment on my socials saying it was harmful to put little kids on a high protein–low carb diet, that we should let babies be babies, other nonsense. She was affecting my brand. I had to make her stop.'

'Paleo babies? Bone broth?'

'We lived for tens of thousands of years as cavemen, dude. Babies too. Didn't do them any harm. Can I go now?'

'Not even close. Where were you between seven pm on the twenty-third of December and six am on the twenty-fourth?'

'At home, watching TV.'

'A neighbour says they saw you leave your house at seven. You weren't at home watching TV—you were out kidnapping and killing your ex-girlfriend.'

Jackson froze. The pedestal fan that had been transported from Stayer's office to the interview room blew a warm wind, lifting Jackson's blond fringe off his forehead. 'Look. Phoebe was a cool girl, and I'm genuinely sorry she's dead, but don't go around pretending like she was this innocent little thing. I'm saying she had a past, man. Like, a proper past. She did something when she was a kid. She never talked about it with me, but there were always whispers. You'll have spoken to her mum by now, right? Well, you've seen where Phoebe came from. It's no surprise where she ended up.'

The figure of Cassie came to him, sitting on the porch of her derelict house, smoking one joint after the other.

'Give us your alibi, Mr Millwall.'

Silence.

'Mr Millwall?'

Still the man said nothing.

Stayer nodded to Constable Walsh, and he resumed reading. '*Silverwater Maximum Security hosts four blocks, A, B, C and D . . .*'

Stayer stifled the urge to smile.

'Fine!' Jackson said. 'I'll tell you whatever you want to know. Just please—stop talking about prison.'

'Your alibi,' Stayer said. 'You left your house at seven on the night Phoebe Glasson died. You said that you were watching TV at home, that is a lie. You were somewhere else.'

'Yes. I'm not proud of it.'

Stayer's phone rang on the table, skidding sideways with the buzzing. It was Sergeant Nichols. He flinched, annoyed at the interruption. He cancelled the call.

'Mr Millwall? What are you not proud of?'

He waited. Constable Walsh, still standing at the door, crossed his huge arms over his chest. Jackson swallowed. A car with loud brakes squealed somewhere outside.

Footsteps were coming down the hallway; Joan from reception appeared. She beckoned Stayer over urgently.

Stayer rose reluctantly. He met Joan in the doorway.

'It's Sergeant Nichols, boss. She's been trying to reach you.'

'I know, Joan. I'll call the sergeant back soon,' he said, annoyed. 'I'm in the middle of interviewing a suspect—'

'Triple zero patched through a call to me this morning,' Joan said. 'Sergeant Nichols checked it out. On the sandhills. Another body's been found.'

10 AM

They moved along the rough-sealed road which led to the Cundra sandhills. Loose rocks and chunks of bitumen crackled under their wheels. Constable Walsh flicked the wheel deftly to avoid a pothole then pulled into the car park.

Stayer trudged up the sandhill for a second time. Constable Walsh moved briskly beside him, looking unbothered by the steep ascent. When they reached the top, they found the pathologist and an assistant already waiting there with Sergeant Nichols, the three of them gathered around the body. Like Phoebe Glasson, the dead woman was fully clothed and lying on her back. She had medium-length brown hair, an average build. Appeared to be in her early thirties.

'I know this woman, too,' Dr Dixon said. 'Not well, but she's local. Her parents work for the fisheries. They're marine biologists.'

The waves boomed in the distance like a thunderstorm.

'No seaweed covering her face,' Dr Dixon continued. 'And no cunjevoi in her hand.' He pointed to the various body parts. The woman's face looked up at them. 'But this is the same,' the pathologist said, squatting and pointing with the end of a ballpoint pen. Stayer crouched with him and looked to the place he indicated.

'Righto,' Stayer said, wiping his brow.

The Jupiter symbol had been carved on the woman's thigh.

'There's also a note, like on Phoebe Glasson.' Dr Dixon handed Stayer a plastic evidence bag, and he peered at the note inside.

She refused to confess. She had to die.
Make the others confess or they die too.

TH

'TH. Tall Harry,' Constable Walsh said.

A seagull flew overhead, hovering, helicopter-like. Its body and outstretched wings sending a shadow over the victim.

'"Thoorgala" means "devil", did you know?' Dr Dixon said. 'In Dharawal—the local Aboriginal language.' Everyone turned to him. No one spoke. 'Almost forgot,' Dr Dixon said, looking at Stayer. 'Merry Christmas.'

'Merry Christmas,' Stayer replied.

•

Dr Dixon slid the body into the refrigerated van and drove off. The back wheels sprayed hot sand onto Stayer's trousers, like shrapnel.

Sergeant Nichols joined Stayer. 'I'm off for two nights, boss. Going up north to see family.'

'Oh.' The words caught Stayer off guard.

'I can stay if you need me,' she said. 'The leave was approved before you started. But I can postpone my trip. Help with this case.'

'Nonsense, sergeant,' Stayer said to Sergeant Nichols. 'It's Christmas Day. You should go and be with your family. Enjoy yourself.' He recalled the image of Sergeant Nichols dropping the body of the first victim, and her silence just now in the presence of the second, and wondered how much of an asset she really was.

'Merry Christmas, boss,' she said and started walking back to the squad car.

'Nichols,' he called after her, 'wait.'

She stopped walking and turned back to him. He jogged over, knees still aching from the second climb up the dune. 'You grew up in Thoorgala, correct?'

She nodded. Her lean frame cut a sharp and tidy shape in the sunlight. 'But I moved away after high school. Studied policing at Goulburn then moved north of the city. I only came back six months ago.' Some alarm beeped on her triathlete's watch. She silenced it with her thumb.

'How would you characterise the town?'

'Characterise it, boss?' She gave him a curious look, like he'd just asked her to tell a knock-knock joke.

'Yeah. Like how you would describe the nature, or the mood. The *feel* of it. I've just arrived here and it's not what I expected.'

'What did you expect?' Sergeant Nichols asked, looking amused.

Stayer shrugged. 'Paradise?' He laughed.

Sergeant Nichols laughed too, but her laugh had bite to it.

The sergeant turned to watch the crashing surf. Finally, she nodded, as though the waves had inspired her to speak her mind. 'Everyone thinks of Thoorgala as this stunning place. But I would characterise Thoorgala as an angry man whose best years were in high school.'

Stayer smiled. 'I think you might be a poet, sergeant. So why did you come back?'

'Pardon me?'

'If you think of Thoorgala as a cranky, has-been place, why did you come back? Why not live somewhere you like?'

She paused.

'I never said I didn't like Thoorgala,' she said at last. 'Thoorgala is my home. I grew up here.'

She went into some private space again and stared at the green water once more.

'Thoorgala doesn't mean devil, by the way,' Sergeant Nichols called after Stayer as he turned to walk away. 'What Dr Dixon said. Common misconception. It is a Dharawal word, but it doesn't mean devil.'

'You seem to know a lot about it.'

'I do,' she said with a proud shrug. 'I'm a Dharawal woman.'

Stayer nodded an apology, cursing himself for his ignorance. 'What does Thoorgala mean, then?'

She smiled. 'It just means man.'

Stayer laughed. 'I see. One last thing, before you go. What do you think of all this about Tall Harry? You're familiar with the guy?'

'Sure,' Sergeant Nichols said. 'Great fun at slumber parties. We'd dare each other to say his name three times. Bang a broom on the window: "It's Tall Harry trying to get in!" Piss your pants from laughter. And fear.'

'People in this town don't actually believe it, right?'

'Of course not. It's an urban legend. Like Bigfoot or the Loch Ness Monster. Although I sure as hell wouldn't say his name three times in a row, not if you paid me. Merry Christmas, boss. See you in two days.'

12.30 PM

Stayer drove wearily along a road that snaked around the headland of Thoorgala peninsula, failing to think of any task less favourable in a police officer's repertoire than the one he was about to undertake. Constable Walsh had accompanied Dr Dixon to the morgue with the body, so he would be performing the task alone.

He pulled up in front of a tasteful pre-war home and walked up a garden path lined with potted ferns. He knocked on the door and a tall, barrel-chested man answered. He had a bushy beard, golden in colour but flecked with grey. Stayer watched the man's face fall as his eyes took in the stranger on his porch and the police squad car parked on the street in the background.

'What's happened?' the man said, his eyes already wet with tears. He spoke in a Scandinavian accent.

Stayer asked if he could come inside, and the man silently, compliantly, waved him in and showed him into a lounge room. He offered Stayer a seat, and the detective took it. Then Stayer explained to the man and his wife—a tall, brown-haired woman with darting eyes who had appeared from the kitchen—that their daughter was dead, initiating them into that special club no one wanted to join, for parents who would outlive their child.

What followed was thirty to forty minutes of what Stayer knew they would only remember in years to come in flashes: words, phrases, and images. Stayer told them where their daughter was found and when, and that the death was being treated as suspicious. A family friend was summoned to the house from a neighbouring town.

A Christmas tree stood in the corner of the lounge room, decorated in the European style, with real candles in thin brass holders. It was an immigrant's home, with the furniture and decor of the old country everywhere: tasteful mid-century wooden furniture, a painting of a fjord, a tapestry of red and blue threads forming owls, foxes and flowers. Among these tokens of their homeland were mementoes which spoke to their new lives and work in Australia: a hand-drawn illustration of a fish skeleton, photos of husband and wife in wetsuits standing atop rocks on the Thoorgala shoreline. Seashells dotted the shelves and windowsills. A giant shark's tooth rested on top of an upright piano, opaque and brilliant white.

Bill Sorgensen explained to Stayer how he and his wife had come to Australia to work at the fisheries, which had been conducting research into the marine algae that was prevalent in the area. They fell in love with Thoorgala, and ended up taking permanent positions at the fisheries as biologists. They had Mikaela sometime later and had raised her here.

'We knew something must have happened,' the father said, after all the details had been conveyed, and many dreadful, stinging tears had been shed, and Stayer had accepted his second cup of tea. Mr Sorgensen had insisted Stayer call him Bill. His Swedish accent was thick, but he spoke in a clipped, refined English, without error. 'We were due at a friend's place for Christmas lunch, and Mikaela was supposed to come here first. We expected her at around nine. I must have left twenty messages on her phone.' Bill sniffed and wiped his nose with his shirtsleeve. His wife, Sabina, wept softly beside him, dabbing her eyes with a balled-up tissue.

Stayer was shown pictures of Mikaela as a child, grinning in brown corduroy overalls; as a teenager standing on rocks by the sea, holding up a large fish. Mikaela blowing out birthday candles on a cake with pink icing, her parents either side, pretending to blow as well, eyes wide and filled with joy. The sadness in the room was like a vapour. The treachery of life.

It occurred to Stayer that the warm decor, stylish fittings, and exclusive location out on the Thoorgala headland could not have differed more from the squalid childhood home of Phoebe Glasson. It was hard to imagine a connection between the two women, let alone one that had seen them both murdered and branded with the same symbol.

He showed the drawing of the symbol that he'd sketched in his notebook to the Sorgensens, asked the same questions about cults and religious sects that he'd asked of Cassie. They shook their heads in the same incredulous way as Phoebe's mother had.

Stayer told them about the note found on their daughter. 'Do you have any idea about what the killer meant? What he might have wanted Mikaela to confess to?'

Husband and wife looked baffled.

Stayer gingerly brought up the charges for civil disobedience laid against Mikaela, which had resulted in two-thousand-dollar fines but no custodial sentences. Bill and Sabina Sorgensen smiled wanly.

'Miki took part in protests against a Japanese whaling company that was seeking a licence to fish in Australia,' Sabina said. 'She has a criminal record for saving whales.'

Stayer asked the pair to describe their daughter and saw them almost wince in pain as they painted a picture of a young woman who was intelligent and kind, always willing to help others. As a child she had taken in stray animals—injured swamp hens, mangy cats from the back alleys behind Thoorgala's restaurants, sick penguins rescued from rocks. Bill and Sabina had indulged her, applauding her sense of duty and empathy, and helping wherever they could to rehouse the animals and quietly euthanising the ones beyond help. Bill's faced glowed, and for a moment he seemed to revel in his recollections, as if Stayer had given him leave to escape there, back to a time when Mikaela was still alive. His face only darkened when it came to talking about Mikaela as a teenager. 'She was bullied in high school,' he said.

Sabina said something sharply to her husband in Swedish and clutched his arm.

Bill replied to her in English, presumably for Stayer's benefit. 'He needs to hear this, Sabi. It may help with the investigation.'

He looked hopefully to Stayer, who nodded for him to continue.

Bill detailed how, on one occasion, milk was poured into Mikaela's schoolbag, ruining textbooks and assignments. Her lunch, often rye bread sandwiches or rollmops, frequently ended up stomped into the asphalt of the playground or smeared across the windows of the girls' toilets.

Bill shook his head. 'It was a mistake sending her to Thoorgala Grammar.'

Stayer's gaze sharpened. 'Your daughter attended Thoorgala Grammar? Did she know Phoebe Glasson?'

Bill and Sabina looked at each other. 'They were best friends in high school,' Bill said.

Stayer straightened. 'Do you have any photos?'

'Maybe,' Bill said, looking to his wife. Sabina had already risen from the couch and was walking to a bookshelf. She located a photo album, flicking through it. She paused on a page. Presented it to Stayer.

Two teenage girls wearing private school uniforms grinned to the camera, arms around each other's shoulders. It took Stayer a moment to process the youthful faces and different hairstyles, but finally he could see that they were Phoebe Glasson and Mikaela Sorgensen. They wore the starched uniforms of Thoorgala Grammar, but both styled their outfits with alternative flourishes: kohl-lined eyes, loosened ties. With their defiant and punkish stares, they looked like outsiders.

'They didn't really fit in around here,' Bill said. 'Why do you ask about Phoebe?'

'Phoebe Glasson was murdered,' Stayer replied shakily. 'Yesterday. Out on the sandhills. Same as your daughter.'

The middle-aged couple reeled. Waves collapsed into the rocks on the shoreline outside the front windows, thunderous and piercing.

Stayer drifted to the other photos on the page. He froze.

'What is it?' Bill said.

'I think that's my sister,' Stayer said. He pointed. It was difficult to tell, as it was a teenage face staring back at him, and taken too far away to make out clearly, but Stayer could just make out the features of Ruby in a smallish-looking girl, smiling softly, standing in school uniform at the entrance gates to Thoorgala Grammar.

'Ruby Stayer is your sister?' Sabina said.

Stayer nodded.

'Miki was friends with her, too.'

•

//Thoorgala. A sandy corner of the internet to discuss all things God's country

HaroldBishop • 12.33 pm

So you're Tall Harry, then?

TallHarry • 12.36 pm

As the name suggests.

HaroldBishop • 12.40 pm

And you committed the murder in the sandhills?

TallHarry • 12.41 pm

I did.

Snookus52 • 12.44 pm

Forgive us if we seem incredulous, bro. Perhaps you could prove it in some way?

TallHarry • 12.44 pm

If you insist. How?

MaryCronin • 12.52 pm

This is disgusting. We shouldn't be talking like this. A woman has died.

HaroldBishop • 12.52 pm

Tell us something only the murderer would know.

MaryCronin • 12.53 pm

Is anyone listening to me?

TallHarry • 12.57 pm

The woman has my mark on her.

Snookus52 • 12.57 pm

Sorry dude. Everyone knows that.

HaroldBishop • 12.58 pm

My dog knows that. Wouldn't shut up about it.

TallHarry • 12.58 pm

The woman refused to admit her crime before she died. Neither did the second one.

MaryCronin • 1.01 pm

Who? There's been a second victim?

HaroldBishop • 1.01 pm

What crime?

2 PM

Stayer stepped back in the squad car and dialled Ruby's number. It went to voicemail. The steaming air of the car engulfed him, stinging his ears, dampening his armpits. He turned the engine on and flicked the air conditioning to maximum, but did not drive away. He stared out the windscreen at the waves colliding with the rocks. His phone rang. It was Dr Dixon.

'What is it, doc?'

'No cause of death again, detective. Mikaela Sorgensen is the same as Phoebe Glasson.'

•

Stayer arrived at the morgue in Solihull. 'We only retrieved the body four hours ago. Why are the results for Mikaela Sorgensen so much faster than for Phoebe?'

'Because I know what I'm looking for now,' Dr Dixon said. 'And everything's the same.' He sat perched on the bench behind the steel gurneys in the autopsy room. Sunlight streamed in through the high windows, bathing the room in rude white light. Mikaela Sorgensen's body lay on the centre steel tray, a blue sheet covering her. The pathologist shook his head. 'Quick bloods reveal nothing. Detailed tox will take several weeks, as you know. No trauma sufficient to cause death. No sexual assault, no semen, no genital trauma. No evidence of drugs or poisons inside the body. No apparent underlying medical conditions. There are bruises on her back again, and wounds on her hands consistent with climbing a barbed wire fence.'

'The killer made her walk out onto the sand again.'

'Correct. She was alive on the sandhills. The killer left her there to die.'

A snap followed by a cheer rose up from a room down the hall. Stayer had seen hospital staff at the nurses' station further along the corridor pulling Christmas crackers, exchanging gifts.

Stayer looked down at his phone and noticed he had seven missed calls from Aunt Carol. He stared at his screen and shuddered. It was the middle of the afternoon on Christmas Day. He was supposed to be at Carol's place for lunch, gifts and backyard cricket.

Stayer turned to Dr Dixon. 'What are your plans for Christmas Day, doc? Expected at a turkey-laden table somewhere?'

Dr Dixon shrugged. 'Not me. The kids are at my ex-wife's family for Christmas lunch.'

Stayer nodded softly. 'How old are your children?'

'Three and five. Two boys. Riley and Danny.' His voice choked as he said their names. Stayer glimpsed the pathologist afresh, his big tummy, his smile strained with emotion. 'Don't mind being called out to work. Something to do.'

'You're welcome to come for lunch at my Aunt Carol's place,' Stayer said. 'She's not really my aunt,' he added, unsure why. 'Me and my sister are going.'

'Nah. Thanks. I want to finish up some paperwork here, maybe run a few more tests. I'll call you if I find anything.' His face was pained, he looked distracted.

'I had a thought about spicy poisons to ask for, in the detailed toxicology request,' Stayer said.

Dr Dixon turned to him. 'Okay.'

'It's not the name of the poison we're interested in, but what it does, right? We're looking for a poison that killed slowly, allowing enough time for the two victims to walk out onto the sandhills before they died. By the time they'd died, the substance had largely left their bodies, to the point that it didn't show up in simple toxicology.'

'Correct,' Dr Dixon said.

'What poison fits this description? A poison which kills slowly, leaves little to no trace, and can't be tested for with simple toxicology. We can ask the lab to test for it.' He looked at the pathologist hopefully.

'A poison that kills slowly, then leaves the body, so it doesn't show up on tests. I know it.'

'Terrific! What's it called?'

'It's called: *the perfect poison*,' Dr Dixon said. 'It doesn't exist.'

2.32 PM

Before he drove to Aunt Carol's house, Stayer sat in the car and rang the superintendent, a brusque man in his mid-fifties who ran the police division for the region from a head office a couple of towns over.

'Hello, sir,' he said, when the man answered on the sixth ring, 'my name is Detective Stayer. This is my second day working in Thoorgala, I was previously in the city—'

'I know who you are,' the super interrupted. He sounded irritated. The noises of a jolly lunch were audible in the background. Glasses chinking, laughter, the excitable voices of children. 'What can I do for you?'

Stayer explained about the two murders on the sandhills. The symbol, the notes, the rumours. The lack of resources. 'I'm sorry to call you on Christmas Day, but I need help. At least three detectives, sergeants minimum. I let one of my cops go up north to visit family—'

'Why did you do that?'

Stayer rubbed his eyes. 'A move I'm now regretting. I'm investigating a suspected serial killer basically on my own.'

'I'm working on it,' the police chief replied gruffly. 'Give me a couple of days. And it's not a serial killer. You need three for a serial killer.'

Stayer couldn't believe what he was hearing. 'Two women are dead and you need a couple of days? I mean, I know it's the holidays, but—'

'It's not because of Christmas,' the superintendent said. 'There's a manhunt to stop the firebug from setting more of the state alight. An area of land larger than England is already burning. They're calling it another Black Christmas.'

'I know. Call in the AFP, maybe?'

The chief sighed. 'Gee, I never thought of that. You should have my job. The feds are looking for the firebug, too. Sorry.' His voice brightened. 'In the meantime, you have a potential detective at your disposal already. Constable Walsh.' He paused, sparking Stayer's intrigue. 'I know what you're going to say. Yes, he's only a constable. But he's very keen, and he's already studied case management and investigative techniques.' A wounded cry of a child rang out in the background, and the chief shushed them.

'I didn't know that. He wants to be a detective?'

'Sure does. Give him a chance.'

'Okay,' Stayer said. 'But I need proper detectives soon . . . You've hung up, haven't you?'

He had. Stayer groaned.

He dialled Constable Walsh's phone. He answered immediately. 'Boss. What's up?'

Stayer explained the situation. The understaffing, the lack of investigative help, the increasingly precarious situation. 'How would you like to step up to acting detective? This is your "dare to be great" opportunity.'

Constable Walsh laughed generously. 'Boss, I'm honoured. But I don't think I'm ready. If I'm honest, this case scares me.'

A middle-aged couple walked across the street in front of the squad car, carrying gifts wrapped in red paper and gold ribbon. They checked their hair and adjusted their clothes before ringing the doorbell of a house next to the hospital. Stayer turned around to look at Ruby's Christmas present on the back seat. It was perfume, purchased from an upmarket department store, on the sales assistant's recommendation. He feared she would hate it, with its sleek glass bottle and gold cap announcing he didn't know his sister at all. 'It scares you. Why?'

'Two women dead,' Constable Walsh said. 'Both climbed a fence and walked out onto the sandhills. This guy is leaving notes and symbols. He's smart. And we've got no leads.'

'Exactly why I need your help, Constable. I agree with everything you said, except one part. Don't call this guy smart. Crooks are far dumber than we make them out be. Their stupidity will astound you. No criminal masterminds, no tortured geniuses. Most people who end up in cells have some form of Antisocial Personality Disorder. They lack empathy and have issues with impulse control, violence and aggression. IQ usually less than ninety. Your ultimate nightmare would be to sit next to them on a long-haul flight.'

'You think this killer is like that?'

'I'd put money on it. Help me catch him?'

'Okay,' Constable Walsh said after a long pause. 'But please, get more help as well, boss. Someone who knows about the symbols.'

'I'll do my best.'

•

Stayer pulled up to Aunt Carol's house: a double-storey, stately home with whitewashed walls like a Spanish hacienda. Old-money Thoorgala. A voluptuous frangipani sprawled across the front yard, its fallen white flowers smothering the grass below. He would poke his head in, wish everyone happy Christmas, give Ruby her present, then make an excuse to leave.

He walked inside and found Carol standing in the hallway, as if to greet him. But she did not wish him Merry Christmas, or embrace him, instead looked past him to the door he'd just walked through.

'Where's Ruby?' she said.

He gave her a confused look. 'She isn't here? I thought she was with you.'

'She's not here. We've called you many times.' She looked frantic.

'I've come straight from work. Ruby told me she was staying with you last night.'

'She didn't! I assumed she'd decided to come with you at lunchtime instead. She missed a hair appointment as well. She said she would meet me at the salon.'

'You didn't call her when she didn't show?'

'Of course I called her!' she snapped, voice straining. 'She didn't answer. I just thought she was mad at me.' Her eyes darted furtively.

Stayer glanced past Carol and saw maybe ten or twelve people seated at an elegantly laid table in the dining room off the hallway. Guests in linen dresses and pearls, chinos and loafers. Turkey and roasted potatoes on silver trays, champagne fizzing in glasses.

'Maybe she went for a run?' Stayer offered feebly.

'On Christmas Day?' Aunt Carol looked outraged. She glanced at her guests, as if to check whether they'd heard.

Of course they had: every pair of eyes was trained on her and Stayer; they were hanging on every word, their expressions concerned and intrigued.

Carol's own face was ashen now. 'Something's happened to her.'

Stayer softened his voice. 'She's probably just at home,' he said. 'I'll go get her.'

•

Stayer returned to the squad car and drove seven minutes to the other side of Thoorgala and pulled up in front of the beach shack at the end of the cul-de-sac.

It dawned on him as he approached the house that he hadn't seen Ruby in over twenty-four hours. And if she hadn't spent the night at Aunt Carol's like she'd said, that meant she hadn't been seen by anyone in more than a day. He crept up the steps leading to the front door and for some reason—call it instinct—drew his handgun.

The door was locked. He opened it with his key and entered, clearing the fibro-walled rooms one by one.

Ruby wasn't there. He didn't know whether to be worried or annoyed. He tried her phone. As it rang, he heard a buzzing. He followed the sound into the kitchen. He must have missed it before, as it was tucked away slightly, nestled between a jar of freeze-dried coffee granules and the wall. But there it was, Ruby's phone, vibrating.

3.01 PM

The home screen of Ruby's phone was a Renaissance painting, *View of Delft* by Vermeer. It was *very* famous, apparently. But Stayer only knew its name by accident.

His sister had scrutinised the original for an inordinate time in a gallery in The Netherlands. They had been there together, meeting up for three weeks while they both backpacked through Europe. Stayer had just retired from swimming; Ruby had graduated uni. They had found themselves both planning European trips separately, and in the rare moments when they had spoken to each other as young adults, they realised they would be in Europe at the same time. Stayer had been quietly excited, hoping this would bring them closer. As it turned out, it had driven them further apart, and it had been mostly down to that painting.

View of Delft hung in a gallery they'd stumbled upon in The Hague. Ruby had sat on the little leather-topped bench they put in front of the artworks and refused to leave. She spent over an hour this way, in silence, almost catatonic, staring at that painting of old buildings on a riverbank, brushing off Stayer's suggestions to move on, get coffee, see the rest of the city.

He'd finally left her, exasperated, and went and got a terrible cappuccino, walked the city, pounding the pavement in too-tight shoes, looking in shops he didn't care about, buying nothing. He'd returned as the gallery was closing, and found her still staring at the painting, in almost the exact same position he'd left her, ultimately leaving only when the guard asked her.

'What were you doing?' he asked her sharply as they were escorted out. He regretted his tone, further spoiling their time together. 'We've wasted almost the whole day.'

She'd started crying and they spent the rest of the day not speaking. Finally, lying in bunks in their threadbare hostel, in the darkness, she'd told him, 'I was trying to work out how he made the light do that.'

'Who?' Stayer had replied, still mulling over the day.

'Vermeer. The artist. That's why I was staring at that painting.'

He'd nodded in the semi-dark, watching the cracks in the water damaged ceiling above him. 'Did you work it out?'

'No.' She'd cried again, small, shuddering sobs in the blackness. He could feel her body shaking in the bunk underneath him. He'd tried to say things to comfort her, suggesting she would work it out, as she was very clever and talented, a great artist, things he didn't know for sure but thought were the right things to say. She eventually cried herself to sleep. Her behaviour had terrified him a little, the sobbing, then the silences, over something that seemed insignificant to him. A ferocious little storm, unpredictable and illogical. In the morning she'd showed up at breakfast fresh-faced and calm, like nothing had happened, and Stayer tried never to think about that horrible afternoon.

On their final day together, wandering through a cathedral in Madrid, he saw that she'd changed the home screen on her phone to that very painting, Vermeer's *View of Delft*. She'd caught him looking, noticing the phone, and for the rest of the day, she seemed to follow him around, as though she wanted to tell him something. Every nave he walked into, every stained-glass window he looked up at, she would be there, standing next to him, mouth open, as though she had something to say. It pained him to think of it, but he had avoided her. He'd feared she would start crying uncontrollably again, and he couldn't handle another scene. He'd made some excuse about feeling unwell and left the church, then wandered the city on his own until it was time to catch his flight home. He'd left Europe without seeing her again, without saying goodbye, just sending her a text from the airport after he cleared border control. She hadn't replied. They had barely spoken since.

It shocked him to see she still had the same photo as her home screen, even now, probably multiple phones later. The picture of the old buildings in Delft faded to shadow on Ruby's phone, as his call to her went to voicemail. '*Leave a message*,' his sister instructed in a dull voice, as though a message was the last thing she wanted.

He hung up without saying anything, his mind speeding up a little. Then his own phone buzzed, an incoming call. He raised it to his ear.

'Matt, it's Aunt Carol.'

She insisted on calling herself that, his aunt, even though it was long established between them that she was no biological relation, and they did not have the type of relationship where she would be called aunt in an affectionate way either.

'Have you found Ruby?' she asked.

His mouth opened, waiting for his brain to tell him what to say. 'I haven't.'

'She's missing,' Carol said. 'I knew it.'

'She's not missing, Carol. She's just not currently present.' He wondered if he sounded as unconvincing to her ears as to his own. 'I'm at her house,' he said, attempting a casual tone and almost achieving it, 'and her phone's on the bench.'

Carol's breathing was ragged. 'I see. And when was the last time you saw her?'

'Yesterday morning, before I left for work. She was decorating the Christmas tree.' He swallowed, aware how this sounded.

'*Yesterday morning?* You haven't seen your sister in over twenty-four hours, and today is Christmas Day, and yet you don't think she's missing?'

'I thought she was with you! I thought she stayed at your house last night. That was the plan.'

'Well, that plan didn't eventuate!' Her voice had risen now, shrill and panicked. Stayer had never heard her like this.

'Let's all calm down,' Stayer said. 'I'm sure there's an explanation.' He tried to think of one, many images and sounds going through his mind, none of them good, the possible connection between Ruby and Phoebe and Mikaela growing harder to disregard.

'She's missing! That's the only explanation. I warned her this would happen, Matt,' she said, almost growling. Stayer was stunned. Some wall had come down to reveal a truer Carol: not the calm, well-turned-out woman who never raised her voice, but a more brutal, angry, tearful version. 'I told her she shouldn't have come back to Thoorgala. She left for good reason. Now look what's happened.'

Before he could reply, she hung up the phone.

3.18 PM

Stayer punched in his password. The computer beeped and a window appeared, announcing an error. 'Come on,' he said loudly.

'Everything alright, detective?' Joan was in the doorway to his office, wearing a Santa hat and a necklace fashioned from tinsel. 'I didn't see you come in.'

She hadn't seen him enter the station because he'd snuck in, slipping past her at reception when she'd turned her back to answer the phone. He hadn't wanted anyone to see what he was doing. He just wanted to keep it to himself for now. He couldn't bring himself to answer if anyone asked what he was doing. He was investigating a possible serial killer. His sister was possibly missing. He felt too stunned to connect those two thoughts. 'It's saying I'm using an incorrect password. It's kicked me off the system.'

Joan walked over. 'You typed in the password I wrote down for you?'

'Been using the same one all day. Suddenly it's not working.' He typed in the password Joan had written out for him. Hit enter. The same error message appeared. 'See?'

'I'm no Bill Gates, but I think you typed eight instead of an asterisk at the end. Try again. Hold shift this time.'

He protested, then checked the note she'd written for him, and checked the keyboard. He did as she suggested.

'Open sesame,' Joan said with a smile. Her eyes narrowed as she read the document on the screen. 'What are you doing, detective? Can I give you a hand?'

'I'm trying to issue a KALOF,' he muttered. 'For my sister.'

Joan looked shocked. 'You're issuing a Keep a Look Out For notice for your sister?'

He nodded sheepishly.

'Your sister is missing?'

'I think so. Yes.'

'How long has she been gone?'

'Around twenty-four hours. Maybe more.'

'My god. It's Christmas Day.' She was viewing him with pity, and a new curiosity.

'What's going on?' a new voice said.

Stayer looked up to see Constable Walsh and groaned to himself. This was exactly what he hadn't wanted.

'The detective's sister is missing,' Joan said. 'He's issuing a Keep a Look Out For.'

Constable Walsh turned to Stayer and offered an expression very similar to Joan's: confusion, compassion, curiosity. He ran a hand through his shiny black hair. 'Shit, boss. I'm sorry.'

'She's only been gone since yesterday,' Stayer said, trying to sound breezy, casual. 'I'm sure she'll turn up.' He had no idea why he said this. He just wanted them both to stop staring at him. 'She will turn up.'

Joan touched his shoulder. 'You think your sister has come to harm?'

Stayer responded sharply. 'Nothing's happened to her. I'm not even sure I should be submitting a Keep a Look Out For.'

Joan nodded diplomatically. 'You haven't completed her date of birth,' she said, motioning to the screen. 'The year is missing.'

'I was coming back to that,' Stayer said sheepishly. 'I have to work it out.'

Joan's voice was kind. 'No problem. How old is she?'

'Thirty, I think. Yes, thirty.' He swallowed as he recalled the birthday party invitation she'd sent him, the half-arsed excuse he'd made not to come.

'Year of birth would be 1995, then,' Joan said.

Stayer thanked her silently and typed the numbers in.

'Her middle name? That's blank too,' Joan said.

'I really don't know that one,' Stayer said, keeping his eyes on the screen.

'No matter. You can file without it.'

'You haven't finalised it—you have to click through to the next page, boss.' Constable Walsh stood over Stayer and pointed at the screen.

People were now asking him things about Ruby, simple, important things, which he should know the answer to, such as her year of birth, her middle name. These could be explained away, as the muddling of an unsentimental, forgetful older brother. Harder to justify were the other things he didn't know, things like her relationships, her friends, her hopes and dreams. Thank god the KALOF did not ask for those things, for they would be left horribly, damningly blank. They had no in-jokes, like other siblings had, no shared stories, no warm memories. All their memories were strangled, and hurtful, and included one sibling turning away from the other.

'I've submitted the form, boss,' Constable Walsh announced, tapping the keyboard for him. 'Sent out to all units.'

'You'll find her, detective,' Joan said, smiling encouragingly. 'The Keep a Look Out For will do the trick.'

Stayer told his colleagues he would go home and promised to call them immediately if he heard anything, they promised the same. Their concerned looks and pitying smiles followed him out of the station.

4.18 PM

He returned to Ruby's beach shack. He went through each room again and established definitively that she was still gone. He called Carol. She answered on the second ring.

'Matt, what's happened?' Her voice sounded urgent, desperate.

'I was calling to see if you'd heard from Ruby.'

'No, I haven't heard from her,' she snapped. 'It's Christmas Day, Matt. Where is she?'

Stayer put a hand to his brow.

They discussed some other places she might have gone: running along the headland, or out by the national park, or along the dirt track by the main road—places Stayer only knew of faintly and had never visited, though apparently Ruby had spent hours, days there. She might have tripped and injured herself and was waiting for someone to find her. Then Carol started sobbing and Stayer could no longer understand what she was saying. He assured her the Keep a Look Out For notice would do its job, that every police officer in the state now had the notice with Ruby's photo and a physical description and her last known whereabouts, but his words were drowned out by her howling. She told him she had to lie down, and hung up on him.

Stayer considered calling her back, but he had nothing to say. So instead he climbed back in the squad car and drove out to the Esplanade, the stretch of pedestrian path that ran around the headland, a place they had just spoken of, and walked from one end to the other. This took him a little over two hours. The ocean that sprayed his face felt warm, like sweat.

Stayer and Ruby's mother had died from ovarian cancer when Stayer was four. Stayer remembered her soft blonde hair and a song about a train whistle blowing that she used to sing. Ruby, one year old at the time, remembered nothing. They were raised by their father. Critical, narcissistic, but worst of all, in a practical sense, a gambling addict, with all the awful and banal details that accompany that. One week there would be furniture, the next week none. Gary Stayer wouldn't turn up to school functions after promising to. He hit Stayer a couple of times, and got a new partner who didn't like the kids very much. Stayer concluded that the only way to find happiness was to get out of there. He was accepted to the Australian Institute of Sport at thirteen. Then he heard in a letter that Ruby had gone to Thoorgala Grammar on an art scholarship. They had written occasionally to each other, in friendly and awkward emails and letters, but then something happened. Sometime before the end of high school, Ruby had decided she wasn't going to communicate with Stayer anymore. The letters stopped; calls weren't returned. Ruby didn't come home for Christmas and holidays. Stayer almost forgot what she looked like. At a guess, he would say Ruby had never forgiven him for abandoning her when she was ten, for leaving her with their father in that awful house. They'd seen each other only a handful of times since high school, with the disastrous trip to Europe being one, their father's funeral another.

He mulled this over as he rounded the headland, staring into the dark water. He found no sign of Ruby, so he drove to the running track in the national park, another place where his sister had apparently liked to run. The sharp, dry scrub scratched his trousers, and his shoes slipped on the packed gravel track. He searched for another two hours there, but again he found nothing. It was the same at the dirt track by the main road.

Darkness finally fell, forcing him to abandon his search. He returned to Ruby's house. Dirt smeared his suit, and his muscles and bones ached so much it hurt to sit down. He stood in the kitchen and stared at the gold clock on the wall. Its gears were exposed, the little brass circles of varying sizes clicking and turning and interlocking as the seconds ticked past. The time on the clock read almost eleven. He had been looking for his sister for over six hours.

Ruby's house had many lovely objects like this clock. It contained no nautical knick-knacks or novelty lifesaver rings to signify this was a beach house, no mounted fish. Art, including her own, hung on the walls instead. All the furniture was second-hand but beautiful. Pots and pans were old French brands. Danish chairs and tables. Eclectic, thoughtful, bohemian. Not curated or showy. It was the house of an artist. He wished he'd asked her about these objects more. It would've been something to talk about.

Stayer's phone rang. It was Carol again, and he answered wearily. 'I tried all those places you mentioned. No sign of Ruby.'

'I just wondered if you'd considered—' She stopped, as though what she was about to say was too painful. She finished in a whisper: 'Maybe she threw herself into the blowhole.'

The house fell quiet; the only sound was the soft whoosh of waves breaking outside and the tick of the clock with the exposed gears in the kitchen.

'You know, Carol, I don't believe Ruby would have done that, and I don't think you believe it either.'

'A few months ago, I got a call from a security guard working at the mall in Garribee,' Carol said. 'He asked me to come and collect Ruby. She had run there. Garribee is forty-three kilometres from here.' Stayer felt his breathing slow. 'When I got there, Ruby was on a chair in the guard's office, damp and doubled over. That night she'd fallen ill, sweating and moaning into the bedsheets, and I took her to hospital. She had sunstroke. She could have died.'

'Why are you telling me this?'

'Ruby's time in Thoorgala hasn't gone well.'

'Carol, how well did Ruby know Phoebe Glasson or Mikaela Sorgensen?'

There was a pause on the end of the line. 'Who are they?'

'They were both found dead in the sandhills at Cundra. They both went to Thoorgala Grammar and were the same age as Ruby. I've been told they were friends. I want to know how close they were.'

Another pause. 'I'm not sure. Sorry.' Carol's voice was vague.

Stayer's shirt was plastered to the chair with sweat. He shifted uncomfortably. 'Carol. This afternoon you said that you'd warned Ruby this would happen, that she should never have come back to Thoorgala. What did you mean by that?'

He could hear Carol breathing again.

'I don't know what you're talking about,' she said. The pained and panicked tone had gone, replaced by something more cautious, more measured. 'I don't recall saying that.' She hung up, again. He called her back; it went to voicemail.

11.41 PM

The first thing she noticed when she woke was the headache. A pounding, throbbing sort, like someone had wound steel wire around her skull and had begun pulling. She sat virtually in blackness, like a starless night sky. The darkness was confounding, suffocating. She could only vaguely make out shapes and silhouettes.

He'd bound her to a chair, securing her wrists to the armrests and ankles to the chair legs. *He*. She assumed her captor was male, so she referred to him in her mind as he. The darkness rendered it impossible to tell anything more than that.

A cat slunk around her bound legs. Its patchy fur brushed her bare skin, the warm hump of its stomach dropped against her shins. The belly had a lumpiness; the cat was pregnant. There was another cat too, a skinnier one, whose protruding rib cage brushed against her calves when it walked past. And a third one, a kitten, whose high-pitched, babyish meows pierced the air. So at least three cats prowled the space with her. She wondered if there were more. She'd woken originally to find a cat licking her hand, the tongue like sandpaper. The smell of them took her breath away. It made her think of a neglected hamster's cage: fetid, moist, fermenting.

The figure emerged again, bounding down what sounded like wooden stairs.

'Who are you? Why the fuck am I here?' she yelled into the void.

No reply.

'You can't keep me down here. I've done nothing wrong!'

He seemed to pause. She could sense him moving towards her. She tensed.

A light flicked on, casting heavenly, wonderful light. It came from a torch. She squinted at first, adjusting to the sudden non-darkness, then opened her eyes wide, eagerly, desperately, glimpsing as much as she could of the space she was in, not sure how long the light would last. She saw some stairs, and a flash of a wet cement ground. Then the light flicked away. The figure turned the torch on himself, and she couldn't repress a scream.

He wore a black cape, and his face was covered in a mask with pointy teeth and a wild grin.

26 DECEMBER

8 AM

Boxing Day. Stayer showered in the open-air wooden cubicle and tried to think of his next move. The sun bore down, the air smelled of smoke. He dressed and moved to the kitchen. A full leg of ham lay uneaten in the fridge. He'd discovered it on the day he'd moved in. Ruby was supposed to take it to Carol's house on Christmas Day, she'd told him. The pedigreed leg of meat remained in the fridge, un-carved, uneaten, triple-smoked, and Stayer realised he was starving.

He toasted some stale white supermarket bread in the grill, then smeared it with margarine he salvaged from an almost empty tub. He carved four pink slices of ham and placed them on the bread. He made himself a mug of instant coffee and sat on the cracked concrete back porch, which overlooked the water. The ham was flaky and soft as butter. It may have been the sweetest meal he'd ever had. He watched the waves softly moving, gentle peaks of white, and understood why Ruby had chosen this place to live.

He opened his laptop and balanced it on his knees. He downloaded the book *Myths and Legends of the Cundra Valley* by Catherine Kelley from an online bookstore. He ate and drank in the outdoors as he read the introduction. The first couple of paragraphs mapped Thoorgala's history since colonisation, including the erection of the

Cape Lighthouse in 1905 that desecrated Dharawal burial grounds and the establishment of the meatworks after World War I, through to the surfing culture of the 70s, gentrification of the 80s, and the current real estate development boom. Eventually it addressed the darker side of Thoorgala, the reason for the book:

> For every hill there is a dell. An underbelly has always existed in Thoorgala, demonstrated by the many people who have jumped to their deaths in the blowhole—prompting the construction of an anti-suicide fence—and the unexplained deaths of numerous backpackers, travellers, seasonal workers, and itinerants. Thoorgala also appears to be an unsafe place for women. This is reflected in the folklore of the area, with its focus on retribution for sinning women, punishment for adulterous and scorned females, and the hunting down of 'witches'.
>
> This book is the result of more than fifteen years of research into the myths and legends which pervade this intriguing place, and interviews with more than four hundred local inhabitants.

Stayer grabbed his car keys.

•

Stayer knocked on Sister Catherine Kelley's door, but there was no answer.

He rang the greasy doorbell. Still nothing.

Pulling out his mobile, he tried her number, but it went to voicemail. He left a brief message then, defeated, headed back to his car.

He was almost to the street when a woman's voice called to him from the external stairs of the apartment block. 'Detective Stayer, this is a surprise. Merry Christmas for yesterday.'

He turned to find Sister Catherine standing on the stairs. Dressed in her nun's habit, she wore a red paper crown over her veil, the kind you find in a Christmas cracker. 'I just listened to your voicemail.' She held up her mobile phone. 'I'm having Boxing Day brunch with a few of the other sisters in a unit downstairs. Would you like to join us?'

'Merry Christmas, Sister. I won't come in, thanks. No time.'

'Can I help you? You didn't say much in your message, just that you needed to see me.'

'You interviewed more than four hundred locals and spent fifteen years researching the area's myths and legends?'

She hesitated, as though trying to catch up with his train of thought. 'I did.'

'You know this region very well then, would you say?'

'I'd say I probably know it better than anyone.' There was a keenness in her expression now.

'You know Thoorgala. I don't. I want you to help me with this case.'

Her eyes flashed. 'You do?'

'I'm not suggesting that we become partners or anything. I just want to ask you some questions. Obviously, I think the whole thing about Tall Harry is a load of crap, but—'

'I never said it wasn't crap.' Her expression hardened.

'Are you allowed to say crap?' he asked.

'No. But if you say it softly, God doesn't mind.' The faintest hint of a smile rose from the corners of her mouth. 'Detective. Tall Harry is an urban legend. You seemed to think I believed it as truth, that Tall Harry was real. You looked at my habit and assumed that because I believe in God, I must also believe Tall Harry to be real, like a child who believes in the tooth fairy or Santa Claus. I wasn't saying that at all, but you left in such haste you did not give me time to explain.'

'Please explain now,' he said.

'I was showing you what I know of Tall Harry because urban legends are important. They are cautionary tales and represent deep-seated fears. They reflect the values of the people who created them. The people of Thoorgala created Tall Harry. Now someone is killing women in his name. I don't believe in Tall Harry, but the individual who has committed murder does.'

'Fine,' Stayer said. 'What do you suggest?'

'Study this folklore. Become an expert in Tall Harry. Someone in the community is pretending to be him. Work out who that is, and why he's doing it, and you will solve the case.'

'Okay. I accept. I want your help.'

'I'm sorry. I don't think so.' She turned and walked away.

'What,' Stayer said. 'Why?'

'I don't think we would work well together. Our perspectives are too different. You are not willing to truly accept what I'm saying.'

'I will. I promise I'll listen.' He groaned. 'Wait.'

'Sorry. My answer is no.' She kept walking, a hot breeze flicking her veil.

He followed her, the metal rail of the walk way ringing as he grabbed it. 'I could offer something in exchange for your help?'

She turned, laughing. 'What could you possibly give me, detective? I need very little, and I want even less.' But then she paused. 'Although there is something you could get for me. The writings of Magda van Aachen.'

Stayer raised his eyebrows. 'Maria von Trapp?'

'Magda van Aachen. She was a thirteenth-century mystic. She wrote about the *Gestim* children.'

'What children?' Stayer was barely following.

'*Gestim* children. *Gestim* is the term given to children who have died. When a child dies, their death is considered so special and sad and tragic that regular heaven is not good enough for them. They go to a special heaven, one just for children. And if you say the right prayer, you can see them again.' Her voice took on a huskiness; she was almost whispering.

'I only understand about every third word you're saying,' Stayer said, 'but please go on.'

'Magda van Aachen wrote about this in her diaries and texts. The works were considered heretical, and she was excommunicated. But she always had a following. Her works were kept secret, hidden away, and passed down from one trusted person to another. People have claimed they've seen their deceased children again, one last time. An Irish nun brought these heretical scriptures to Australia in the 1990s—or tried to. She was stopped at customs and Magda's writings were confiscated. They've been in a police evidence vault ever since. You could get them for me.' She gave him an imploring look. The breeze lifted the edge of her veil again.

Stayer stared at her. 'You want me to break into a vault and steal police evidence for you?'

'You wouldn't need to break in. Police are allowed into the vault. And it would be borrowing, not stealing. I just want to read the writings and then you could put them back. No one will miss them.'

He laughed. 'That's okay then. So long as no one would miss them. Why do you want to read them?'

'My interest is academic,' she said quickly, looking defiant. 'Linked to my work.'

'I'm sorry.' Stayer could hear the desperation in his own voice. Sweat dripped between his shoulder blades. 'I just don't know if that's possible.'

'Then we don't have a deal,' she said.

She turned away from him, and took the stairs once more.

He opened his mouth and spoke aloud the fear he had been trying so desperately to repress. 'I believe the individual who killed those women might have my sister,' he said.

She turned back. 'Your sister is missing? Why didn't you tell me this earlier?'

'She *might* be missing. I don't know her well enough to know if she's just gone off to think, or if someone's taken her. We're not that close.'

'How long has she been gone?'

He swallowed. 'Almost two days.'

The nun touched his arm, her small fingers curling softly around his elbow. 'And does she have any connection to the woman who was found dead on the sandhills?'

'Women. There's been two now. And Ruby knew both.'

The nun leaned on the rail. 'I said there would be more.' She turned and walked past him, continued to her own apartment and disappeared inside.

She returned moments later carrying her handbag, a battered black box with a faded strap. 'Let's find your sister, detective.'

10 AM

Catherine had tried to hide her delight when the detective had shown up at her door for a second time. She believed she had hidden it well, and she hoped the detective had not seen the smile which she felt continuously creeping across her face. This was a busy time of year for people in her line of work, but to be honest, this was by far the most exciting thing that had happened to her in years. The urban legend she had written about, studied, researched, could be linked to real life murders. She felt like she had swallowed fireworks.

The detective led Catherine to a squad car, a white holden commodore with Thoorgala Police Area Command emblazoned on the bonnet in blue letters. They drove down the highway, passing malls and mega supermarkets. There was an awkward silence, as though they were two colleagues on a work trip who had never spoken outside the office. As they stopped at a red light, a man walking his dog slowed and performed a double take, seemingly at the sight of a nun in the passenger seat of the squad car. Catherine saw the scene through the dog-walker's eyes. She glanced at the detective in the driver's seat. He wore an anxious expression; he had seen the dog walker too.

'Everything alright, detective?' she asked.

'Perfectly fine,' the detective replied. He shifted in the driver's seat. He was taller and leaner than he had appeared in the swimming races on television.

'Nonsense. You're regretting your decision. You're noticing the looks people are giving you and thinking you've made a mistake in asking for my help.'

'Do people stare at you often?'

She laughed. 'I'm a thirty-three-year-old nun. All I get is stares.'

'This was a bad idea. Too dangerous for a holy woman. I should take you home.'

Catherine panicked. This was the last thing she wanted. '*Yea, though I walk through the valley of the shadow of death, I will fear no evil: for thou art with me; thy rod and thy staff they comfort me*,' she said. 'I do not fear danger, detective. I want to find your sister.'

Her last line seemed to convince him. He nodded and returned his eyes to the road and they drove on in silence.

'So how will this work?' she said after a time.

'How do you mean?' he asked, veering right to exit the freeway.

'Will I be an honorary police officer?'

'I'm not giving you a gun, if that's what's you're asking.'

She chuckled. 'Of course not.' She pictured herself holding a firearm. 'I meant . . . do I come with you when you are interviewing witnesses, family members?'

The detective looked uncomfortable. He spoke firmly. 'You are only here to observe. You're not to speak to witnesses or family members. Certainly do not speak to the media. And not a word to your lunatics on the internet. Understood?'

'Understood,' she said quickly. She was just happy to be there. 'The people on the internet may be eccentric, but I would not discount them so quickly,' she added. 'They may end up being the key to everything. They may give themselves away.'

The detective glanced across at her. As they turned a corner, an angry orange sun slanted through the window like the glow from a bar heater, and she caught the freckles, maybe half-a-dozen, scattered across his nose.

'You haven't, by the way,' she said, watching as he flicked the indicator with a large hand.

'Haven't what?'

'You haven't made a mistake in bringing me on board. You never know, detective. I might solve the whole case.'

•

Catherine was aware of two staff members, both in uniform, staring at her intently as she entered the police station by the detective's side.

'Good morning, detective,' the older woman said to Detective Stayer. 'Who's your friend?'

'Joan, this is Sister Catherine Kelley. She's an expert in the local area who's going to be helping us with the murder investigation. Sister, this is Joan Wilson, receptionist.'

'Okay,' Joan said cautiously. 'Welcome, sister,' she added, offering her hand.

'Thank you, Joan,' Catherine said, careful to say the woman's name.

'I'm sorry, sister. It's just that the detective here wasn't exactly singing your praises earlier, now he's brought you in to help on the case.' Joan shot a cheeky look to Detective Stayer, and he glared back.

'I can understand why, Joan,' Catherine said. 'Detective Stayer deals in evidence. I am asking him to delve into an urban legend. But I truly hope to help solve these terrible crimes.'

The younger man in uniform stepped forward. He was hugely tall and muscular. 'Constable Walsh,' he said, holding out his hand. Catherine shook it, it was like shaking a bear paw. 'Welcome, sister,' he said enthusiastically. 'I'm a big fan. I've read both your books and look forward to hearing your ideas.'

The detective looked at the constable in surprise. 'I had no idea you were such a reader, Walsh,' Detective Stayer said.

'I'm not,' the constable said modestly, 'but *Myths and Legends of the Cundra Valley* is a classic.'

Catherine tried not to beam with delight.

'Would you like a cup of tea, sister?' Joan offered.

'I would love one,' Catherine said, 'but I will make it myself, if you would point me to the kitchen. Thank you, Joan.'

They made their cups of tea in the kitchenette, which contained an extremely Thoorgala-esque vending machine selling nothing but protein bars, then Detective Stayer showed Catherine to his office.

'May I see the photos of the Jupiter symbols again?' she said, as soon as he had closed the door behind her.

The detective looked at her curiously. 'You mean on the victims?'

'Yes, the symbols that were carved into them.' She hoped she did not sound too abrupt.

The detective located the photos and laid them on his desk. They showed the first victim's hand and the second victim's leg.

Catherine inspected them, flicking back and forth between the two images. She sipped her tea. She felt alive. 'Just as I thought. They are both pointing at moles.'

She motioned to the photos. The detective came around to her side of the desk and took in the symbols more closely.

'Do you see?'

The detective's expression showed he agreed with her. The reddish stem of the four ended at a brown mole on each victim's skin. The more they looked, the more obvious it became. 'What's your point?' he asked her.

'The seemingly random location of the two symbols—one on the hand, the other on the thigh—is not random at all. Moles mark the body in a way that has fascinated and repulsed people for centuries. Before science and reason took over. People have always speculated as to their meaning.'

'Science and reason, huh? You're a fan of those things? Moles don't mean anything. Except too much sun sometimes.'

'We know that now. A mole is a perfectly normal growth which occurs when melanocytes cluster on the skin. But they had never heard of melanocytes in medieval times. Back then, moles were called "the devil's mark". During the Spanish Inquisition and witch trials, moles were used to identify women who practised dark arts. There's a whole chapter dedicated to moles in the *Malleus Maleficarum*, or *The Witches' Hammer*, a sort of textbook for witch hunters.' She motioned to the crime scene photos again. 'Whoever did this is calling these women witches.'

Detective Stayer seemed incredulous. 'Witches. With pointy hats and cauldrons, green faces and broomsticks. In Thoorgala: a town with lifesavers and longboard competitions, which holds the record for Australia's largest sausage sizzle. A bit ridiculous, no?'

'A witch doesn't necessarily have a broomstick and a green face, like in *The Wizard of Oz*,' Catherine said. 'Historically, a witch was a woman who didn't live according to the accepted norms. A woman who practised medicine, for example, or was gay. And I don't think it sounds ridiculous at all. Not to me. I think a witch would very likely be found in a place that thinks longboards and sausage sizzles are the best life has to offer.' She nodded emphatically and looked at the crime scene photos again. She couldn't believe she was seeing this. The more she looked, the more she felt convinced.

'You know a lot about witches, sister?' Detective Stayer asked. 'Isn't that something the Catholic church would frown upon?'

Catherine offered him a crooked smile. 'On the contrary. There's no greater expert on witches than the Catholic Church. Responsible for the majority of burnings at the stake in world history. We can divide the witches of history into two groups: firstly, the branded witches. Herbalists, midwives. Spinsters who preferred their own company to that of tiresome men. These women were viewed with suspicion, and in turn, vilified as witches. Many a woman was burned at the stake simply for knowing how to read, or how to bring down a fever. Burned for not knowing her place.' She hoped she wasn't speaking too fast in her excitement.

'And the second group?'

She smiled. 'The real witches. Women who performed spells. Who worshipped pagan gods and goddesses, ancient female deities, and pre-Christian idols. They dabbled in black magic, occasionally wishing others harm. These women were the real witches, so to speak, and even though their magic may not have been real, they thought it was. They would cast love spells, brew potions, place curses. This second group consisted of women who felt powerless in the society they found themselves in. They might have been abused, sexually or physically, for example, by husbands or family members. They might have been scorned or humiliated by townsfolk. Ironically, these women from the second group, the ones who practised witchcraft, were caught and burned at the stake far less than the midwives and healers of the first group, who were executed and tortured with alarming regularity. This is because the real witches from the second group concealed their identity, and operated in secret, making them harder to catch.' She could feel her veil slipping back on her head. The room was stifling, and she was sweating. She used two fingers to bring the fabric forward slightly.

'Witches and witchcraft are mentioned many times in the Bible. Take Leviticus 19:26, for example. The Old Testament. It says, *Non exerceas maleficia*. That's Latin: "Thou shall not practise witchcraft." During the Inquisition, women from that second group, the real witches, would use these words as a code to identify themselves to each other as witches. Women still quote those same words today. They always use the Latin, too, never the English—because Latin is the tongue of Catholicism. So who better to take an interest in witches than a Catholic nun?'

The detective seemed satisfied with this explanation. 'Fine,' he said. 'The killer is calling these women witches. Branding them. Why would he do that? And how is this going to help us catch him? We need to find him before he hurts Ruby—if he hasn't already.'

Catherine smiled gently. She wanted more than anything to help Detective Stayer find his sister. 'They must have done something to warrant the branding in the killer's eyes. The individual impersonating Tall Harry believes that these women have committed some crime and wants to let us know. And they used witchcraft to commit it.'

A strong wind had begun blowing outside, making the palm fronds swing in the trees out the window. She glanced over at the detective. He seemed to be thinking. 'Would you call witches an urban legend?' Detective Stayer said.

'The marking of women in possession of knowledge as suspicious and evil?' Catherine said. 'I would call witches the oldest urban legend of all.'

Joan knocked on the door and entered. 'Sorry to disturb, detective.' She seemed to hesitate. Her expression was morose.

'What is it, Joan?' Detective Stayer said.

'There's another body in the sandhills.'

Catherine felt as if an electric current ran through her. The detective inhaled sharply; he looked terrified. The room seemed frozen, no one knew what to do.

'Is it my sister?' Detective Stayer asked at last. Catherine wanted to melt into the wall, feeling like she shouldn't be there.

Joan was shaking her head. 'I don't know, detective. It might be. No description or ID given. Same situation as before, a member of the public has found a body and dialled triple zero. That's all I was told. Dispatch allocated to us, and now I'm telling you.' She stood there quietly. They both seemed to have forgotten Catherine was in the room.

'I'll come with you,' said Constable Walsh, appearing in the doorway. 'We'll get there quicker if I drive.' He was already reaching for the keys to the squad car.

'Wait here,' Detective Stayer said to Catherine.

'Let me come with you,' she said instinctively. She wanted to help wherever she could.

'Not a chance. It's not the place for you.'

Catherine nodded. 'Good luck.' She touched his arm briefly as Detective Stayer and Constable Walsh hurried from the room.

•

Joan told Catherine that they would probably be a while, and suggested she take a walk. Catherine agreed gratefully, gathered her handbag and walked outside. The air was stifling, and she sweated under her veil and habit. She walked only a few metres down the palm tree-lined main street of Thoorgala before she felt like she might faint. She was looking for somewhere to sit down when a voice sounded behind her.

'Sister. This is a surprise.'

Catherine turned. A man in his forties stood there. She didn't recognise him.

'Name's Dan.' He held out his hand. Catherine shook it, wincing slightly at the wetness of his sweat-drenched palm. He was missing half his index finger, and the smooth nub had tickled her palm. *Never show disgust to one of God's creatures.* 'You don't know me. I'm on the Thoorgala Forum. I so enjoy your posts.'

'Oh. I haven't posted lately.' Catherine felt squeamish, she had shown hubris in those posts, she saw how it must have looked to the detective, and now his sister was missing.

'What are you doing near the police station?' Dan said. 'Are you helping with the case?' he looked excited.

'I can't say, I'm sorry,' Catherine said. She wasn't sure how much she was allowed to share.

'Would be fabulous if you were. You could set them all straight. Ever heard of a guy called Stanley Lacey? The artist?'

Catherine shrugged. 'Possibly. The name rings a faint bell.'

'Maybe look him up. You're a smart lady.'

'Okay.' She smiled politely. She became aware that he was moving closer to her. She stepped backward to keep a distance. They moved further inside the little area she'd walked into, a small dead-ended laneway at the end of a public garden. She scanned the space; no one else was around, it was just the two of them.

'Has Detective Stayer read your book, *Myths and Legends of the Cundra Valley*?'

'I believe he's read parts of it,' she said warily. She looked around for an escape. Thick bushes lined the area, there was only one way out, past the man who now stood in front of her.

'And how about the other one?' He had a cheeky look.

'I beg your pardon?'

'*Witches, Sirens and Unusual Women.* Your other, less well-known book. Has Detective Stayer read that weighty tome?' He grinned mischievously.

'I don't know.'

'Are you going to tell him about it? About the Black Heart Rite?'

'What did you say?' Catherine felt nauseous. 'I'm not sure I follow.' The man was blocking her exit.

'Don't you think you should tell the detective?' Their eyes met.

A crash sounded behind Dan; he turned at the sound. A rubbish bin had upended in a gust of hot wind, hitting the concrete path with a clang. Catherine took her chance and ducked by him before he could stop her. She walked away, ignoring his calls for her to come back, to answer his questions, to keep talking. She hoped to never see that man again.

11.30 AM

With the lights and sirens on, they sped through the traffic. As cars moved to the sides, Stayer saw drivers glancing at them, watching, looking intrigued, maybe even excited. He figured police cars did not speed through Thoorgala often, and everyone must have known where they were heading.

Constable Walsh sat quietly in the driver's seat, steering precisely. He opened his mouth several times, seemingly looking for some words to say. Finally, as they approached the turn off to the sandhills, he spoke. 'I know there's nothing I can say to make this any better, boss,' he said, voice pained. 'I'm sorry. I wish—'

'It's okay, Walsh,' Stayer replied, grateful. 'I know. Thank you.'

They arrived at the car park, and Walsh slotted the squad car into a space. They moved up the giant dune for a third time. Stayer clawed at the hill as it steepened, like he was climbing a ladder. The sand felt hot and sharp in his hands, like glass. He could hear Constable Walsh ascending beside him with strong legs. Stayer was almost on all fours when he reached the summit. He pulled himself onto the flat and saw a black-haired woman lying dead on the sand.

Walsh arrived beside him. He spoke softly between ragged breaths. 'In the picture you put on the Keep a Look Out For, your sister had blonde hair.'

'Not my sister,' Stayer confirmed.

'Thank god, boss. We'll find her.'

They stood in silence for several moments, studying the dead woman with black hair lying on the sand, until Stayer had the unnerving feeling they were being watched. He turned and discovered a large group of men and women, mostly men, standing at the southern end of the sandhill. They had an audience.

The onlookers wore running shorts and singlets, with digital watches and colourful, hi-tech shoes. They had the cranky, tanned, underfed look of people who took their fitness seriously.

'Everyone stay back,' Stayer yelled. 'Who are you?'

'Thoorgala Running Club,' one of the men answered. 'We found the body.'

'This is a crime scene,' Stayer said. 'I won't say it again. Stay back.'

'A professional now, eh?' the man said, hands on his hips. 'Where was that professionalism earlier? How about you return our calls. I phoned the police station two days ago with information. Never heard back. Now another woman is dead.'

Groans and shouting followed, as the crowd surged forward. Stayer and Constable Walsh both raised their arms.

'Hey! Stop that!' Constable Walsh said. Stayer looked over. Walsh marched towards a man who was holding up his phone, pointing it at the dead body. Walsh almost tackled the man, reaching for the phone.

'Get your hands off me, lurch!' the man exclaimed. 'I'm a lawyer. Want a civil suit?'

'Let him go, Walsh,' Stayer said. Both men were sweaty, with muscles tensed. Stayer didn't know what to do, he had nothing to shield the victim with. He couldn't physically cover her with anything, to risk losing evidence. Finally he removed his suit jacket and held it up like a screen, covering most of her torso. As his jacket came off, his shoulder holster was exposed. The sight of his gun seemed to subdue the crowd, their shouts and cries becoming mumbles, whispers.

'My kid goes to Thoorgala Grammar,' the man who'd announced he was a lawyer said. 'Archie was at the end of year assembly when the girl said the Tall Harry rhyme on stage. Why didn't you investigate that? Why didn't you arrest her?'

'I'm sorry,' Stayer said. 'I'm not sure what you're asking me. You know that he isn't real, right? Tall Harry is an urban legend.'

The lawyer rested his hands on his hips. He wore a running singlet emblazoned with the logo of a local realtor on the chest. 'Are you being sarcastic with me? This is a nice town, no crime, everyone works hard, does what they're told. Now there's three dead bodies, pal. All since you showed up.'

'I know this is stressful,' Stayer said.

'Stressful? Stressful is missing a plane, working under a shitty boss. This isn't stressful, this is horrific. Stumbling across the local pharmacist's dead body on your morning run.'

Stayer shot his eyes to the man. 'You know the victim?'

'Everyone does. That's Jessie Phan. She owns the chemist on Beach Road. Have you looked into what the women might have done to deserve this?'

'I beg your pardon?'

'No one is murdered like this for no reason. It might help solve the crime if you know why they've been killed.'

Stayer couldn't find any words to respond. Walsh stepped forward. 'Gents, give him a break. Don't you know his sister is missing?'

Stayer snapped his head to Constable Walsh. He could feel his face growing hot. The runners all turned to Stayer. Expressions now increasingly familiar greeted him once more: pity, intrigue, curiosity.

'What's his sister's name?' a voice from the crowd said. Stayer couldn't tell who, but it was a woman's voice. A horrible moment passed.

'Ruby Stayer,' another woman's voice said. Nadia Traurig appeared, the woman who had approached Stayer at the petrol station, claiming a schoolgirl friendship with Ruby. Stayer blanched. Nadia wore hot pink running shorts and a crop top, and her hair was tucked under a baseball cap.

Looks of recognition moved through the crowd. Everyone peered at Stayer. 'Okay. We're going to speak with all of you. Form a line, Constable Walsh will take your statements.'

Walsh interviewed the witnesses, one by one. Stayer remained by the body, holding his jacket up like a screen. Everyone basically had the same thing to say—they ran up the hill and came across the body. Once everyone had finished giving their statements, they returned to crowding around Stayer, staring and whispering.

Then the crowd began to part, and Dr Dixon pushed towards them. 'Please get out of the way,' he announced sternly. Black boxes weighed down his shoulders, and he panted heavily over the sand. The crowd let him through. Stayer eyed him gratefully and ushered him to the woman's body. Seagulls cruised overhead, as though this were any other day at the beach. Stayer lowered his suit jacket to allow Dr Dixon to properly see the body. Once again, the dead young woman with black hair became visible to the crowd of runners, waiting bossily on the sand dune.

Dr Dixon knelt by the body and took the victim's left leg in his gloved hands. 'I think I see something,' he said. He placed one hand on the victim's left calf and the other on the thigh and gently bent the limb upwards at the knee. The leg creaked and resisted, gripped by rigor mortis, but after much gentle straining, manipulating, easing, the pathologist was able to bend it. He pointed to the underside of the leg.

Stayer crouched down in the hot sand to see. On the underside of the woman's left calf was a mole, and next to it a Jupiter symbol had been carved into her skin. 'One of the runners said her name was Jessie Phan?'

'Yes,' Dr Dixon replied. 'It's Jessie Phan. Local pharmacist.'

Then the sound rang out, and Constable Walsh ran towards it but was too late. A camera took a picture. One of the runners had his phone pointed at the dead body.

12.46 PM

A woman outside the hospital where the morgue was located grabbed Stayer and Walsh as they walked inside and begged them to help find 'Tall Harry'. The guard beside the reception desk said the same.

It had gone mainstream now. Despite Walsh taking the runner's phone, the photo of the victim's body had somehow already been uploaded to //Thoorgala. A cropped, pixelated version of the same photo, showing not the whole body but just a close up of the symbol carved into her leg, had then appeared in the news sidebar of a tabloid paper's online version. A broadsheet then picked up the story, adding a small write-up of the basic facts, but no photo, to its website. In less than an hour, news of a third dead body with a symbol carved into it found in the sandhills of the suburban beach paradise had made it into the establishment press. Every national newspaper in the country had called the police station in turn, asking for statements for their evening editions. A broadcast news van for a commercial television network was also apparently attempting to break through the bushfire line to travel to Thoorgala.

Joan had relayed this information to Stayer in a series of excited phone calls. Stayer had listened, head in hand, saying nothing.

Medical staff in green scrubs and trainers and patients shuffling with IV drips watched Stayer and Walsh as they walked down the corridor towards the lifts which would take them to the morgue. A patient in a full body cast was wheeled down the corridor by a hospital porter, his arms and legs encased in white plaster, so he looked like a mummy. Stayer felt like asking if they could swap places. He scrolled through the //Thoorgala forum on his phone and viewed the photo of the victim's body, the original which had been snapped on the sandhills. The image featured the outline of the victim's chin, and the curve of her nose, lightly visible in the background. Stayer stopped walking.

'Walsh. Get to the victim's family.'

Walsh halted beside him. 'Boss?'

'This photo gives a glimpse of the victim's face. Someone who knows her—'

'They could identify her from this photo. They could tell the family. I'll go now.' Walsh turned and walked back out of the hospital. Stayer kept going towards the morgue.

Sister Catherine was waiting for Stayer near the lifts. 'Everything okay?' she asked.

'Spectacular,' Stayer replied. 'What are you doing here? I told you to wait at the station.'

'I want to see the body.'

'No way,' he said stiffly. 'You shouldn't have come here. Do I need to say it again? You're here to advise me, that is all. You're not an investigator on this case.'

A flash of gold appeared on the nun's forehead, catching Stayer's eye. He realised: a lock of her hair had escaped from her veil. It ran dark blonde and curly, a little frizzy. She began tucking the lock away, and Stayer coughed and looked down, pretending he'd seen nothing.

'I understand,' she said, smoothing the edge of her veil onto her forehead. 'Will you please just tell me if there's a symbol carved into the body?'

'There is. A Jupiter symbol under her calf. Pointing to a mole.'

The lift arrived at their floor, the tarnished stainless-steel doors sliding open.

'I'll be back soon.'

Their eyes met again as the doors closed.

Dr Dixon was waiting for Stayer in the linoleum hallway of the basement. Stayer entered the secure area, and a technician brought out the body that had been transported in the refrigerated van from the sandhills.

'Records formally confirm her name is Jessica Phan,' Dr Dixon said. 'Thirty years old. A pharmacist. Lived in Thoorgala all her life. I've only performed a cursory exam at this point, and simple tox still pending, but as before, no physical evidence of poison, no obvious trauma. In other words, I don't know what killed her. Hand wounds and back bruises as with victims one and two. Consistent with being made to climb the fence, walk out onto the sand, and then left there to die.'

Dr Dixon wore the same fixated look, the same stiffened posture, as when he'd been examining the first victim, and the second.

'I'm still thinking of poisons to test for in a detailed tox screen,' Stayer said. 'The perfect poison. We'll find it.'

'More women will be dead before then,' said Dr Dixon.

The words stunned Stayer. They spoke awkwardly for a few minutes about when to expect test results, and what their next steps might be, and then Stayer left the morgue.

He collected Sister Catherine on his way back out of the hospital.

A woman stopped them in the foyer. 'Is the person in the morgue another victim of Tall Harry?' she asked Stayer urgently.

Linoleum squeaked below them. A cleaner wiped down a row of chairs by the wall, head cocked to them, pretending not to listen.

The woman who stopped them wore green scrubs. Stayer recognised her as the technician who assisted Dr Dixon. 'I saw the symbol,' she said. 'Same as the others.' Her eyes darted wildly.

'Tall Harry is an urban legend,' Stayer replied, regarding the technician blanky.

'Please catch him,' the woman begged. Her black hair was scraped back from her face into a bun so tightly it must have been giving her a headache.

Stayer pictured Ruby the last time he saw her, on Christmas Eve, sweaty and distracted, decorating that tree. Something caught in his throat. Was she still alive? He thought about calling Carol and getting a group together. They should have people out there looking for Ruby. He could feel Sister Catherine's eyes on him, standing beside him in the foyer. 'We're doing everything we can,' Stayer said as he strode through the door. He dialled Carol's number. It went to voicemail. He left a message telling her to call him.

3.15 PM

Ha Long 88 was a Vietnamese restaurant in the main street of Thoorgala. They entered a dining room heaving with people. Young families, groups of jolly older men, and what looked like a rugby team sat at bamboo tables, devouring curries, noodles and stir-fries. Beer bottles sweated onto the tablecloths. Waiters in black trousers and red bow ties moved swiftly.

Jessica Phan's sister, a lawyer wearing a pearl necklace and sensible heels, collected Stayer at the front of the restaurant and led him towards the back, where her parents were waiting. Sister Catherine waited at the front of the restaurant, taking a place between a coat stand and a fish tank.

'Boxing Day banquet,' Violet Phan said to Stayer as they passed through the at-capacity dining room. 'The lunch service was already underway when we were notified . . . about Jessie.' She had a dazed, shocked look. 'We decided not to interrupt it; I'm not sure if that was a mistake or not.' She dabbed her eyes with a crumpled tissue.

They walked down a narrow tiled corridor, past crates of carrots stacked against the wall, dirt-caked and woody. A grassy smell of herbs wafted. Knives tapped chopping boards; pans clattered. Ladles clicked on woks.

Stayer found Mr and Mrs Phan sitting on a couple of overturned milk crates in a storage room at the back of the kitchen. Constable Walsh sat next to them; his huge frame looked ridiculous perched on a milk crate. He nodded a greeting to Stayer. The victim's parents were staring into space, with red-rimmed eyes, dripping noses, slumped backs. Mr Phan wore a shirt and bow tie: he had been waiting tables before Constable Walsh had shown up. Mrs Phan wore a silk shirt and pearls and hugged a photo frame to her chest.

Stayer explained gently about the symbol that had been found on their daughter, in the same way he'd done for Cassie and for Bill and Sabina Sorgensen. He showed them the line drawing of the Jupiter symbol in his notebook and watched their disorientated faces as he asked them if they recognised it. Violet spoke with her parents in rapid-fire Vietnamese, pointing to the symbol. Mr and Mrs Phan shook their heads violently, angrily, and spat words back to her. 'They know nothing about that symbol,' Violet said, translating. 'We're Catholics. Jessie was in no cult.' Her voice was steely, her expression hard.

Mrs Phan stood suddenly and offered the photo she was holding to Stayer. He accepted it with a nod.

The photo was a school portrait showing Jessie as a teenager. A slim face with dark hair and shining black eyes. She looked animated in the picture, smiling widely, revealing a row of small white teeth.

Stayer leaned forward. He recognised the uniform immediately. 'Jessie attended Thoorgala Grammar?'

The mother stared up at him blankly. A gas flame *whooshed* from somewhere behind them in the kitchen.

'She doesn't speak English well,' the sister said to Stayer. 'Yes, Jessie went to Thoorgala Grammar. I did too. Mum and Dad worked in this restaurant seven days a week for thirty years to send me and Jessie there. They put us through university, too.'

'Did Jessie know Phoebe Glasson, or Mikaela Sorgensen?'

'I knew of Phoebe Glasson,' Violet said, not even asking her parents. 'She was a rebellious girl. Jessie wasn't friends with her. I remember Mikaela Sorgensen, too. A kind girl, but an outcast. Jessie wasn't friends with her, either.'

'Are you sure?'

'I'm sure. Jessie did not hang out with girls like that.' Her gaze was steely.

Stayer paused. 'How about Ruby Stayer? Did Jessie know her?'

Violet's demeanour changed, her face softened. 'Ruby was her best friend,' she whispered. 'Why do you ask?'

Stayer absorbed this in silence. He inhaled, feeling Constable Walsh looking his way. He forced his breathing to slow and explained about the other victims found dead on the sandhills, and how Ruby was missing, presumed taken also. He watched Violet's face fall. Mr and Mrs Phan looked to their daughter expectantly, confused, and Violet spoke to them in more speedy Vietnamese, with Stayer catching the names Phoebe, Mikaela, Ruby, and Thoorgala Grammar. Mr and Mrs Phan took in the new information, shaking their heads, looking at the ceiling. Mrs Phan took back the photo of Jessie from Stayer and began cradling it once more.

'Why are you only coming around to us now?' Violet asked Stayer, turning to him with tear-stained eyes. 'Jessie's been gone for two days. We came to the station and reported her missing, but you did nothing. And it's only now that she's dead you come to us with questions?'

A glass smashed in the dining room, and the three Phans all turned towards the sound. Drunken and cheerful apologies rose up from the tables. A waiter rushed down the corridor, dustpan in hand.

'I wasn't aware you'd reported her missing,' Stayer said. He looked to Constable Walsh, who shook his head also.

'Are you calling us liars?' Violet demanded.

'Of course not. I just didn't know. I'm sorry.'

The mother spoke again in Vietnamese, crying now and pointing at Stayer. He looked to the still-living daughter to translate, though he had a good idea of what she was saying.

'We went to the police station. We spoke to a police officer.'

Stayer shook his head, feeling desperate. 'Who did you speak to?'

Her eyes moved upwards, like she was searching her head for the name. 'Sergeant Nichols.'

4 PM

'The Phans came in two days ago,' Joan said. 'They spoke with Sergeant Nichols.' They had returned to the station and were standing around Sergeant Nichols' desk. Stayer had rung Sergeant Nichols' phone three times, each time getting voicemail.

Constable Walsh sat on the office chair at Sergeant Nichols' desk and logged in to her computer. His fingers moved deftly over the keyboard and mouse as he pulled up various files, faster than Stayer's eyes could follow.

'There's no KALOF here,' Walsh said finally, pushing the chair back from the desk. 'Nichols didn't make one for Jessie Phan.'

'Perhaps she made one, and forgot to hit submit? Or the system crashed, and she lost the file without realising?' Joan offered.

Walsh shook his head. 'It saves automatically. Even if the system had crashed, a draft would still be here.'

'Why wouldn't she issue a KALOF?' Joan said. 'Doesn't make any sense.'

The room fell quiet. Stayer scanned Sergeant Nichols' desk, hoping to glean some hint of her personality, her character, from the objects that lay on it. A clean and sparse space lay before him, with no photos or personal items of any kind. The only object of any sort, aside from the computer and keyboard, comprised pens and pencils resting in a white mug bearing the NSW police insignia. The desk possessed no personality at all, as difficult to read as the person who seemed to occupy it. Stayer felt like he had a pretty good gauge of Joan Wilson as a person, with her dry humour, her smoking, her fine-tuned police skills lurking quietly under the surface. And he was sure he had pinned Constable Walsh's character down, the gentle giant keen to impress, desperate for approval, like a sad puppy, flashes of ambition in his face betraying him periodically. But as for the third member of his reduced staff, Sergeant Nichols, Stayer could safely say with stark and depressing clarity that he had no idea what made her tick, and had given up any opportunity to find out by letting her leave on Christmas Day. He was beginning to suspect this might come back to bite him.

Sister Catherine glanced at Stayer, as if reading his mind, and offered only a shrug. The bell rang at reception, and Joan went to answer it. She returned a few moments later with a confused expression.

'Excuse me, detective, the mayor is coming to see you.'

Stayer was momentarily thrown; of all the things Joan could have said to him, this had not made the list. 'The mayor? Am I expecting them?'

Joan professed to have no idea of the reason for the visit, and before Stayer could protest, a fit-looking middle-aged woman with an impressively blow-dried helmet of blonde hair walked through the station and into Stayer's office. Stayer had no choice but to follow her in there. He closed the door behind him, leaving Joan, Walsh and Sister Catherine to watch on from outside.

'Matt Stayer, it's an honour,' the woman said. 'Robin Yarden. Mayor of Thoorgala. I'm a huge fan—watched all your races.' She held out her hand, and Stayer felt he had no choice but to shake it.

'What can I do for you, Mayor Yarden?' Stayer said finally.

'I came to make sure you were swimming in the race this afternoon. The Black Island Classic.'

A fly buzzed around Stayer's head, slow and loud. He shooed it away with a sweaty hand. 'Sorry, I don't know what that is.'

'It's a swimming race? One kilometre. Around Black Island. It's famous! Held every year on Boxing Day. It's for charity and there's a five-thousand-dollar prize for the winner.' She looked at Stayer expectantly, as though waiting for him to catch on.

'I don't think I can. You might have heard; three people have been murdered.'

The mayor waved her hand dismissively. 'But it'd be a great draw for people. To watch you in the race, a former Olympian. Yes, there have been some unfortunate events. But seeing you swim will buoy everyone's spirits.'

'I'm really sorry,' Stayer said, trying to sound as emphatic as he could, 'it's simply impossible.'

'You can't back out now!' the mayor said, looking panicked. 'You're on the promotional material. Thoorgalans are expecting you to swim. We had flyers printed with your photo on them.'

'What? I didn't give permission for that. I never said I would swim in the race. I'd never even heard of it until you told me just now.'

'You entered weeks ago!'

'I did not.'

'You did. Your sister submitted the entry form.'

Stayer looked at her, baffled. His mind swam.

'I apologise for any misunderstanding,' he said, when he had recovered his voice, 'but I'm afraid I won't be participating.'

After several more rounds of Mayor Yarden imploring and Stayer declining, the mayor finally left, angry and tearful, muttering about severe disappointment and potential in lost revenue. Stayer resumed brooding at his desk, his mind fixed on an image: of Ruby entering him in the race, for reasons she had not explained, scratching his name into an entry form without telling him.

'I think you should swim in the race, detective.'

He raised his head to find Sister Catherine in the doorway to his office.

'You can't be serious. In the middle of a murder investigation? You think that's a good use of my time?'

'I do. The whole town will be there. You might find out something significant or discover something we've been missing. I overheard the mayor in your office. She said Ruby entered you in the race. Why do you think she did that?'

He shrugged. 'I really don't know.'

'Could it have something to do with this case?' Sister Catherine offered him a kind smile.

'Fine. I'll go in the race. But I burned all my speedos when I retired,' Stayer said.

The nun's face brightened. 'That won't be a problem.'

'And I'll need something to eat. Walsh? You there?'

The constable appeared in the doorway, his frame casting a shadow over the nun. 'Boss?'

'I'm going to the beach. You stay here and keep trying Sergeant Nichols' phone. Call me the second you get through.'

4.30 PM

Arriving at Cundra beach, with its glare and heat and smell of sunscreen, Stayer instantly regretted agreeing to the swim. Hundreds of people packed the shoreline, and they all turned to look at Stayer as he walked onto the sand in his suit and leather shoes. He had no idea what he was doing there; he racked his brain for some reason why Ruby might have entered him.

The hot wind churned the waves. Ink green water rose and crashed then was sucked back out to sea. Stayer scanned the beach, looking for anything out of the ordinary. He felt wired and on edge, like he'd drunk too much coffee. Which he almost certainly had—he'd stopped counting after his eighth cup.

Sister Catherine ran up and handed Stayer two bags. One was made of plastic; the other was a small paper bag with a circle of grease beginning to bloom from its corner. 'A swimsuit and a sausage sandwich.'

Stayer tore open the paper bag and shoved the sausage sandwich into his mouth. The fatty sausage hit his teeth, making him feel nauseous.

He ducked into the change rooms and donned the pair of borrowed speedos. He returned to the beach and Sister Catherine approached.

'You look sporty,' she said.

He glared at her. 'They're leopard print!' he said. 'Where did you get them?'

'It was all they had at short notice. An old pair left over from a charity show. Some of the boat crew danced like in *The Full Monty* and one left their costume in the lost and found. What is it, detective?' she added, seeming to notice his discomfort.

'I don't know what I'm doing here. I shouldn't be racing. I should be out looking for Ruby, investigating the case. I don't know why she entered me.'

'Does the reason matter? Maybe your sister remembered how much you used to love it. Maybe she just wanted to see you race. You're here now. Make of it what you can.'

He joined the group of racers on the sand. Someone tapped Stayer's back. He turned. A boy of about ten stood behind him.

'Here,' the kid said, holding out a pair of goggles. 'Sister told me to bring you these.'

'Thanks,' Stayer said, putting the goggles on his head. They had sea creatures on them. 'Kid. What do you know about surf swimming? I don't care about winning, I just don't want to die out there.' He stared at the churning surf.

'Get down low when the waves come,' he said. 'And stay out of the other guys' wash.'

Stayer listened intently. 'Anything else?'

'Yeah: catch a wave on the way back in. The guy that gets the wave wins the race.'

A man holding a starter's pistol called all competitors to a line drawn in the sand. He explained the rules: they were to swim around the buoys which snaked around the back of Black Island and return. 'First over the line wins.'

Twenty or so men placed their toes on the line and crouched. Stayer glanced over the beach one last time but saw nothing out of the ordinary. The gun went off.

The men launched themselves forward. Their late-teenage and early twenties frames hit the surf, tanned legs and muscular shoulders disappearing into the green water. Taut bodies, sinewy, they bloomed with speed and fitness. Stayer lumbered behind, pale, heavy, the wrong side of thirty, in a borrowed swimsuit and goggles meant for children.

They reached the breaking water as a group and began diving under it. Stayer, already lagging, arrived at the waves a few seconds later and threw an arm over, stroking instinctively like he was in the pool, and found a churning wash of white foam fizzing in his hands. He looked up and sucked salt water into his mouth and nose. It stung. He remembered what the kid had told him—'Get down low when the waves come'—and realised his error. The next wave built and came for him, and this time, instead of hanging on the surface and trying to swim through it, he dived down low, under the water, aiming for the sand, and waited for the wave to pass. He snuck a look upwards as the wave thundered over the top. The water became a terrible, rolling-cloud sky above him, and he decided this was what being buried alive must feel like.

More breakers came and he ducked under these too, until finally he had cleared the white surf and found himself floating in open water. He looked ahead and discovered his initial mistake had cost him dearly. The other swimmers were far ahead of him, swimming in a pack, and he was coming dead last.

The sight woke a long-dormant beast inside of him.

He hurled himself into the loneliness and difficulty of swimming, water filling his ears and nose, bubbling, gurgling, swishing, making the world both deathly quiet and noisy as hell. He remembered how much he hated and loved this. He sucked a deep ball of air into his chest, then shoved his head down and stroked twenty times—*twenty*: enough to swim the length of an Olympic-sized swimming pool—without drawing breath. He began to feel the satisfying tingle and burn of pumping muscles and stretching limbs, doing something they hadn't done in a long time but had done many, many times before.

He swam on and his fingers brushed something cold and wriggling; he recoiled, thinking he'd finally touched a shark, but then he raised his head and saw that he'd reached the swimmer at the back of the pack, and realised he'd skimmed his toes. He remembered the kid's second piece of advice—'Stay out of the other guys' wash'—and made a left turn, swimming across the bodies, until he reached a clear stretch of water, away from everyone else.

The pack arrived at the string of buoys which bobbed around the back of the island. Stayer followed around the edge, watching as some of the men got tangled in the ropes. Their bodies wrestled and struggled, fast and heavy. He swam on and reached the end of the buoys and turned once again. He now faced the beach.

He looked ahead for the pack of swimmers but couldn't see them. He glanced over his shoulder and saw them, a cluster of froth and churned water, a few metres back. They were behind him. He was in the lead.

He turned back to face the beach saw the flags marking the finishing line. A dark figure stepped out from the crowd. It wore a black cape. It was difficult to see much from that far away, but it bore a resemblance to the image of Tall Harry that Sister Catherine had shown him at their first meeting.

Stayer's head slammed forward, and he realised that a wave had hit him from behind. He had been treading water, stunned, watching the figure, and had not anticipated the wave coming. Salt water scoured his throat and nose like vinegar. As he resurfaced, the black figure melted into the crowd on the sand. Stayer had to get back to the beach.

He resumed swimming but discovered that he was growing very, very tired. He could feel his stroke slowing; it was like swimming through butter. He remembered the kid's final words of wisdom: 'The guy that gets the wave wins the race.' He didn't care about winning, but the advice still applied; a wave would get him to shore as fast as possible.

He turned to see one swelling behind him. What chance did he have of catching it? Some of the guys behind him had missed the wave already, and they were practised surf swimmers. And then it was upon him, the force of it like an explosion, propelling him forward. He straightened his back like a rod and rode the wave and felt elated. Then suddenly his knees grazed sand, and he'd reached the beach.

He pulled himself to his feet awkwardly. Another swimmer had caught the wave with him, and was beginning to stand too, a dozen or so metres down the beach. The other swimmer picked up his pace and began surging towards the finish, his face contorting with the effort. But while the younger man wanted to win a swimming race, Stayer's mind was only on catching the black-clad figure. He groaned, hating sand yet again, the way it made his legs feel like lead, and with a last, undignified, lung-busting gasp, threw his fleshy, leopard print-speedoed form towards the crowd. He reached the finish line and kept on running, past the marshals offering him bottles of water and congratulations. He ran into the crowd, ignoring the praise and laughter. 'Well done, mate, but you can stop now. You won!' He kept forcing his way through.

Sister Catherine found him. 'Well done, detective!' Her face was damp and happy.

'Someone's here,' he said to her, slowing to a stop. It hurt to breathe.

She nodded. 'Who? Where?'

'I saw him while I was in the water. He was in the crowd. Don't know what I saw exactly. It was a figure, dressed in black. Wearing a cape.'

'Like Tall Harry?'

Stayer shrugged and said nothing. He put his hands to his hips, trying to suck more air into his lungs.

Sister Catherine nodded again. 'Go right. I'll go left.'

She disappeared into the crowd.

Stayer turned in the other direction and resumed pushing his way through the people. They slapped his back and praised him for winning the swimming race. He offered a few curt smiles, if only so people would let him through. He moved his eyes left and right, up, and down, looking for any hint of a black outfit, a cape. He reached the edge of the crowd and was spat out onto a hot patch of sand at the end of the beach. He swivelled his head, searching. The sand felt like burning metal under his feet.

He turned back and made his way back to where he and Sister Catherine had parted.

She appeared a few moments later, holding her hands out in an empty gesture.

'See anything?' he asked.

She shook her head. 'Sorry, detective. Nothing.'

5 PM

A presentation ceremony followed, where the Mayor of Thoorgala, looking overjoyed, presented Stayer with a medal and a novelty cheque for $5000. They had escorted him to a podium in front of the surf club. He'd agreed to go only when he'd realised that on the podium he'd be raised above the crowd and afforded a view of the entire beach. He continued to scan the surrounds as the ceremony proceeded. There was no sign of the black figure in the mask.

The mayor gushed about what an honour it was to have a former Olympian competing and asked Stayer about the wave he'd caught to seal his win. Stayer answered absently, eyes fixed on the spot where he had first seen the masked figure. Then he and the mayor posed for a photo for the local newspaper, the mayor flushed and sweating in ceremonial robes and wearing a cartoonishly large medallion and chain, Stayer in his leopard-print speedos. As he leaned in to pose for the camera, a flash of black slinked across the back of the crowd. It was the caped figure from before. Not only was he wearing a cape, but he also had a mask covering his entire face: with sharpened teeth and a devilish grin. The figure waved at Stayer.

Stayer jumped from the podium.

Baffled, amused, and angry faces met him as he pushed through the crowd once more. He ran down the path leading away from the beach. The caped figure was about twenty metres ahead of him. Stayer had no shoes on—no clothes, either—and as he ran, every rock, twig, and bottlecap stabbed the soles of his feet. The black figure lolloped up a seaside path, away from the crowds, and Stayer ran after him, lungs and legs feeling like lead from the swimming race. The path sloped upwards and curved around a hill. Coastal heath lined one side, their brown and green needles scratching Stayer's bare skin. The other side of the path dropped steeply towards a swell of emerald ocean below.

The path climbed higher, tracing the cliffs above Cundra Beach's southern side. Stayer felt like he might faint. The figure, still running, disappeared around a bend. When Stayer caught up he saw the figure at the top of the cliff, waiting. He stood at the mouth of the Thoorgala Blowhole.

They stayed like that for several moments: Stayer on the path, gasping for breath, and the figure motionless at the clifftop. Stayer was too far away to get an accurate idea of the person underneath the costume.

Stayer stepped forward, and in response the figure stepped backward, now dangerously close to the cliff's edge. Stayer held his hands up to indicate he wouldn't go any further.

'Who are you?' he called out. 'Can we talk?'

The figure cocked his head, as though finding Stayer a curious specimen. He raised an arm and pointed at something beside the blowhole, then took off along the path running down the side of the cliff to the caves below. Stayer took off too, but when he reached the clifftop, the figure had disappeared. He was still standing there, looking, when something hit him from behind with incredible force. He fell forward, smacking his head on the ground. Water rushed into his ears and mouth.

He leaped out of the way as the blowhole geared up to explode again. The force of the spurting water shocked him; it was like being struck with a plank of wood.

Then someone grabbed him and pulled him backward. He turned to see Sister Catherine gripping his arm.

'Move away before it blows again,' she urged.

She held his elbow and guided him to a wooden bench beside the viewing platform. Stayer's chest hurt. His left eye felt sticky and warm. 'You're bleeding,' the nun said.

She moved his hand away and pressed something dry and scratchy to his eyebrow. It was the bottom of her veil. The rough wool prickled his skin.

'You must have hit your head on the rocks.'

Stayer tried to stand, but Sister Catherine forced his shoulder down gently. 'Wait a few moments. You might have a concussion.'

'I want to find the guy in the mask,' Stayer said, his voice weary. 'He was right here.'

'He's gone,' the nun said regretfully. 'I saw him running away across those rocks, then he disappeared. I'm sorry, detective. Maybe Constable Walsh could come from the station and drive down Peninsula Way, the road that snakes around the headland. It's the only route in or out.'

Stayer turned towards where she was pointing, saw a line of rocks and caves in the distance. He couldn't see the masked figure.

'You need stitches,' she said. 'I suggest we go back to your squad car.'

Stayer reluctantly agreed, and Sister Catherine helped him to his feet.

'Did the masked figure say anything to you before he disappeared?' she asked him.

Stayer shook his head. It sounded like the inside of a car wash. 'He pointed at something.'

'We should go back together and take a look,' she said.

He led Sister Catherine carefully to the blowhole and stopped where the masked figure had stood before vanishing.

A small marble plinth lay next to the blowhole. Its face hosted a brass plate that commemorated a person who had died there fifteen years earlier, apparently by falling into the blowhole. The man's name was Stanley Lacey.

5.30 PM

Stanley Lacey: enfant terrible, Casanova, rock star artist. That's how he was described in the online encyclopedia which Stayer now read on his phone. The blazing sun made the screen almost impossible to read; he had to hold the phone at an angle to see the words.

He was sitting in the driver's seat of the squad car, the door open, his feet planted on the sandy bitumen of the Cundra Beach car park. Stayer had called Constable Walsh and told him to search for the figure on Peninsula Way, then had dressed hurriedly by the side of the car, putting his trousers and shirt back on over the speedos. He made a mental note to return them, though he doubted someone was desperately missing the leopard-print swimwear. He still had sand in his hair and under his fingernails from the ocean swim. His skin felt dried out and hot, his mouth was pasty and white with salt. He longed for a shower, a drink of water, but instead kept reading about the life and achievements of the artist called Stanley Lacey.

He had no idea why he was reading about this man or what he should be looking for, but he kept scrolling. After detailing the usual biographical items—place of birth, early education, family members—the entry spoke at length about an early artwork called *Sunset*, the painting that heralded Stanley Lacey's entree into the art world. An image was included in the article. Stayer enlarged it, hoping it would shed some light on what was so far seeming like a futile exercise.

The painting was not of a sunset but of a decrepit old man, splayed naked on a chair, grinning lasciviously. It had won the Doug Moran portrait prize, apparently, and was Lacey's most lucrative early sale. Mounds of flesh, wrinkles, and a limp and oily penis slunk between dimpled thighs. The subject smiled at the viewer, his mouth a wet and angry red slash. Stayer found this all mildly interesting but proceeded to scroll faster and faster through the article, scanning the words with urgency, trying to find something, anything that would connect the artist with the murders on the sandhills and with his sister's disappearance. He read on, feeling increasingly dejected.

The portrait called *Sunset* was used on the album cover of a giant 1980s rock band and had made Stanley Lacey a superstar, Stayer learned. He straightened a little in the driver's seat as this single detail jolted him. He recalled this album. Yes, he remembered holding it once over his father's turntable, the paper rustling as he removed the record from inside the sleeve, the bark of his father from the living room to be careful. He had pulled the album cover out from the shelf now and then as a kid, staring at the oily penis with horror and fascination.

The encyclopedia entry listed a few other paintings by Stanley Lacey: mostly minor works which had not done as well as *Sunset*. By the 2000s, it seemed Stanley Lacey had fallen out of favour or just wasn't cool anymore. He married and adopted a son and moved his studio to a suburban mansion called Eveleigh. He had sessional gigs teaching oil painting at regional art galleries and did artist residencies at private schools. Then, in 2010, he enjoyed something of a major resurgence, primarily to do with a new painting called *Sea Bitch*. This new work had won the Archibald Prize and been lauded internationally, touring galleries around the world.

It was celebrated primarily for inventing a new painting technique to depict waves in an impressionist style. Stayer had no idea what this meant, but according to the online article, the technique was now so synonymous with the artist that it was forever after known as Laceyism. Stayer scrolled further down the article, looking for a photo of *Sea Bitch*, but couldn't find one. After Stanley Lacey's death, the article said, the painting was withdrawn from public display.

Stayer closed his phone and stared at the pounding surf, baffled. He knew of no connection whatsoever between the artist Stanley Lacey, who had died fifteen years ago, to the three women who had been murdered in the sandhills. He began wondering if he might have made some terrible mistake, that the person in the Tall Harry costume had not been pointing to the memorial by the blowhole at all.

Sister Catherine appeared, carrying a first-aid kit. Stayer had refused to go to hospital and the nun, having seen his desperate and stubborn expression, agreed to go looking for something to treat his head wound. 'I convinced the lifeguards to give it to me,' she said as she approached the car. 'Shall I do the honours?'

'Thanks.'

On the car's dashboard she laid out some swabs, a small brown bottle of antiseptic solution, and thin plaster strips. 'I'll touch you now, if you'll permit me.'

He baulked at the strange and polite request, then suddenly, for some reason, he felt nervous. He nodded anyway. As she moved the swab, now soaked in the disinfectant, towards his face, their eyes met briefly, and they shared a look Stayer couldn't categorise exactly. He sat in silence as she pressed the swab to his eyebrow with her small, fine fingers. The brown ointment felt cool and damp on his skin and smelled pleasingly clinical.

'What did you find out about Stanley Lacey?' she asked, dabbing the cut.

The breaking waves of Cundra Beach sounded behind them, like white noise from an old television.

'He was an artist,' Stayer said. 'A successful one.' He told Sister Catherine about Lacey's wild reputation, his prize-winning artworks. He showed her the picture of *Sunset*, the naked old man lying spread-eagled, grinning.

'Oh, yes—the album cover,' she said. 'Not my style of music, but I remember that image. Quite famous at the time.'

'What's your style of music? Let me guess: death metal? Gangster rap?'

'Metallica made some great songs in their day.' She finished with the antiseptic solution and removed the adhesive strips from their backing.

Stayer told her about the other painting, *Sea Bitch*, how it was even more lauded than *Sunset* but no longer displayed in public.

She shook her head. 'I'm not familiar with that one.' She pressed another strip to his brow. The skin of her finger felt smooth. Stayer closed his eyes. He listened to her breathing. Soft, small inhalations, slightly shallow.

'Finished,' Sister Catherine said. She stepped back. 'That should hold the wound closed.'

Stayer inspected himself in the rear-view mirror. A neat line of strips lay across the gash on his eyebrow. A thin line of red remained the only sign of the wound. 'An excellent job. Thank you.'

Sister Catherine smiled, looking quietly proud with herself. 'Did the article say how Stanley Lacey died?'

Stayer clicked his phone back into life and scrolled. 'It says he fell into the Thoorgala Blowhole. The plaque by the blowhole said the same thing. A coroner ruled the cause of death as accidental.'

He switched over to another tab in his web browser, where he'd opened a different article on Stanley Lacey. He scrolled through, scanning for any other information on the artist's death. He paused.

'What is it, detective?'

'This article says that Stanley Lacey undertook several artist residencies in the years leading up to his death. It lists the schools and organisations he worked at. Stanley Lacey completed an artist's residency at Thoorgala Grammar, the year the three murder victims were in year ten at the school.'

5.41 PM

Stayer and Sister Catherine began the drive back to the station, passing the beach again on their way through. The crowd that had gathered for the Black Island Classic had dispersed, leaving empty plastic bottles on the sand. A beach tent with a snapped pole lay crumpled and abandoned next to a full rubbish bin. The rough wind had picked up again, blowing chip packets across the footpath by the side of the road.

A traffic light went red ahead of them and Stayer halted the squad car. An elderly woman with a walking frame began to cross. As she came in line with them, she turned and began walking directly towards the squad car. She knocked on Stayer's window, making a winding motion with her hands. He opened the window.

'Please get off the road, ma'am,' he said. 'You could get hit by a car.'

'G'day detective,' she said. 'Can you give me a lift home?'

'I'm sorry, that's not possible.'

Sister Catherine shot him a dismayed look. The woman was wheezing and appeared faint.

'It's important,' the old woman said. 'I must tell you something. The three women found dead on the sandhills. I taught them in high school.'

•

Sister Catherine helped the old lady, who'd introduced herself as Mrs Button, into the back seat while Stayer loaded her walking frame into the boot. Stayer turned the engine over and they departed.

'Tell me, Mrs Button. You taught the victims?'

'I taught English at Thoorgala Grammar for forty-two years. Phoebe Glasson, Miki Sorgensen, and Jessie Phan. I taught all three of them. About Shakespeare. About Jane Austen.'

Stayer's breath quickened. 'What can you tell us about them?'

'Mikaela always used a grocer's apostrophe. Like putting an apostrophe to show ownership on subjects that didn't own anything. CDs, DVDs, et cetera. Very distracting. Other teachers said it was because she spoke Swedish at home, and that using the two languages got things mixed up in her brain. I don't see how that could have been the reason, because the Swedish language doesn't use apostrophes that way either. I suspect she had dyslexia, though it was less diagnosed in those days. Phoebe was brilliant, but a wild girl. Clever, but spent too much time smoking and drinking and sneaking around with boys to reach the highest heights. She still did fine in any case, went to uni, made something of herself. Jessie loved poetry, which was unexpected. I think she liked the imagery, the metaphors. I still collect my prescriptions from her, at her pharmacy. Collected . . . I can't believe they're dead.'

She went quiet, looking out the window.

'Thanks for that extensive info, Mrs Button,' Stayer said, trying not to sound ungrateful. 'Did the victims have anything to do with Stanley Lacey at the school?'

'Who?'

'He was the artist in residence at Thoorgala Grammar around the time they were in year ten.'

'Oh yes,' Mrs Button said. 'Leather pants man.'

'I'm sorry?' Stayer said. He shot a look at Sister Catherine.

'Stanley Lacey. He used to walk through the school grounds in absurd leather pants. I think he thought he was Jim Morrison. Do you get that reference? Jim Morrison. You are one of those millennials. He might be too old for you.'

'I get the Jim Morrison reference. Did the girls have anything to do with him? Stanley Lacey, that is?'

'I wouldn't think so,' Mrs Button said. 'I don't remember any of those girls in his seminars. None of them studied art. The art rooms were right next to my classroom. I never saw them go in there.'

'Do you have any information about anything other than their English abilities, Mrs Button?'

'I'm sorry, that's all I know. I thought I was being helpful.'

Stayer could feel himself deflating.

'You've been very helpful, Mrs Button,' Sister Catherine said, turning to smile at her. 'Thank you.'

They rode on in silence. Stayer's head felt heavy and sore. The sun made red sparks inside his eyelids. Maybe he truly did have a concussion from the blowhole, like Sister Catherine said.

Then he opened his mouth suddenly and asked another question.

'Did you teach Ruby Stayer, Mrs Button?'

Mrs Button turned her head to him slowly. 'Ruby Stayer was the best student I ever had.'

•

They arrived at Mrs Button's house, and while Sister Catherine helped her out of the car, Stayer fetched her walking frame. Its legs grazed the lip of the boot, making a chinking sound. He handed her the frame and she leaned on it gratefully. The skin of her hands was thin and papery.

Stayer and Sister Catherine walked either side of Mrs Button as she inched towards her house, throwing the walking frame in front of her in tiny increments. 'A girl with the devil of genius in her, Ruby Stayer was. Quiet and clever, with a brilliant mind. Most of the time you can't recall your students' names within a year of them leaving. But Ruby was one of those kids I could never forget. She won the English prize every year—no contest. She read every text I set, and wrote beautiful essays. And she was a spectacular painter. Never seen anything like it. Her paintings moved me to tears.' She stopped for a moment to rest, leaning on her frame.

Stayer felt a lump in his throat. He had never heard anyone speak of his sister this way.

'Like looking at the work of an old master, Ruby's paintings were,' Mrs Button continued, 'such beauty and sadness. You got lost in them. Van Gogh reincarnated in an Australian teenager. Then one day, something darkened in her.'

Sister Catherine stepped closer, the dry grass crunching under her feet.

'What happened?' Stayer heard himself say. He strove for a casual tone which he didn't think he achieved.

'I don't know,' Mrs Button said. 'All I know is that she changed. Some light went out. Might have just been teenage-girl stuff—I saw it happen often enough. Around fifteen or sixteen, in girls of a certain type, a light goes out. It's sad, but then so are a lot of things. Why do you ask about Ruby Stayer?'

'She's my sister.'

'My goodness,' Mrs Button said, eyes brightening. 'You must be so proud. Does she still do her art?'

'She's—she's missing,' Stayer said.

The old woman's face fell. 'I don't understand. She disappeared? How long ago? Why?'

'About three days ago. Her disappearance might be linked to the murders in the sandhills,' he added. 'So, if you remember anything significant from when you taught her, anything at all, please tell us.'

Mrs Button's face seemed to darken. The frangipani tree behind her swayed in the hot breeze. The wind knocked flowers to the ground, white petals stained with brown at the edges. 'You asked about Stanley Lacey before,' Mrs Button said. 'Ruby went to his art seminars. Those other girls had no connection to Stanley Lacey, but Ruby certainly did. I mentioned I saw a light go out in Ruby? If you ask me, it had something to do with that man.'

Stayer froze. 'What happened?'

'I don't know what, exactly. It was hushed up.'

'If it was hushed up, how did you know about it?' Stayer asked. He heard the sharpness in his voice.

Mrs Button shrugged. 'I asked about it at the time. No one would tell me anything. I'm sorry. I wish I could help you, but I've told you everything I remember. Can I go inside now? I need to sit down.'

Stayer felt like grabbing her and shaking her.

'I'll help you inside,' Sister Catherine said. She took the old woman's arm and led her down the path. Heat rose from the concrete like hot coals. Stayer watched the two women walk away from him, feeling rooted to the ground.

•

'Can I show you something?' Sister Catherine said, entering Stayer's office. They had finally returned to the station, driving there from Mrs Button's house in mutual silence. He followed her into his office and watched as she collected three files and spread them across his desk. They were the autopsy reports for the three women found in the sandhills.

'These are the times and dates each woman went missing, and the times and dates they were found on the sandhills. Does anything stand out? Phoebe Glasson, time of death between two and four am on December twenty-fourth. Mikaela Sorgensen, time of death between two and four am on December twenty-fifth. Jessie Phan, time of death between—'

'Between two and four am, December twenty-sixth,' Stayer said, leaning forward. He felt his breathing quicken.

'It is now almost six pm on December twenty-sixth. If Tall Harry is keeping to some kind of system—'

'He is going to dump another body on the sandhills,' Stayer jumped in, 'about eight hours from now.' His breath had grown wild and his eyes darted over the autopsy files. He felt jittery and desperate. The body the killer could dump on the sand was Ruby's, but Stayer couldn't bring himself to say it, to speak his sister's name.

Sister Catherine handed him his phone. 'Send Constable Walsh out to the sandhills,' she said. 'He can stand sentry. Watch for anything untoward. If someone tries to dump a body, he will see it.'

Stayer accepted the phone gratefully and dialled.

Constable Walsh answered quickly. Stayer explained the plan to him over the phone, and Walsh agreed eagerly. 'I'll drive out to the sandhills now,' he said.

Stayer exhaled. 'Thank you, Walsh.'

'Tall Harry vanished into thin air, by the way,' Constable Walsh added. Stayer heard a car engine start down the line.

'I'm sorry?' Stayer said.

'The guy at the blowhole, wearing the Tall Harry costume. I drove around Peninsula Way, up and down. Took the squad car all around the headland. Nothing. Sorry boss.'

'Oh. Never mind. Thanks for looking.' He hung up and turned to Sister Catherine, who offered him a nervous smile.

Stayer's phone rang again and he answered swiftly. It was Dr Dixon.

'Detective, I know it's late. But could you come back to the morgue?' He sounded agitated.

'Why? What's happened?'

'Victim two has victim three's blood on her.'

6.02 PM

Stayer and Sister Catherine waited by the lift to take them down to the morgue. The wall lights came on in the hospital corridor, glowing yellow. Stayer pressed the call button, a small silver disc which lit up blue. 'Wait here, I won't be long,' he said to Sister Catherine.

'I want to come with you, detective,' she said. 'To the morgue.'

He sighed. 'We've been through this, several times. You can't come to morgues, to interview witnesses, to crime scenes—'

'I hear what you're saying. Things have gone too far now.' Her gentle tone silenced him. 'We both heard what Mrs Button said, about your sister's connection to Stanley Lacey. Your sister is missing, and the individual who has killed these women has probably taken her too. Every minute that passes takes Ruby one minute closer to being killed, if she's even still alive. You need all the help you can get, detective. Let me. You relay the information to me afterwards anyway, it saves time if I just come with you.'

The lift doors opened; Stayer stepped inside. Sister Catherine watched him hesitantly. 'Are you coming or not?' he said.

She jumped inside the lift.

Dr Dixon's office adjoined the morgue. A long, built-in desk stretched across one wall, hosting a filing tray, pens and pencils, pathology request forms, and a desktop computer with three screens. A poster of Leonardo da Vinci's *Vitruvian Man* hung above the desk. A glass window formed the opposite wall. It looked out onto the steel gurneys of the autopsy room.

Dr Dixon gazed curiously at Sister Catherine as she entered the room. He turned to Stayer expectantly. 'Doc, this is Sister Catherine Kelley,' Stayer said. 'She's an expert in folklore.'

A flash of recognition dawned on Dr Dixon. 'I've read your book, sister. Dane Dixon.' They shook hands.

'It might seem unorthodox to bring her down here,' Stayer began.

'Actually, it's the first smart idea you've had,' Dr Dixon said good-naturedly. 'Come in, sister. Welcome.' He turned to his desk.

Sister Catherine stood beside Stayer. The fabric of her veil gently brushed his shoulder. Dr Dixon pointed to a series of numbers and codes on the first computer screen.

'I collected a blood sample from the second victim, Mikaela Sorgensen, which wasn't hers and wasn't in the police database. Female blood. I catalogued it but couldn't identify it. After analysing Jessie Phan, the third victim, I found it was Jessie's blood on Mikaela Sorgensen. Jessie had a bloodied nose. The spray must have landed on Mikaela when the injury occurred.'

The pathologist shifted his weight from foot to foot. The computer screen glowed, making his face blue.

'Where is he keeping them?' Stayer said.

'I can't answer that,' Dr Dixon said. 'But I did find something else. In all three victims' hair, I've found granules. Here . . .'

He passed Stayer a small, clear evidence bag.

Stayer studied its contents. 'This looks like sand,' he said. He rolled his fingers under the bag. Particles sparkled like tiny jewels. 'Is it from the sandhills where their bodies were found?'

'I thought that at first, too. It has similar properties to sand, but it's chalk.'

'The caves around the Cundra Valley contain chalk,' Sister Catherine said.

'I found these chalk particles in the hair at the back of each woman's head,' Dr Dixon said. 'Near the crown. As though their heads were resting against the chalk.'

'He's keeping them in a cave,' Sister Catherine said.

'Not exactly,' said Dr Dixon. 'Because mixed in with the chalk, I found particles of cement.'

'I'm at a loss, doc. What does a mix of cement and chalk mean? He moved the victims to multiple locations before killing them? A construction site? A school?'

'I don't know,' Dr Dixon replied. The room fell quiet. The fan on the desktop computer whirred.

'When they built many of the waterfront houses around the Thoorgala headland, they cut a basement into the earth,' Sister Catherine said. 'Chalk comprises most of the rock in that area. Chalk can crumble and become unstable, so they reinforced these spaces with concrete. This would explain the chalk-cement dust on the victims. The killer could be keeping them in one of these basements.'

The two men turned to the nun. 'How do you know this?' Stayer asked her.

'When I wrote my book, I interviewed over four hundred local people. Many of them lived in those very houses. With these types of basements.'

The energy in the room seemed to shift. Stayer smiled. 'I think you might be on to something, sister. How many houses are there along the headland?'

'My grandmother used to live down that way, before she went into a nursing home,' Dr Dixon said. 'Her address was one ninety-eight Peninsula Way. It was the second last house on the road.'

'In other words, there're about two hundred houses,' said Stayer. 'If we search them one by one, we might find Ruby.'

The plan was formalised, a map accessed. House numbers drawn up in a list and divided, weapons and ammunition checked. Dr Dixon nodded to Stayer. 'Good luck.'

Stayer called Constable Walsh back to tell him the plan.

Constable Walsh listened eagerly. 'Great plan, boss,' he said down the phone line. 'I hope your next call to me is with your sister.' Detective Stayer slid the clip inside his service weapon and pushed it into his shoulder holster. He went to hang up his phone when Constable Walsh spoke again.

'By the way, boss. Did you find anything out? From that guy dressed as Tall Harry at the blowhole?'

'Oh,' Stayer said, thinking back. 'Sort of. The guy in the costume was pointing at the commemorative plaque for Stanley Lacey.'

There was a pause down the phone line. 'Right,' Constable Walsh said finally, 'I remember now. The artist. He painted the album cover with the old naked guy on it.'

'That's the one. He died at the blowhole.'

'Yeah. It's coming back to me now. There were rumours about that guy,' Constable Walsh said. The computer's fan stopped whirring. The screens flicked to a screensaver.

'Rumours?' Stayer said.

'Yeah,' Walsh said. 'That his death wasn't an accident.'

6.30 PM

The figure paced back and forth. He had the torch with him again, and the beam moved as he swung his arms slightly. She followed the light as it flicked into corners, onto walls. She saw the room in flashes: shelves, a cabinet, wine bottles, cats' eyes. A concrete wall, a wooden staircase, a climbing frame for cats covered in rotting carpet. She could now pair images to the smells: the ammonia and other hamster cage odours were coming from a large area dedicated to her feline companions: kitty litter trays, plastic food bowls, dishes of water. The wet, earthy smell came from the concrete. She was in a basement; she was sure of it now.

7.40 PM

Stayer and Sister Catherine—who had, once again, insisted on accompanying him—drove directly to 2 Peninsula Way, the first house on the road which snaked around the Thoorgala headland. Stayer used his lights, no sirens, moving deftly but calmly through the traffic.

As they exited the car, he caught his reflection in the glass and shuddered. He was still in his rumpled suit with speedos underneath and smelled like the ocean. 'I wonder if I should have showered and changed first,' he said, 'before we go knocking on rich people's doors, asking to see their basements.'

'Or maybe your desperate appearance might work in our favour,' Sister Catherine replied helpfully, 'people might take pity on you?'

'Fingers crossed,' Stayer said.

They walked up a gravel drive towards a house of un-showy wealth, a sandstone and brick, split-level, mid-century home.

Stayer knocked on the door, heart thumping.

A man in his early seventies dressed in a Ralph Lauren polo shirt and jeans answered. He wore the pleasant and gracious expression that came from owning a seven-bedroom waterfront on the Thoorgala headland.

As Stayer showed his badge and explained their far-fetched predicament, the old man's eyes flicked to Sister Catherine, who nodded reassuringly. Stayer was beginning to realise how useful it could be to have a nun on your side. When he sensed they'd won the old man over, Stayer finally asked, 'Could we see your basement?'

The man did not hesitate, welcoming them inside. Stayer and Sister Catherine stepped into an air-conditioned, open-plan living-dining-kitchen area, surrounded by floor-to-ceiling windows looking out onto the gently undulating waves and moored dinghies of Port Joseph Bay. The view took Stayer's breath away.

'I'll take you down to the basement,' the house's owner said in a friendly baritone. He explained that they had indeed built the basement by cutting into the rock of Thoorgala headland.

Stayer felt a zap as they descended a spiral staircase into the chalk-and-concrete basement.

'We use this as a storage space and wine cellar,' the owner explained. Racks held dusty bottles stacked neatly on one side. The man showed Sister Catherine some bottles of Grange from the 1960s. The nun smiled politely and admired the labels. A disused treadmill, suitcases, and golf clubs lay against the other wall. The owner clearly held no women down there. He showed no sign of participating in any criminal activity at all.

It was time to move on to the next house.

They knocked on the door of 4 Peninsula Way, the next house along. A similarly unshowy display of wealth greeted them: mid-century design, sandstone, at least three storeys built into the rocks.

They waited. No one answered the door.

Sister Catherine knocked again. Nothing. 'I'll look around the side.' She began walking off.

'Wait,' Stayer said, grabbing her small wrist. 'Look.'

The nun peered up to where he'd pointed. A large, expensive-looking CCTV camera pointed directly down at them. 'This house has a security system to make ASIO jealous. Multiple cameras, probably a nuclear warhead in the back somewhere. We have no probable cause to enter the property, no warrant, and a judge certainly wouldn't give us one. We can't go further.'

'Okay,' she said reluctantly. She hesitated before finally leaving the driveway.

The next four houses were all the same. No answer when they knocked. Security systems that would catch a spider sneezing. Each property knocking him sideways with their wealth, their size.

The next house, 14 Peninsula Way, stunned Stayer. Vines covered the house, in its entirety; they emerged from the ground, thick and green, and climbed up the walls and over the flat roof, as though they roped the house to the ground. The house would have been fashionable once, all rounded angles, like something the Jetsons might live in. Now it looked like a cardboard box left out in the rain until it rotted and was reclaimed by nature.

They knocked and waited. No one answered.

Stayer had a skin-crawling feeling as they stood on the porch, the overripe smell of the vines hitting him. He knocked again. No answer.

'Let's go, detective,' Sister Catherine said to him. 'I can see CCTV cameras on the roof.'

It took considerable cajoling from the nun before Stayer finally agreed to leave. He vowed to return as soon as he could and keep returning until he caught the owner at home.

They continued knocking on doors down Peninsula Way. Wherever they found residents at home, they were more than willing to welcome them inside. People were in a festive mood, off work, and were idle and curious, hot and bored. Offers of sherry and Christmas cake abounded. Stayer and Sister Catherine saw basements in use as wine cellars, home cinemas, and one that had been converted into a bowling alley. None housed Ruby Stayer.

The more doors they knocked on, the more it seemed that the grand plan might be turning into a fool's errand. Half the residents were not home, and those who were had been all too willing to show them around. Stayer couldn't see any situation in which an owner of one of these grand, easy-life houses would dress up as an urban legend and kill women.

Stayer sat on a brick fence bordering a playground halfway along Peninsula Way and turned to Sister Catherine. 'I'll drive you home. There's nothing more we can do here tonight.'

She protested for a time, suggesting they check a few more houses, or return to other doors they'd already knocked on, to see if the owners had just been out to dinner and now come back, but her face bore a look like she felt the quest was as futile as he did, and eventually she relented and accepted the offer of a lift home.

They drove quietly back out to Garribee, sporadically discussing the enduring hot weather, the bushfires, and remarking on the sizes of the houses they'd encountered on the headland. As they reached the nun's block of units and she exited the car, she paused, holding the car door.

'What do you think about what Constable Walsh said?' she asked Stayer. 'About Stanley Lacey's death not being an accident.'

Stayer absorbed this. 'I knew you were going to ask that.'

She leaned down, further into the car. Her handbag strap slipped from her shoulder. She replaced it softly. 'If it wasn't an accident, what then?' she said.

'If Stanley Lacey's death wasn't an accident, then someone killed him.'

27 DECEMBER

6.30 AM

Stayer woke with a woolly head and a sandpaper mouth. He called Constable Walsh, cursing himself for falling asleep.

'Sorry, boss, nothing to report,' Walsh said, his voice weary. Stayer had spent the night calling Constable Walsh at hourly intervals. And now morning had come and nothing had happened. No bodies had shown up, on the sandhills or anywhere else. After three straight days when bodies had been found, this was the first day without one appearing. And Ruby was still missing.

Stayer showered in the open air then drove to the police station, arriving a little after seven, even though his shift didn't start until eight. Once he got there, he wondered why he had rushed. He had nothing to go on. He sat at his desk, the photos of the symbols carved into the victims' bodies splayed out before him, angry red marks on purplish skin. He read internet articles about Stanley Lacey and Tall Harry. The more he read about artworks and wild parties, about witches and urban legends, the less he knew. He felt wiped out and nauseous, as though hungover. Ruby had been gone for three days now, and they were no closer to finding her than they had been in the first moments he realised she was missing. He tried not to think about the statistic every cop knows, drilled into them at the academy and during training, and confirmed firsthand out in the field: that if a missing person, particularly a woman or child who has vanished under suspicious circumstances, is not found in the first four hours, they are almost certainly dead. Some people say twenty-four, or even forty-eight hours is the magic number—the point at which it becomes evident the person is likely dead—but cops knew different. The number was horrifyingly, terribly lower than that. You had four hours to find a woman or child who had been taken. No more. And by the time Ruby had been gone for four hours, Stayer hadn't even known she was missing. This fact came to him almost constantly.

Stayer's phone rang, and he was grateful for the shrill noise it made, providing him with something to do with his hands and brain, other than pore over symbols, pictures of cadavers, statistics. He assumed it was Aunt Carol calling again for an update, but it was a number he didn't recognise. 'Detective Stayer,' he answered.

A polite male voice came on the line. 'Hello, detective. My name is Warren Nichols. I'm Jenny Nichols' father. Joan gave me your number.'

It took Stayer a moment before he realised the man was talking about Sergeant Nichols. 'Yes, of course. Mr Nichols. What can I do for you?' He leaned into the phone.

'Please, call me Warren. Jenny was supposed to fly up to Lismore on Christmas Day, after her shift. I went to the airport to pick her up at the arranged time, but she wasn't on the plane. I was wondering if you'd heard from her?'

The pedestal fan in Stayer's office made a crunching sound then stopped. A steamy heat seeped into the room instantly. Stayer walked to the fan and clicked the power button off and on. The fan didn't start.

'I haven't heard from Sergeant Nichols since Christmas morning,' he said.

Stayer recalled her silhouette in the hot sun, her watch beeping, her odd, disparaging words about Thoorgala. Then he recalled her dropping the body.

Stayer followed the fan's cord to the outlet and knelt down. He flicked the power off and on again. The fan remained off.

'I texted her early on Christmas morning to confirm that I'd pick her up at the airport,' Warren Nichols said. 'I texted again later to ask if her plane was on time, but she never answered. I've called many times, but I keep getting her voicemail. I've spoken to some of her friends and acquaintances, but no one's heard from her. We're a little frantic up here.' His voice cracked.

Sister Catherine entered his office, waving a greeting.

Stayer straightened. 'Don't worry, Mr Nichols. Warren. We'll find her.' He hung up with the promise to call him back.

'Everything okay?' Sister Catherine said.

•

After checking for the sergeant's address in the personnel files, Stayer—with the nun riding shotgun—drove to a neat two-bedroom apartment near the train station. They took the stairs to the second floor and knocked on the door of 2D. As Stayer's knuckles rapped on the door, he felt the unnerving sensation of no pressure, of the door giving way. It was already open. Stayer drew his weapon and heard Sister Catherine inhale behind him as he did.

'That's a gun,' she said, motioning to the Glock pistol in his hand. He felt her quick breath on his shoulder.

'Yes. I'm a policeman,' he said. 'Stay here.'

She nodded and he left her in the corridor. He crept down the apartment's hallway and cleared rooms methodically, pointing his weapon into a bedroom, then a bathroom, another bedroom, the living space, and finally a kitchen. Everything appeared untouched. Cups and saucers were stacked neatly in the cupboards or on the drying board by the sink, a towel hung on the rail in the bathroom, long dried. Nothing seemed out of place: no books overturned, no pillows sliced open, no signs of forced entry or exit. He called for Sister Catherine to come inside, and she looked around the apartment in silence.

Then he saw it: Sergeant Nichols' phone, resting on the coffee table.

•

They spent several hours searching Sergeant Nichols' apartment. Dr Dixon arrived and they helped him catalogue every finger and foot print. After much searching, discussing, photographing, documenting, they reached the conclusion that they had found absolutely nothing.

'I don't believe it,' Dr Dixon said, standing in Sergeant Nichol's tidy kitchen, the red sun streaming in through a window above the sink. 'I'll wait for the lab to confirm, but as far as I can see, there's only one set of footprints and one set of fingerprints in this whole place. Good money says they all come from Jenny Nichols. The person who took her either never entered the apartment, or has covered their tracks very well.' He wiped his brow.

Joan met them in the car park as they arrived back at the station. 'Detective, I think I've got something.' She handed him her phone, looking anxious. 'I found this.' It was a picture taken at a party held in someone's backyard. Two people stood inside cardboard boxes decorated to look like skyscrapers. A plastic model airplane protruded from one of the buildings.

'Why are they dressed like buildings?' Stayer asked.

'It's a costume party,' Joan explained. 'They're the Twin Towers.' Yellow and orange cellophane flowed from the sides of the buildings, as if to show they were burning.

Stayer screwed up his face. 'That's in poor taste.'

'That's the theme,' Joan said. 'It's called a Bad Taste party. You invite people to come dressed as something rude or derogatory or offensive. See?'

Joan swiped through more photos of people in costume. One woman dressed as a retired Hooters employee, pendulous boobs with saucer-sized nipples dangling out the bottom of a tiny Hooters t-shirt. Another photo showed a little kid dressed as Hannibal Lecter strapped to a board in a straitjacket and mask. His parents stood behind him dressed as cannibalised victims, with fake intestines spilling out of their stomachs. Another guest was Michael Jackson, wearing one glove and sunglasses, accompanied by a ventriloquist dummy in the shape of a young boy.

'Who are these people?' Stayer said.

Joan scrolled through the images. 'An assortment of Thoorgala's finest.'

'Look at this,' Sister Catherine said, leaning across them and pointing to another post: a photo of a person wearing a black mask and a striped shirt. 'The hands,' she added. The party guest wore novelty gloves with plastic blades emerging from the knuckles. 'He's come as Tall Harry.'

Stayer stiffened.

'Look at the caption,' Catherine said.

'*Tall Harry at #BadTaste*,' he read. 'Oh lordy. Have these people no decency? Someone has come to this abomination of a function dressed as the person who has supposedly murdered three of this town's people?'

'Disgusting,' said Joan. 'Some of these costumes are so clever. But disgusting.'

'Is this what you came to show me, Joan?' Stayer said. 'I thought you said you had something about Sergeant Nichols.'

'I do. Sorry. I've gone in back to front, detective. I'll scroll down. Here. This is what I wanted you to see. This party took place on Christmas Eve, so three days ago . . .' Joan scrolled to another picture. Stayer had to squint. Sister Catherine gasped.

In the foreground, people posed for the photo, but in a darkened corner almost out of frame, the person in the Tall Harry costume was talking with a woman. She was dressed all in green, with green streamers flowing from her head, as though she had come to the costume party dressed as some kind of vegetable. The woman pointed her finger at the Tall Harry man. Her posture rigid. They seemed to be arguing.

The woman in green was Sergeant Nichols.

Stayer flicked eagerly through the pictures in the same series. A familiar face looked back at him from one of the photos. 'That's Jackson Millwall.' Phoebe Glasson's ex, the gluten-free bread enthusiast, was wearing a pirate costume: black hat, eye patch, striped shirt, fake parrot on shoulder. He still hadn't provided an alibi for his whereabouts on the night Phoebe was murdered.

1 PM

Stayer and Sister Catherine drove to Jackson's address, a leafy cul-de-sac of manicured lawns, complicated hedges, European SUVs. Constable Walsh, who had been home catching up on sleep, met them there. A gardener mowing the lawn out the front of a double-storey mock-Tudor home informed them that Jackson wasn't home. 'Gone surfing,' the man said, sweating under an Akubra hat and overalls. 'Try Cundra.'

They drove two minutes down the road to Cundra Beach and found Jackson standing in the car park, fully clothed in a flannel shirt and torn tracksuit pants, one shoeless foot perched on the paling of a low fence, watching the waves smash the sand. Women sunbaked solo in bikinis, hats over faces, books cast aside. Two surfers tiptoed across the sand towards the water, boards tucked under their armpits, wetsuits black and smooth.

'Why do you watch the surf but never go in?' Stayer asked.

Jackson swung around at the sound of Stayer's voice and groaned when he saw the two policemen and Sister Catherine walking towards him.

'Do you even own a surfboard?' Stayer continued.

Before he could say any more, Jackson sprinted away, the soles of his bare feet flashing white behind him.

'Hey!' Stayer shouted.

Jackson ran towards a line of buildings which dotted the road behind the beach. He paused in front of the Thoorgala Returned Serviceman's League then darted inside.

Stayer chased after him. 'I'll go around the back,' Constable Walsh called out to Stayer. He peeled off, heading towards the laneway running behind the row of buildings.

'Stay here,' the detective told Sister Catherine, calling behind him to where she was standing.

'No chance!' she said, launching into a run. 'I'll go left.'

She parted from him, running towards the other end of the row of buildings. She was surprisingly speedy, her legs swinging rapidly in their black tights.

Stayer ran towards the RSL. A building in two parts stood before him: on one side, a handsome whitewashed building which read *AD 1924* across the top in raised concrete; on the other, a brown brick box squatting in the grass, with *Thoorgala Returned Servicemen's League* sprawled in neon cursive. Stayer ran inside the first side, entering a bistro area. He weaved around people sat at little square tables. Smells of chicken parmigiana and steak with Diane sauce wafted.

He scanned the room. He'd lost him.

Then, across the way, in the brown brick box section of the building, flannelette fabric flickered behind a pokie machine. It was Jackson, sneaking a look at Stayer. Machines lit up and beeped. Every player wins. Stayer ran towards the flannelette, and Jackson jumped out from behind Jewel of the Nile and towards a fire exit. He slammed the metal bar down on the emergency door and jumped into a laneway, where Constable Walsh was waiting.

He almost leaped into the policeman's arms, as if embracing him.

Stayer caught up to them. He removed his cuffs from his shoulder holster and dangled them in front of Jackson. 'Do I need to put these on you?'

'Don't cuff me, please,' he said, puffing. Sister Catherine arrived in the laneway, cheeks flushed.

'Why is there a nun here?' Jackson said.

'She's here to give you the last rites. Why did you run from us, Mr Millwall?'

The man shrugged and said nothing.

'You're coming with us to the station, Mr Millwall. We need to talk.'

'Fuck no. You can't make me.'

'Actually, I can. You still haven't given me an alibi. That's reason enough to bring you in. In addition to that, you're in a photo with a missing policewoman. You were one of the last people to see her before she disappeared. Not to mention that you just ran away from two policemen. Not good. Come down the station for a chat. Constable Walsh can tell you some more about Silverwater prison.'

'Please, not that again,' Jackson begged, eyes frightened now.

'Give us your alibi,' Stayer said.

Jackson's eyes darted back and forth nervously. 'I'm cheating on my new girlfriend, Cheyenne.' He hung his head guiltily. 'That's where I was that night when Phoebe died.'

'With whom?' Stayer said.

'Does it matter?'

'Yes,' Stayer and Walsh said in unison.

'Natalia Garibaldi,' Jackson said. He hung his head. 'That's her name.'

Stayer offered his notebook to Jackson and a pen. 'Write her name and phone number here.'

Jackson scrawled a name and number on the page and handed it back to Stayer.

'I'll check it, boss,' Walsh said. Stayer ripped the page from the notebook and handed it to him, and Walsh walked away, phone in hand. A seagull pecking at discarded chips by the rubbish skip in the laneway was joined by more seagulls. A scuffle broke out. Screeching, orange beaks snapping.

Constable Walsh returned. 'Alibi checks out, boss. Natalia Garibaldi confirms she was with Mr Millwall on the night of the twenty-third, and that he stayed at her dwelling until six the following morning. Apparently, the CCTV in the foyer of her apartment building will confirm this. She sounded like a lovely lady,' Walsh added, 'too good for the likes of him.'

Stayer shook his head. 'Baffled, Mr Millwall. Why didn't you tell us this earlier? We could have ruled you out of the inquiry two days ago.'

'You'd better not tell anyone about Natalia,' Jackson said, meeting Stayer's gaze. 'Please don't tell my mates.'

'Why do you care so much about what your mates think, Mr Millwall?'

He inhaled, as though about to divulge some terrible secret. 'Natalia works at a storage place out near Garribee. Drives a Yaris. She came to the races once on a hens' day and we randomly hit it off. She's quite buxom. Doesn't eat clean. Not the type I usually go for.'

It took most of Stayer's strength not to laugh, and the rest of it not to despair. 'Refusing to give an alibi? Running away from police? All because a woman you're seeing doesn't look a particular way. Mr Millwall, I feel sorry for you.'

'You don't know what it's like here, man. How you look matters.'

The seagulls fighting over the chips near the rubbish skip had finished the last crumb of potato. They looked around, irises like red pins. They lifted their wings and flew off.

The laneway's end afforded a glimpse of the crashing waves of Cundra beach. Jackson stared at them longingly. 'Can I go surfing now?'

'First tell us where the party was on Christmas Eve. The Bad Taste Party.'

Jackson rolled his eyes. 'You're not much of a detective if you can't work that one out. It was at Greenie's. Michael Green's place.'

•

'I shouldn't have let Sergeant Nichols go,' Stayer said. They were walking back to the squad cars, parked in front of Cundra Beach. Water and white foam rolled furiously, crashing like a spider milkshake into the yellow sand. 'But after she dropped the body of the first victim on the sandhills—'

'Wait,' Constable Walsh said. 'Nichols dropped the body?' He turned to look at Stayer.

'It was understandable. I didn't realise it at the time, but that was her first dead body. She was in shock. Walsh? What is it?'

Walsh wore a hardened expression. 'That's not right, boss.'

'What?' Stayer said. 'That Sergeant Nichols dropped the body?'

'Not that. She told you it was the first dead body she'd responded to? That's not true. Not even a little bit. Sergeant Nichols has attended dozens of callouts for dead bodies: suicides, accidents, people dying at home, family violence, the occasional murder or manslaughter. Many in my company.'

Stayer was taken aback. 'Strange. Why would she lie about that?'

'No idea,' Walsh said.

1.42 PM

When Stayer, Walsh and Sister Catherine arrived at Michael Green's house, they found the Bad Taste Party still going, despite it being almost four days later. Party guests wandered around, looking greasy and exhausted, lolling on sofas and smoking on the balcony. The carpets bore stains of unknown origin. Legs had snapped off chairs.

Entering the lounge room, they found a young woman in a platinum blonde wig cut into a bob, wearing a blue tracksuit and a gold medallion, lying listlessly on a sofa, phone in hand. A cigar dangled from her mouth.

'Who is she supposed to be?' Stayer said.

'No idea,' Constable Walsh replied.

'I believe she's come as Jimmy Savile,' Sister Catherine said quietly, 'that paedophile who presented shows on the BBC.'

'Okay then,' Stayer said. 'She's mastered the theme.'

The young woman was flicking through songs on a music app, playing each song for five to ten seconds before seeming to decide she hated it and selecting another track. The music blared from big, old-fashioned speakers, so loud that the floor vibrated beneath Stayer's feet.

'Pick a song and stick with it,' Stayer said.

The woman gave him a *the-fuck-you-think-you-are* look, so he flashed his badge. 'Do it,' he said. 'I won't ask again.'

The woman nodded nervously, looking terrified, and put down the phone. The song she'd landed on was Cher's 'Gypsys, Tramps & Thieves', and the tinkling of the carnival calliope rang out as they walked through the room. Once Stayer had shown his police ID, people began to scurry. People wearing hockey masks like the one worn in *Friday the 13th*, dressed as terrorists, as the microbe emoji that symbolised Covid-19, and Jesus, darted from the room. A man dressed like Marilyn Monroe in *The Seven Year Itch*, in a white dress, carrying a bottle labelled *Barbiturates*, with red lipstick deliberately smeared from his lips across his stubble, emerged from a dark corner and bolted. Stayer shouted after him to point in the direction of the party's host, and the guy motioned upstairs as he fled.

'Not so fast,' Constable Walsh said to a woman dressed as an Amish person, in a black bonnet and hooped skirt, who tried to run past him while carrying a giant bong. 'I'll question these ones, boss,' he said to Stayer. 'You take upstairs?'

Stayer agreed, and he and Sister Catherine climbed a set of carpet-covered stairs, then followed a hallway down to what appeared to be the master bedroom. A middle-aged man snored face down on top of a four-poster bed. He drooled onto the brocade bedspread. His trousers had scrunched down, revealing a hairy bum crack.

'Are you Michael Green, the owner of this house?' Stayer asked the man.

The guy didn't stir.

Stayer asked him again, this time stabbing him in the shoulder with his finger.

'Alright, fuck, yes,' the man replied. He rolled onto his back.

'This your party, sir?'

'You betcha.'

'Are you aware there were drugs consumed on these premises?' Stayer asked.

Green chuckled. 'I should certainly hope so.' Then he opened his eyes. 'Who the fuck are you?'

'I'm Detective Stayer, and this is Sister Catherine Kelley. She's a nun. Please don't swear in front of her.'

Green grasped the bedhead and hauled himself up into a sitting position. 'Any chance those are fancy dress costumes?' he pointed to Sister Catherine's habit.

'Afraid not. We've seen photos of this party posted to social media on Christmas Eve,' Stayer said. 'It's now the twenty-seventh of December. Has this party really been going on for four days?'

'Impressive, right?' Green said. 'Some people went home to be with their families on Christmas Day, but the hardcore stayed. Backpackers, mostly. Nowhere else to go.'

'You don't think it was inappropriate for guests to come dressed as Tall Harry, when a local woman had been murdered that morning?'

Green didn't answer.

Stayer showed him the photo of the party with Sergeant Nichols in the background. 'Do you remember this woman?'

Green studied the picture. 'Jenny. She's a family friend. Quiet girl usually. But that night . . . not so quiet.'

'How do you mean?' Stayer asked.

'Oh shit,' Green cried, 'get out of my way.'

He ran into the ensuite, slamming the door shut behind him. The sounds of vomiting came from the bathroom; lurching, wet, obscene.

'Explain the appeal of a Bad Taste party to me, sister,' Stayer said to the nun, perching on the bed. 'Because I just don't get it.'

A groan then a howl echoed from the bathroom as the contents of the party host's stomach were ejected. There was a pause, and silence, then the vomiting resumed.

'You see the symbolism in everything,' he went on. 'I challenge you to find the profound meaning in this.'

Sister Catherine opened the window. A warm but fresh breeze blew into the sour-smelling room.

'The desire to offend and outrage lives in all of us,' she began. 'Humans are pack animals. Most of the time we behave ourselves, we obey society's rules, to avoid being cast from the group. We flatter our incompetent boss; we say please and thank you to the obnoxious employee at the roads and transport office. But the more we bend the knee, the more we yearn to lash out. We dress up outrageously, with a desire to transgress, to offend as much as possible, when we can. Yes. I see profound meaning here.'

'And tell me, what did Sergeant Nichols come as, in her all-green ensemble with the great stalks coming out of her head? As you're the expert.'

'Coriander,' Sister Catherine replied. 'Certain people have an aversion to it. The smell receptors in their nose identify it as soap. Hence, it's a "bad taste", perfect for a Bad Taste party.'

The toilet in the ensuite flushed and Green emerged. 'She's right,' he said as he stumbled towards the bed. 'Jenny came dressed as coriander. We all thought it was very clever.'

'And classier than what the rest of you were wearing.' Stayer said. 'What's your costume supposed to be, by the way?'

The man had a model of a mountain, brown and green and furry, like from a train set, taped to his chest.

'I'm that German pilot who flew the passenger jet into a mountain,' he said, lying back down. 'Not my best effort.'

'What did you mean by not so quiet?' Stayer asked.

'Pardon me?'

'When describing Sergeant Nichols—Jenny—you said she was not so quiet at the party.'

'Have you got any paracetamol? I need something for this headache or I'm going to die. I think my skull might explode. You're a cop, right? You must have a gun. Just shoot me. Put me out of my misery.'

'I would but the paperwork would be substantial.'

'I'll get you some if you tell me where they are,' Sister Catherine offered.

'Thank you,' Green said gratefully, as though she'd offered him water after a month in the desert. 'In the ensuite. Medicine cabinet.'

Sister Catherine left the room and returned seconds later with the tablets and a glass of water. Stayer watched her hold Green's head as he drank the water. Such an intimate action, to touch someone's face, like seeing them naked, yet Green let her do it.

'You were saying?' Stayer asked. 'About Sergeant Nichols? You said she was quiet, then not so quiet. What did you mean?'

'It's hard to explain.'

'Try. Start from the beginning. What time did she arrive?'

'About nine pm? Ten?'

'And you said she's a family friend?'

'Yeah, Jenny's the daughter of a good mate of mine. Her dad used to bring her to my Christmas parties when she was a kid. When I heard she'd moved back to town, I invited her. For old times' sake.'

A loud crash came from downstairs. Someone called out 'sorry'.

'Fuck. What was that?' Green sighed and pulled himself off the bed. 'Better go see.'

He walked out of the room and down the stairs, and Stayer and Sister Catherine followed him.

Downstairs, the woman dressed as Jimmy Savile had knocked one of the speakers over.

'What happened here?' the party host asked, despairing.

'Sorry, Greenie,' she said. 'I dunno.'

Green picked up the speaker, which seemed to have Cher on repeat, and put it back on its low shelf with a prolonged groan. 'That's it—everyone out,' he said.

People muttered their protestations, but Green was clearly not in the mood. The remaining guests gathered their belongings and slunk out.

A weary stillness settled over the house. Green sunk into a chair.

Stayer asked his question yet again. 'Jenny Nichols. You said she wasn't quiet for long?'

'Yep. I looked over a few times at her through the night, checking that she was having a good time. She was just sitting outside on a deckchair, nursing the same drink, speaking to no one, just watching people. But then I went into the kitchen to get some more blood dip and—'

'Blood dip?'

'Yeah. It was just taramasalata, but we added some red food colouring to make it extra red.'

'Jesus, mate,' Stayer said.

'Yes, yes, I'm a terrible person. Can I finish my story? I need to lie down again or I think I really might die.'

'Finish, please,' Stayer said. 'Do us all a favour.'

'I come back out and she's having a full-on screaming match with one of the guys dressed as Tall Harry.'

'*One* of the guys?'

Green nodded. 'There were a few.'

'Okay. What were they arguing about?'

'No idea. But they were going back and forth like a married couple. I thought Jenny was going to punch him at one point.'

'And then what happened?'

He shrugged. 'She disappeared.'

'Disappeared?'

'Yeah, she just left. Puff: vanished.'

'Did she leave with anyone?'

'Dunno.'

'I'm going to need the names of everyone who came to the party,' Stayer told him.

Green snickered. 'Good luck. This went off. Biggest party in Thoorgala, if not Australia. I didn't know half the people coming in or out.'

'Start with people dressed as Tall Harry. Cough up their names.'

'Why do you care so much about Jenny?'

'Because she's missing.'

'Fuck me. Does her dad know? Makes sense, maybe.'

'What does? What makes sense?'

Green ran his fingers over the mountain taped to his chest. 'Nothing,' he said. 'I'm just talking crap.' He opened a notes app on his phone and showed the screen to Stayer. 'Here's my original guest list. The people I invited. Three of the guys on this list came in Tall Harry costumes. Fair warning, though, I think there were about ten more.'

'Thirteen people came dressed as Tall Harry?'

Green looked uninterested. 'A popular costume this year.'

Stayer took a photo of the list.

•

Michael Green trudged back upstairs, and Stayer and Sister Catherine showed themselves out. Walsh met them in the front yard. 'A few people remember Sergeant Nichols, but none of them spoke to her,' he said. A woman was sitting on a low brick fence with her head bowed. Stayer recognised her as the one who'd been controlling the music. She'd lost the cigar and wig and removed her blue tracksuit top. 'Did you speak with her, Walsh?' He motioned to the same woman.

The constable shook his head. 'Didn't catch that one.'

They all walked over. 'What happened to your wig, Jimmy Savile?' Stayer said.

'Not a good look to be dressed like a paedophile in broad daylight,' she said. 'I'm waiting for my Uber.' She spoke in a soft English burr, from the West Country maybe.

'Do you realise "Gypsys, Tramps & Thieves" is still playing in there?' Stayer pointed back towards the house.

She nodded. 'The speakers are still connected to my phone.'

'What's so special about that song? You must have played it fifteen times already.'

'I was too scared to flip to another track. You told me not to change songs.' She put her head in her hands. 'I feel awful. I miss my parents. Don't know what I was doing, coming to Thoorgala for Christmas. I should be with my family. Or just people who are nice, at least.' She suddenly looked tiny, like a bird, with her bony elbows and thin neck. 'I'm in Australia on my gap year.'

'Do you recognise this woman?' Stayer showed her the photo with Sergeant Nichols in the background.

The woman looked up reluctantly and studied the picture. Her expression changed. 'People were talking about her.'

'What were they saying?'

'This is me.' She motioned to a blue sedan that had pulled up to the kerb and began moving towards it.

'What were people saying about her?' Stayer yelled after her as she opened the rear door of the car and greeted the driver, smiling and nodding like he was an old friend.

She turned back to Stayer reluctantly. 'That she was a cop. And that she killed someone when she was in high school.'

She slid into the back seat and pulled the door closed behind her. The car drove off. Cher sang a few last bars before cutting out abruptly as the girl's phone moved out of range.

Stayer, Walsh and Sister Catherine watched the car move away in silence.

2.30 PM

Michael Green's house lay in a peculiar development known as Cundra Hills Beach—a masterfully planned suburb consisting of entirely new houses and streets, built over bulldozed sandhills. Rows of gleaming double-storey dwellings were stacked closely, almost on top of one another. Each seemed to possess identical amounts of glass louvered windows, cement render, and slate tile cladding. Looking left, Stayer glimpsed the start of the Cundra sandhills. He was less than a kilometre from the murder sites of the three women.

Constable Walsh exited the house and jogged over to where Stayer and Sister Catherine were standing. 'Okay. Clearer picture now,' Walsh said. He was lightly puffing. 'I went back in and asked around. At the Bad Taste Party on Christmas Eve, the guy dressed as "Overdose Marilyn Monroe" saw Sergeant Nichols accusing a guy dressed as Tall Harry of stirring up trouble. They argued openly, causing a small scene in Green's backyard. Nichols left the party. The guy in the Tall Harry outfit went round afterwards, telling everyone that Sergeant Nichols and her friends killed Stanley Lacey when they were in high school. He'd been doing some digging, he said. Found some things out. A few other people I spoke to confirmed this version of events. Quite a few.'

A woman exited the house next door and began mowing the small patch of lawn out the front of her house. It took her only one turn back and forth to cut the whole patch. The smell of cut grass rose up, sweaty and sweet. Stayer was aware he had a stunned expression and tried to conceal it. He glanced at Sister Catherine and saw she had a strange look too.

Stayer told them he had a call to make and walked down the road a little. He dialled the number for Warren Nichols.

Jenny's father answered on the first ring. 'Detective Stayer—you have news of Jenny?' his voice was eager, strained. Stayer realised he'd probably been waiting, phone in hand, for the detective to call.

'I'm sorry, Warren, I don't. And I've got reason to believe she's missing.' He explained about finding Sergeant Nichols' phone in the empty apartment, the Bad Taste Party, the argument she'd had with the other guest. 'We've got everyone working on finding Jenny.'

'Thank you,' Warren said. 'I appreciate that.' His voice cracked again.

Stayer paused. 'Warren, Jenny grew up in Thoorgala—what high school did she attend?'

'Thoorgala Grammar,' Warren said. 'Why do you ask?'

The woman mowing her lawn next door took her little pile of grass clippings and tossed them into a green bin. The hot wind caught them, flicking a small clump into her mouth, which she spat away in horror.

'Jenny is thirty years old,' Stayer said, 'so she would have been in the same year as three women called Phoebe Glasson, Mikaela Sorgensen and Jessie Phan. I'm asking you to cast your mind back, but any chance you recall if Jenny was friends with these women?'

'Hmm . . . Yes, Mikaela was a friend. Jessie, too. And I think I remember a Phoebe in the mix.'

Stayer tried to stay calm. 'And how about my sister, Ruby Stayer?'

'Ruby's your sister? Yes, she was in the group too.'

A silence echoed over the phone line, awkward, like dead air on a radio show.

'What is it, detective?' Warren said.

Stayer glanced back at Green's house and saw Sister Catherine perched on the front yard wall, watching him. 'Warren, it's possible Jenny has been taken by someone who wants to punish her for a crime they believe she committed when she was a teenager. Not Jenny alone, but her and the other four girls I've just mentioned.'

'A crime? What kind of crime?'

'I don't know. If I had to guess, I would say it's to do with a rumour that, as teenagers, Jenny and her friends were responsible for the death of an artist who was working at their high school. A man named Stanley Lacey.'

'I've heard of him. Good grief.'

'Is there anything you can tell me about that time?' Stayer asked. 'Jenny would have been about fifteen. Do you recall anything going on with her, anything out of the ordinary?'

'Out of the ordinary?'

'Yes. A change in Jenny's behaviour around that time, for example.'

The silence down the phone line caused pain in Stayer's ears.

'Mr Nichols—Warren, anything you can remember might be helpful. If we can understand *why* Jenny was taken, we have a better chance of figuring out by who.'

'You mean Jenny and your sister.'

'Yes. My sister is missing too. So anything you can think of—'

'Son, I truly can't think of anything.' Warren Nichols' tone was still polite, but there was a hardness in it now. 'I could be wrong, but what you're implying is that my daughter committed murder as a teenager. That's not even in the same universe as Jenny.'

Warren Nichols ended the call soon after, saying he was needed elsewhere. Stayer reassured him they were doing everything they could to find his daughter. He sounded quieter and smaller as he made his goodbyes, promising in what seemed like a half-hearted tone to call Stayer if he thought of anything, and Stayer knew he wouldn't be hearing from him again unless he called him first.

•

'Everything okay, detective?' Sister Catherine said as he returned to the front yard of Green's house. A dog barked nearby. Children squealed from a shade-cloth covered playground across the road.

Stayer relayed to her and Constable Walsh the conversation he'd just had.

Sister Catherine listened with bright eyes, nodding. 'Nichols is the fifth victim,' she said once he'd finished. She pulled a folded piece of paper from her pocket and handed it to Stayer. It was a photocopy of the note they'd found on the first victim.

The nun read aloud. '*They shall confess. Or four more*. That's what it says. *Or four more*. That means five victims total. Phoebe Glasson, Mikaela Sorgensen, Jessie Phan, who have already been killed. And unless we can stop him, Ruby Stayer and Jenny Nichols will be the fourth and fifth. Tall Harry is taking revenge on these five women.'

They both seemed to be thinking the same thing. They jumped in the car and drove out to the sandhills, to the place where the bodies were found. Stayer parked in the little car park and they ran out onto the sand, puffing and straining in the sun and climbing the sandhill in silence. They reached the top and walked out onto the flat. They found nothing. Stayer scanned the sand, squinting in the horrible sun. 'I really thought we might find something this time,' he said, feeling himself slump. Sister Catherine placed a hand on his arm.

'I just realised,' Stayer said, 'Sergeant Nichols dropped Phoebe Glasson's body, not because it was her first time handling a dead body. It was because she knew her.'

3.06 PM

Back at the station, Stayer, Constable Walsh and Sister Catherine sat around Stayer's desk.

'I think we need to look into Stanley Lacey's death,' Sister Catherine said. 'It may reveal some information we've missed. It's possible the individual impersonating Tall Harry thinks these women killed Stanley Lacey. If we investigate his death, it may reveal some detail which leads us to this individual. And if we can find him, we find Sergeant Nichols, and we find your sister.'

'She's right, boss,' Walsh said. 'Looking into Stanley Lacey's death is a smart idea. We might find out why the killer has done this. He must have a reason.'

'Okay,' Stayer said at last. 'Look into it how?'

'We could start with the coroner's report,' Walsh offered. 'The autopsy?'

Stayer picked up his phone. After three rings, Dr Dixon answered.

'Doc, I need the autopsy report for a Stanley Lacey, who died fifteen years ago. Can you access it?'

'Could you spell the surname?'

Stayer did, and the sound of computer keys tapping rang out. 'We have it,' Dr Dixon said after a few seconds. 'Emailing now.'

Stayer thanked him. 'While we've got you, could you tell us the cause of death?'

Again Dr Dixon's fingers tapped, a mouse clicked.

'Multiple catastrophic skull fractures consistent with falling from a height. Anything else?'

'That's all. Thanks, doc.' He ended the call.

Stayer checked his inbox and printed copies of the report for Sister Catherine and Constable Walsh.

He watched Sister Catherine's eyes as they moved across the page, reading terms like *subdural haemorrhage*, *multiple disabling soft tissue injuries*, *liver rupture*, *spleen rupture*, *aortic transection*. The final page of the report contained a colour photo of the body in the location it was found, on the rocks beside the Thoorgala Blowhole.

'He's wearing a tuxedo,' Sister Catherine said.

Stayer nodded. 'He had attended the Thoorgala Grammar year ten formal the night he died.'

Stayer glanced at the picture of the body again. The man had spiked his hair with gel in a style which reminded Stayer of a Backstreet Boy. There was an oddness to it, a childish vanity. An adult putting gel in his hair and wearing a tuxedo to a student dance.

'I think we should look at the blowhole again,' Sister Catherine said.

'I think we're wasting time on this,' Stayer said. 'We should go back to knocking on doors down Peninsula Way. See if any of the owners who weren't home yesterday are now there. We should have someone watching the sandhills too.'

'Let me do that, boss,' Walsh said. 'I'll check out basements while you go to the blowhole. We can meet up afterwards and exchange notes. We don't all need to be there, but it makes sense for at least one of us to read the autopsy report at the crime scene.'

•

'Blowholes have been feared and celebrated for millennia,' Sister Catherine said, looking out the window to the choppy surf of the Pacific Ocean as Stayer drove. 'There's tremendous meaning in them.'

'Meaning.' Stayer's voice was dry. 'In a blowhole?'

'There's meaning in everything, detective,' the nun replied. 'In the way you're driving to the way you comb your hair to selecting the blowhole as a place to die.'

'There's no meaning in the way I comb my hair,' Stayer said. 'It was pointing in multiple directions, now it just points in one.'

'There's meaning. You are saying to the world, *I am not a slob*.'

They arrived at a small car park in front of sandstone cliffs. Faded white lines marked the parking spaces, and windblown scrub provided a wall on three sides. They could hear the ocean but could not see it. The thick bush had been parted in one place, allowing for a narrow dirt path. Stayer and Sister Catherine walked down it, and stepped out into the light. Below them were the rocks and the thundering ocean, whirling and sucking, moving in and out of the giant blowhole. The sight was mesmerising, and terrifying. A huge swell of water tipped then disappeared into the caves beneath them, vanishing for seconds, then reappearing as a rocket of water shooting upwards, emerging from the blowhole like a projectile.

'There's a wave coming,' Sister Catherine said perfunctorily, as though this needed to be announced, motioning to a swell moving towards the rocks.

Stayer watched. He waited. Another tremendous spurt of sea water exploded into the air like a cannon. The force took his breath away.

'And there's the explosion,' Sister Catherine said.

Even though they were behind a fence, salt water still hit them, roughly splashing water on them both.

'I'm all wet!' Stayer said. He stepped back and wrung out his shirt.

'I think it's refreshing,' Sister Catherine said.

'I don't see any meaning in this. There's no symbolism in being hosed down.'

'It's not the water that holds meaning. It's the blowhole itself, the hole through which the ocean passes. Look.' She pointed to the gap in the rocks in front of them.

'No thanks,' Stayer said. 'I don't want to get saturated again.'

'You won't. There are no waves coming.'

Stayer walked gingerly around the fence and peered into a yawning mouth of jagged rock. It fell away into darkness, a bottomless abyss. He imagined the artist, Stanley Lacey, falling into the hole, how effortlessly the blackness would swallow him, how sharp the rocks would be.

He returned to Sister Catherine, still standing behind the fence.

'What did you think?' she asked him. 'Do you understand now?'

Stayer shrugged. 'All I understand is that falling into that thing would be a horrible way to die.'

Sister Catherine retrieved the autopsy report from her handbag and began reading. 'Let's retrace the steps. The coroner's report says that Stanley Lacey was seen walking erratically along these rocks at around one am on the night he died. Two backpackers who had been drinking on a bench beside the beach path leading up to the blowhole saw him staggering. The light of the Thoorgala lighthouse was making a strange flickering in the distance, they surmised he might have been distracted by it. They testified that they called out to warn him he was walking towards the blowhole, but he did not respond. They said he just kept walking, his arms stretched out in front of him. Next thing they saw was water exploding out of the blowhole. It hit Stanley Lacey, he tripped and either fell into the blowhole or was sucked into it by the retreating water.'

Stayer joined Sister Catherine back behind the fence, reading the report over her shoulder. 'And these witnesses—the backpackers: were they cleared of any wrongdoing? Ever suspected of foul play?'

Sister Catherine shook her head. 'Cleared. Two women aged twenty and twenty-two at the time. German tourists. Their DNA wasn't found anywhere on Stanley Lacey nor around the blowhole. Stanley Lacey had no signs of violence inflicted on him by people or weapons, no evidence he was pushed or assaulted prior to his death. His only injuries came from the rocks inside and around the blowhole.' Sister Catherine kept reading, then paused.

'What is it?' Stayer said.

'His blood alcohol level was point one two,' she said. 'A huge amount.'

'I'm surprised he could even put one foot in front of the other.'

A pelican flew above them, its beak pink, its wings alarmingly huge. It swooped the water and ducked under the surface, hunting some fish only it could see.

'So the two witnesses saw Stanley Lacey stumbling, walking towards the blowhole, and when they tried to warn him, they couldn't get through to him,' Stayer said. 'And he had a blood alcohol level that should have rendered him unconscious.'

'I believe we've both reached the same conclusion, detective.'

The pelican emerged from the salt water, beak empty. It had either failed to catch the fish or had eaten it already.

'The only thing you can conclude: Stanley Lacey was stumbling along these rocks, drunk as a skunk, with no one else around, and he tripped and fell into the blowhole where he died. His death was overwhelmingly, resoundingly, an accident.'

4.32 PM

They returned to the station. Sister Catherine went to the kitchenette. Stayer sat at his desk and stared out the window. Ash from the bushfires had begun collecting on the windowsill like black confetti. Rarely in his life did things fall into his lap, but as he glanced through the window, Stayer saw the schoolteacher, Mr Catton, walking down the footpath across the street from the police station.

Stayer felt groggy and woolly-headed after several nights of non-existent sleep, but somehow one or two of the brain cells left in his skull pulled together and assembled a thought. Stayer suddenly became aware of Mr Catton's right index finger, which was missing. He hadn't thought about that distinctive digit since the schoolteacher had shown up at the station.

Stayer swiped his phone from the desk and opened his photos, finding a screenshot he'd taken of the social media post that showed Sergeant Nichols at the Bad Taste Party. Stayer flicked the image to enlarge it, zooming in on one detail: the right hand of the person in the Tall Harry costume. He couldn't believe he'd missed it before. The costumed figure was missing the top of his right index finger.

Stayer leaped from his chair.

'Mr Catton,' he shouted, once outside.

The schoolteacher looked around, then began walking faster.

'Mate, not a good look, running away from a police officer,' Stayer called.

Mr Catton stopped walking.

'I wasn't running,' he said as the detective approached. He didn't meet Stayer's eye.

'You were dressed as Tall Harry at a party at Michael Green's house on Christmas Eve,' Stayer said. 'You were seen arguing with Sergeant Jenny Nichols.'

Mr Catton opened his mouth as if to protest, but Stayer seized the man's right wrist and held it up. 'Unless you can produce another six-foot individual with the top of their finger missing, I wouldn't bother denying it.'

He showed Mr Catton the photo on his phone. 'I don't get it, Mr Catton, you came to my office expressing your concern about Phoebe Glasson, begging me to do something, warning me more women would be killed. Then later that night, you show up at a party dressed as Tall Harry, the very monster you'd warned me about! Which is it, Mr Catton—are you concerned about the women who have died or are you celebrating their killer?'

'I was concerned.' He snatched his hand back. 'At first. Then I went online. Read the forums, did some digging. There's more to this story. There's more to those women. I started to think for myself.' He wore a proud look.

'Going online and thinking for yourself? Those two tend to be mutually exclusive.'

Mr Catton glared. 'I read about the symbol, and the note. People aren't killed like that, in that way, randomly. Phoebe must have done something—'

'What were you and Sergeant Nichols fighting about?' Stayer asked him. 'At the Bad Taste Party.'

'I think you already know, detective,' the teacher said. 'Jenny Nichols was blaming me for spreading rumours about her and her friends.'

Stayer said nothing.

'I told Jenny she was accusing the wrong person. If she was looking for a guilty party, she should look in the mirror.'

A woman emerged from the supermarket behind them, wheeling a trolley towards the car park. The hot wind blew her skirt into the back of her legs, like a mould.

'Was that you on the beach yesterday?' Stayer demanded. 'Dressed in a Tall Harry costume and leading me to Lacey's memorial plaque by the blowhole?'

Mr Catton smiled broadly. 'That wasn't me. I would have happily done that if I'd thought of it, but I didn't.'

'Who was it then?'

The schoolteacher shrugged. 'Beats me. Maybe it was the real thing.'

'You're coming dangerously close to getting arrested, Mr Catton.'

'Steady on. Why?'

'Let's see. First you come to my office, telling me about that student saying the Tall Harry rhyme, setting the creature from an urban legend loose. Then you dress up as that very same creature and have an argument with Sergeant Nichols—who has since gone missing.'

'I haven't done anything wrong. You have no reason to arrest me.'

'How about the murder of three women? I've never asked you for your alibi on the days they went missing.'

Mr Catton looked irritated. 'On the twenty-third, I was at home with my wife and kids. On the twenty-fourth, I went to Greenie's Bad Taste Party, then went home to my wife and kids. On the twenty-fifth, my wife and kids and I stayed the night at my in-laws. Call my wife, call my in-laws, for confirmation. My in-laws, especially. They hate me and think I'm not good enough for their daughter. They wouldn't lie for me.'

Stayer glared, and Mr Catton glared back.

'I didn't kill those women. Whoever did kill them had good reason. Jenny Nichols and her friends murdered an innocent man as teenagers. There's proof out there, if you know where to look.'

'If you have all this proof, why haven't you told me directly?' Stayer said. 'Why didn't you return to my office and show me your evidence? Why wouldn't you try to help me in my investigation?'

Mr Catton looked indignant. 'Because I didn't want to help you. Once I discovered the truth, I didn't want you to catch him before he'd finished his work.'

Stayer flinched. 'How dare you. You know my sister is missing.'

'That's what makes this so sad,' Catton replied. 'You're still not getting it, detective. *She* does, though.' The schoolteacher was pointing over Stayer's shoulder.

The detective turned. Sister Catherine walked down the footpath towards them, the wind pushing her black veil back from her shoulders and making it fly. The nun smiled at Stayer, then her face fell, seemingly at the sight of Mr Catton.

'Hello, sister,' Mr Catton said. 'I was just telling the detective that he's been wilfully ignoring important elements of this case. We can't entirely blame Detective Stayer though. How can he understand when he doesn't have all the information? He doesn't know, for example, that you have been keeping things from him.'

Sister Catherine said nothing but nodded slowly. Her expression was hard to read.

'Those schoolgirls got revenge on that artist because he humiliated one of them. So she and her friends killed him. Isn't that right, sister?'

Stayer saw the nun stiffen. Her face was grey. Her veil continued to flap behind her in the hot wind, like a black flag.

'I don't know what you're talking about,' Sister Catherine said, though her expression indicated the opposite.

'You know exactly what I'm talking about. The Black Heart Rite. *Witches, Sirens and Unusual Women.*'

Stayer turned to Sister Catherine. 'What's he on about?'

'I don't know,' she replied. Her voice shook.

'She's lying to you, mate,' Mr Catton said. 'Look it up yourself. New comments. Online. Now you've found a worthy suspect, detective, I'll leave you to it.' He strolled off, looking pleased.

Sister Catherine wouldn't meet his eye.

'I haven't lied,' she said. 'I just haven't been entirely truthful.'

'What haven't you been entirely truthful about?'

Sister Catherine's face fell further. 'Something in one of my books.'

4.53 PM

Catherine held her computer in her lap, screen closed. Both hands lay on top, as though she needed to physically hold it shut. The moment she had been dreading for days had finally arrived, and she didn't know what to do. She wanted to sink into the floor, or run away, but instead she just sat there, feeling foolish.

They had returned to Detective Stayer's office and were sitting on either side of his desk. The detective was gazing at her with a look which scared her, a piercing look, as though he saw straight through her.

'Can we see what he's talking about?' the detective said, motioning to her laptop.

Catherine shook her head.

'I need to see, sister,' Detective Stayer said, firmer. 'It could help us find Ruby and Sergeant Nichols.'

Catherine had no choice but to speak. 'I want you to remember that things you read on the internet do not necessarily translate into real life. Do you agree?'

'What's going on?' he said, looking baffled. 'Now you're scaring me. Please. Open the computer.'

She relented. She placed her laptop on the desk. It suddenly felt heavy and hard to carry, like a lead bar. She reluctantly opened the //Thoorgala forum. She knew what she was going to find there. She could hear her breathing grow faster, but she couldn't stop it. She watched the detective's eyes move across the words.

//Thoorgala. A sandy corner of the internet to discuss all things God's country

HaroldBishop • 1.53 pm
The cops are looking for you Harry.

TallHarry • 2.47 pm
Let them look. They won't find me.

HaroldBishop • 2.48 pm
Why not?

HaroldBishop • 2.49 pm
Hello?

MaryCronin • 2.49 pm
This joke is getting out of hand. Impersonating a killer is disgusting. People have died.

PeterJoplin • 2.54 pm
I agree it's getting out of hand. But I would like to know the truth as well.

HaroldBishop • 2.57 pm
Are you worried cops are watching this thread? That's why you've gone quiet?

TallHarry • 3.08 pm
I'm not worried. They won't find me. In fact, I hope they read this thread. It contains pertinent information.

HaroldBishop • 3.08 pm
Which information's that?

TallHarry • 3.09 pm
This. A quote from a local expert.

Catherine moved the cursor over the underlined words and clicked on the link. Her hand shook.

A new page opened which contained an image with text arranged like a quote.

The Black Heart Rite has its origins in the descriptions of Witches' Sabbath rituals held in the late Middle Ages and at the time of the Inquisition. Women were said to gather in a group of five to honour the pentagram and chant a spell. It was believed that, through the performance of this rite, balance would be restored to Eros, the god of sexual energy.

One of the women had been scorned in love. She was infatuated with a man who did not return her affections. She had employed all her wiles to attract him, offered her body to him, and still he spurned her, finding her wanton and desperate. The woman was humiliated, her vanity wounded, and thus the women gathered to bring about the destruction of the man.

First the women would link hands, forming a pentagram. They would chant to Venus—the Roman goddess of beauty—in Latin: *Igne natura renovatur integra*. 'Through fire, nature is reborn whole.'

In this way, the women would summon the devil. The following day, the man in question would be found to have had an accident. The woman whose vanity had suffered would be restored, her black heart whole again. There would no longer be a man walking the earth who did not return her affections.

Catherine Kelley, *Witches, Sirens and Unusual Women*, 2023, p22.

'Well?' Detective Stayer said.

Catherine had said nothing for over a minute. She kept her eyes on the computer screen, refusing to meet his eye.

'Do you know who's behind the Tall Harry account?' Stayer said.

'No,' Sister Catherine replied.

'It's not you, is it? A fake account you've set up to promote your books or something?'

'Of course not,' she cried. 'How could you even think such a thing?'

'Why didn't you tell me about this?' Stayer said.

'I didn't think it would come up! I hoped it wouldn't,' she said. She made a scoffing, pained noise. 'It's not so bad, is it? Whoever has posted this has taken my words out of context—they've cut out the part where I explain that this is *folklore*! I was writing about things people believed in years past; I was *not* writing about Ruby or those other women. This story about a "scorned" woman seeking vengeance was invented by local farmers.' She changed her expression to one of amusement, to prove how ridiculous she found the whole thing. 'I am writing about superstitions! About legends and rumours. Women were branded as witches to control and censure them.'

'I get that,' Detective Stayer said. 'But this passage in your book basically confirms to every conspiracy theorist what they want to hear: that Ruby and her friends killed that artist because one of them was infatuated with him and he rejected her.'

'But we know that isn't true! We read the coroner's report,' Catherine said to him, hearing her voice rising. 'We went to the blowhole. It states unequivocally that Stanley Lacey died by misadventure. He was drunk and stumbled off a cliff.'

The detective spoke softly, which upset her more than if he'd shouted. 'What you've written is folklore. I know it. You know it. But people who are scared will believe anything that helps them feel safe. And if that means blaming the victims for their own deaths, then that's what they'll do.'

'But it would never stand up in a court of law—'

'Of course it wouldn't. No judge is going to cite your book as hard evidence that Ruby and those other girls cast a spell.'

'I'm so sorry,' she said. She could feel the tears slipping from her eyes. 'I didn't know it would be interpreted this way. Please forgive me. What can I do to make it right?'

'Help me find my sister and Sergeant Nichols.'

He handed her a box of tissues. She felt awful. She took a tissue and dabbed her eyes. 'Of course I will. I'm already doing that. I'm so sorry, detective. We'll find them.'

Outside, the wind lashed the trees.

'Let's get some rest and start first thing in the morning,' the detective said.

Catherine met his gaze, feeling shocked. He looked determined. 'Of course,' she said. 'You're right.' She located her faded handbag and swung it over her shoulder, feeling cast down. 'I'll go home then. You'll call me if something comes up?'

He dropped his gaze. 'Certainly.'

'Goodnight then. See you tomorrow.'

'See you tomorrow, sister.'

She walked out of the station, feeling wretched.

6 PM

Stayer had watched Sister Catherine leave the police station, then satisfied she was gone, he collected his keys and bag and exited the station himself. But he did not go to his car to drive home. Stayer crossed the street and walked through the plaza to the strip of shops on Beach Lane. He entered the florist and found Nadia Traurig arranging a bouquet of tall yellow flowers.

'Detective Stayer,' Nadia said. 'Nice to see you. You're lucky to find me here. Usually I'd be closed by now, but I'm preparing an arrangement for a special client.'

Bunches of large-petalled flowers, lilies maybe, lay spread on butcher's paper on the counter, their wet stems dripping. The shop smelled damp and overripe, almost rotten, like a rainforest on a steamy day.

'Last time we spoke, you said something happened to Ruby when she was a teenager,' Stayer said. 'I want to know what that was.'

Nadia slipped her fingers into a pair of heavy silver scissors. The metal clicked against her painted nails. Behind Nadia was a giant glass vase containing birds of paradise; from where Stayer stood, it looked as if they were taking flight, escaping from her head.

She raised the scissors and began slicing the stems of the lilies one by one. 'You didn't sound all that interested before,' she said in a sweet voice.

'I am now.' Stayer shifted his feet, his legs still achy and stiff from the swimming race the day before. 'Please tell me.'

'So what do you want to know?' she asked.

'I want to know about Stanley Lacey, the artist. And Ruby.'

'Are you sure you want to hear this?' She leaned forward and met his eye, seeming aroused by the prospect of telling him.

Stayer looked away. 'I'm sure.'

Nadia tapped her chin thoughtfully. 'Where should I begin . . . Well, Ruby was always a wilful girl. Wilful and spoiled, as I'm sure you'd know. A champion runner, captain of the netball team and volleyball too. On top of that, she won all the academic awards. The teachers always gave her the highest mark. Not because she deserved it, you understand; she bullied them into it. She would cry when she didn't come first.' Nadia paused, covering her hand with her mouth theatrically. 'I'm sorry. Should I stop? You probably don't want to hear unflattering things about your sister.'

Stayer resisted the urge to glare. 'Please go on,' he said.

She nodded portentously. 'Very well. Ruby was intense. She had obsessions. A compulsive girl, sneaky. She would fixate on something, then she had to have it. She had a nervous breakdown in year ten. Were you aware of this, detective?'

She finished snipping the ends off the stems and looked up at him. In the silence, Stayer heard a cat meow outside.

'Go on,' Stayer said. He tried to sound casual, as if this was not news to him.

'She had to be hospitalised. In a psychiatric ward.'

Stayer stared at the flowers but he could feel Nadia Traurig's eyes on him.

'She only returned to school two weeks before the formal. And of course, the night of the year ten formal was when Mr Lacey died. It's still a habit, you know, to call him Mr Lacey, even though I'm grown up now, an adult, running my own business. Funny.'

'And was Ruby a student of Stanley Lacey's? Was she friendly with him?'

'Friendly?' The woman smiled triumphantly. 'Oh, they were much more than friends. So much more it would make you blush.' Stayer heard himself let out a small gasp. He didn't know what to say.

Nadia fetched another vase from the shelves behind her and put it on the counter.

'Ruby was obsessed with Mr Lacey. Infatuated. Not with his paintings. With *him*. Ruby went to every class he offered. Every single one. She wasn't a very good painter; her artworks were very weird. Sorry, I know she's your sister, but it's true. Her paintings made you uncomfortable to look at.' She shivered theatrically.

'Ruby got all confused in her head,' Nadia went on, 'and decided that there was something romantic between them. That his kindness and patience was meant as seduction. The poor man had a wife and a son, you know—but that didn't stop Ruby. She had to have him. And when he told her gently that nothing was ever going to happen between them, she lost it. Said she was going to harm herself. That's why she was put in hospital. Then she returned to school and acted all breezy, as if nothing had happened.'

She looked at Stayer. 'Detective? Are you listening?'

'Do you have any idea how ridiculous this all sounds?' Stayer said. He was beginning to feel desperate again, and baffled at what he'd heard. 'You're saying my sister was hospitalised because the artist in residence at her high school rejected her advances?'

The florist wiped her hands with a towel. Green sap from the flowers streaked the cloth like grass stains. 'You don't know what it's like to be a teenage girl. Everything is fireworks. Being desired and loved is the sum of your existence. If you're not that, you're nothing. To be rejected is worse than death.'

A superior smirk raised the corner of Nadia Traurig's mouth. 'And don't tell me you don't believe Ruby is obsessive. I feel like you don't know her very well, but surely you must have noticed that.' An image came to Stayer, of Ruby scurrying around the dead Christmas tree. Nadia Traurig placed the scissors on the bench. 'If you don't believe me, look at the painting.'

'What painting?'

'His most famous work, detective. The one that won the Archibald Prize. *Sea Bitch*. Ever seen it?'

Stayer shook his head.

Nadia sniffed. 'You really must see it. Look into the model's eyes. See the desperate expression on her face.'

'Where is the painting? In a gallery? I read it was removed from public display.'

Nadia laughed. 'Correct. It's in storage. His widow detests it. She had it removed from the gallery after he died and refuses to show it. No one has seen it in years. Once you've seen it, you'll understand why. No one knows where it is, but I do.'

Stayer groaned. 'Where is it?'

'Apparently Mrs Lacey keeps it in her husband's old studio behind the house. She left his studio untouched. You could go there. It's that grand old place, Eveleigh, on Peninsula Way.'

'If the widow doesn't want the painting on public display, what makes you think she will show it to me?'

Nadia's smug expression made Stayer's eyes hurt. 'When you tell her the reason for your interest, detective, I think she will be very keen to show you.'

'What's the widow's name?'

'Barbara Lacey.'

At first the name only pinged with a vague familiarity for him, then realisation hit him like a slap. He couldn't believe he'd never made the connection before. Barbara Lacey was the woman who had visited him at the station wanting to report the murder of her cat.

6.45 PM

She worked out she had twenty minutes before he returned.

Twenty minutes. Like a REM cycle. That was how long it took his brain to reset. It had only been forty-eight hours, but she was beginning to know him, like a long-suffering housewife who'd learned to predict her husband's moods. Twenty minutes and he would be back. He'd cool down, then come up with a new plan. The new plan would involve violence. Hitting, yes. Stabbing, perhaps. If he brought a gun down here, it would all be over. Did he have access to a gun? Maybe. But she had twenty minutes before they got to that point. So she went to work.

She began with the tape that bound her wrists to the armrests of the chair. He'd wrapped them tightly; tight enough that her fingers felt swollen with blood. She lifted her elbows to see if that might loosen the tape, but it only seemed to make the bindings tighter.

After several minutes, she gave up and slumped in the chair. She would not get free this way. And she had wasted probably five or six precious minutes finding this out. She still had her watch on, and it beeped every fifteen minutes, an old lap setting for time trials that she'd forgotten to switch off. It had annoyed her previously, this beeping, but it came in handy for the present situation, for it helped her keep track of time. Only fifteen minutes left.

She could hear him overhead, pacing.

One of the cats wound itself around her legs again and she tried to brush it away by wriggling her toes furiously, the only part of her feet she could move. Her toes flicked up and hit the cat; it growled and leaped away.

She cocked her head. She heard the cat jump, but she didn't hear it land. She peered into the dark, trying to see where it had gone, and her eyes landed on the metal shelving lining one wall. The type of shelves you would find in a garage or basement, where people put old kettles, unwanted golfclubs, worn clothes.

She guessed she had about ten minutes left.

He'd wound a piece of tape around her chest as well, meaning she couldn't bend over to gnaw the tape at her wrists. Trying to strain against the tape gave her a panicky feeling, but the thought of gnawing had given her an idea. Perhaps something else could be teeth. She needed to get to those shelves.

She heaved and felt the exciting sensation of lifting off the ground, heard the chair legs scraping. She'd moved maybe half a centimetre.

She gritted her teeth and hurled herself forward in a bunny hop. She would win no prizes for elegance.

After another minute of lurching in the chair she estimated she had moved about five centimetres. This had taken about five minutes. She now had maybe five minutes left.

At this rate, she wouldn't make it in time. She needed to increase her pace. Throwing her body forward, she inched closer to the shelves. She lurched frantically and then realised she had rocked too far forward; she was tipping over. She tried to right herself, but to no avail. Her chair crashed into the metal shelves as she went down, the clanging noise echoing horribly. She winced.

The muffled footsteps upstairs suddenly stopped.

She lay there in terror. Her shoulder ached where it had hit the ground. Her knees and hips felt like they were on fire. Maybe he hadn't heard anything, she told herself. But then the footsteps resumed, quicker now, and getting closer.

A dark silhouette appeared at the top of the stairs then hurried down them. He was wearing the black cape and mask.

'Silly bitch,' he said, the first words he'd spoken to her.

Her ears pricked up. Did she recognise the voice?

'Water,' he said.

There was that voice again. Where did she know it from? She searched her brain to make the connection.

He offered her a water bottle, and she opened her mouth greedily, her tongue so dry it burned. But then she noticed how her captor was standing: he seemed to be straining with anticipation. She shut her mouth before the bottle reached her lips.

'What's wrong?' he said.

She clamped her lips tighter.

'Drink the water,' he said. He shoved the bottle towards her roughly and she could sense the heaviness of his arm in the air, the strength of him. She took the neck of the bottle between her teeth and shook her head violently. The bottle came free from his hands and flew. It fell to the ground beside her. He rushed to the bottle and scooped it up quickly, like he was trying to save the liquid inside. She knew then. There was something else in that bottle. It wasn't just water.

'I'm definitely not drinking it now,' she said.

He moved towards her, looking stiff and tense. 'Drink it.' He shoved the bottle at her mouth again, gripping the back of her head with his other hand.

'No,' she managed.

He slapped her across the head, dazing her. She wasn't known for much, but she did have a talent for timing. She was a patient woman, essentially, and she also knew when to seize the moment. Noticing he was off guard, looking down, she hit him with that wrench she had found on the shelves. She hit him again, and again, drawing blood on his upper arm. He stumbled, seeming shocked, both from the impact and from surprise.

In the seconds before he'd descended the stairs, she'd rubbed the tape at her wrist furiously along the shelves' steel edge. It had finally worn through as he'd leaped from the bottom stair into the basement. She had just managed to grab the wrench and conceal it between her thighs before he reached her.

She hit him a fourth time, a fifth, on the side of the head, the little wrench ringing as it met his skull. He doubled over and staggered forward, and she threw her arm out. She grasped the mask covering his face.

She pulled. The mask came free.

He fumbled, trying to return the mask to his face, but failed. The torch he'd been holding was flung to the ground. The beam illuminated his face, now exposed.

She felt her mouth drop open with shock.

'Fucking hell,' Sergeant Nichols said. 'It's you.'

7 PM

Stayer drove to Peninsula Way, the Pacific Ocean on his left looking grey and choppy in the dusk light. He pulled up in front of a grand but decrepit old house. It looked like a centuries-old mansion which had fallen into disrepair. Built in the Edwardian style, it had gables, turrets, verandahs, and bay windows, all painted in various shades of green. It sat high on a hilltop and looked over the headland, as though imposing its will on everything around it. He knocked on the front door, a giant oak slab painted mint green, but there was no answer. The lights were out; it seemed no one was home. He tried Barbara Lacey's mobile phone for a second time. It went to voicemail.

He considered leaving, but the urge to find out something, *anything*, that might help him find his sister made him desperate. He spotted a path running down the side of the house, lined with overgrown oleander trees; evidently someone liked this plant, as hundreds of them lined the path, covering half of it. The hardy leaves, coming to a sharp point, stabbed and scratched Stayer as he walked past. The delicate pink flowers seemed to dissolve on his clothes. Several cats prowled around, following him down the path. He counted at least four—he recalled Mrs Lacey telling him she owned seventeen. He passed a swimming pool with jade tiles, the water glowed lurid green. He reached what must have been the artist's studio: a fading, neglected brick building built in the same ornate style as the main house. Sash windows, stained glass, painted brickwork. It even had a chimney. Stayer peered through a window but couldn't see much in the dark space. Trying the door, he found it locked. He returned to the window and noticed that the old-fashioned sash fastener was missing. He looked around in the semi-darkness and then, when he was sure the cats were his only witnesses, slid the window upwards and climbed inside.

Stayer flicked his torch into the corners of the room. He was indeed in a painter's studio, long disused. An old wooden table stood in one corner, on which sat numerous glass jars filled with paintbrushes. Circles of dried paint of varying colours crusted on palettes. Rags, greying and paint-stained, rested haphazardly on windowsills and tables.

A series of canvases lay stacked against a wall. Clenching his torch between his teeth, Stayer flicked through them. The first few paintings were purely abstract works: foggy squares and rectangles in various shades of red. They didn't mean much to him. Next in the stack lay sketches: of hands, buildings, bodies, drawn in what looked like charcoal. Then there were more paintings of trees, leaves and beach scenes, all mostly unfinished, followed by two completed paintings of waves, which Stayer found haunting and beautiful, and different in style from the rest. He'd almost reached the end and had begun to despair of finding anything useful when his eyes lit on a lock of hair, an arm, belonging to a finished painting towards the back. His heart picked up speed. A figure lay in the ocean of the painting, surrounded by waves. Removing it from the stack, Stayer propped it against the wall then lifted his torch.

In the painting: a young woman lay, nymph-like, in a tidal pool, surrounded by a wash of waves. She wore a slip, so sheer that her nipples were faintly visible. The sight sent Stayer stumbling backward a little, and he heard himself gasp. He couldn't believe what he was looking at.

He took a photo of the painting with his phone, aware his hand was shaking. At the same moment he heard a crash, like someone had dropped a ceramic pot. Stayer looked towards the sound that had come from the back of the studio. He peered into the shadowy area. He couldn't see anything. Another crash rang out.

Heart pounding now, Stayer clambered back through the window of the studio and ran, feeling like someone was chasing him.

He sprinted down the path, scratching his arms on the overgrown oleander, sap bitter and stinging. He'd left the artist's studio in disarray—canvases rifled through, window still open—but it was too late to go back.

Legs aching, lungs burning, he lurched through the wrought-iron front gate and out of the property, sure that someone was in pursuit. He ran to the squad car, parked at the end of the gravel road, and slid into the driver's seat and locked the door. Panting, he scanned the street. The hot wind ruffled the silvery leaves of a giant gum tree above him. Nothing.

He gazed up at the rambling old mansion, expecting to see a light on inside. But the house was dark and still.

Stayer leaned back in his seat and closed his eyes, waiting for his breathing to calm. It took several minutes of panting, scanning, reassuring himself that no one was there, for his regular heartbeat to resume.

When it finally did, he fished his phone from his pocket and pulled up the photo he'd taken of the painting.

Stayer's breath caught once again. It was her. She was young, maybe fifteen years old, and Stayer had never seen a photo of her at that age, but it was her. There could be no doubt that this was the painting Nadia Traurig had been talking about. The subject of Stanley Lacey's most famous portrait, *Sea Bitch*, winner of the Archibald Prize, was his little sister, Ruby.

Sea Bitch. He took the image in once more, dumbfounded. His sister as a teenager, the devouring waves around her. He opened a web browser and typed the painting's title into the search bar. He needed to know if any of the articles and critiques mentioned Ruby. He found the same biographical article he'd read earlier and scrolled down to the section on *Sea Bitch*. From here he clicked a link that took him to a critique of the painting.

The critic wrote:

> Water is one of the most difficult elements to portray without slipping into cliché. Turner did it. Monet managed it, sometimes. How to show something which is translucent but whole? Immaterial, yet comprises 70% of the earth and 60% of the body? But Lacey has done it. Those waves are that wordless sermon, the reason why humans paint. The near-naked woman in the foreground is almost non-entity, a cliché, swallowed and subsumed by the force of nature. As if to say, look at the impermanence of human life and the permanence of the world around it.

Funny how the critic referred to Ruby as a woman, Stayer thought; she was fifteen when the portrait was painted. He flicked back to the photo he'd just taken of the canvas in the artist's studio. The art critic was right: the rendering of Ruby was quite ordinary, even to Stayer's philistine eye. But the waves . . . They were something else. Stayer was no art expert, but even he could tell. The artist had painted them so skilfully that they appeared to be moving.

Stayer read a few more articles but found no mention of Ruby by name. She was simply the model: unidentified and unimportant.

•

Stayer pulled up to the home of Aunt Carol and, noticing the quiet street, bashed on the door loudly.

After some minutes, Carol answered, wearing a silk dressing-gown.

'Matt,' she said, her face surprised and tone unwelcoming.

'Ruby was the subject of Stanley Lacey's painting,' he said. 'But you knew this already, didn't you?'

Carol said nothing.

'What are you not telling me, Carol?'

'Keep your voice down,' she said sharply. She looked around, as if to check if anyone was watching, then said, 'If you insist on making a scene, you'd better come inside.'

She led the way to the kitchen without speaking.

'Did Ruby have a nervous breakdown when she was fifteen?' Stayer said. 'Was she sent to a psychiatric facility?'

Carol threw her head back and laughed. 'You're not serious, Matt, surely?'

'I'm repeating what I've been told,' Stayer said. 'Is it true? Carol, Ruby is missing and almost certainly in danger. You were the closest person to Ruby while she was at Thoorgala Grammar. You need to be honest with me.'

'What were you doing while Ruby was at boarding school, Matt? The reason I am the only one who knows anything about this is because you weren't here! You're her *brother*, her only sibling, and you probably spoke to her a handful of times all the years she was here!' She gave him a look of such coldness he turned away.

'What about Stanley Lacey, the artist? Was Ruby infatuated with him?'

Carol glared at him. 'How dare you. Whatever else may have occurred back then, I can say with confidence that Ruby was *never* infatuated with that man.' Her eyes were narrowed, and she was almost hissing. Stayer had never seen this poised and polished woman, with her manicure and blow dry, lose her composure in this way.

'Carol, if you want me to find Ruby alive, you need to tell me what you know.'

She looked at him with a quivering lip, as though she might burst into tears. 'You don't understand,' she whispered.

'What don't I understand?'

'I should have protected her, Matt,' she said, tears appearing.

'Protected her from what? From whom? What are you talking about, Carol?'

Carol sank to the floor of the kitchen, the silk of her dressing-gown squeaking against the paintwork. She sobbed on the Italian tiles, refusing to speak. Stayer reached out to touch her, but she batted his hand away.

'Carol,' he said softly. 'Talk to me. What should you have protected Ruby from?'

She stood and ran out of the kitchen. Stayer followed her, pleading for her to come back. She fled to her bedroom and shut the door. He pleaded, cajoled, knocked. He received no reply. After half an hour, he gave up. 'I'll come back,' he said through the door. 'We'll discuss this some more later.'

She gave no answer.

28 DECEMBER

6 AM

Stayer spent a terrible night staring at the ceiling, falling occasionally into fits of sleep. He rose a little after six, lurching from the bed. He showered, drank a coffee, then did the thing he'd so far avoided: he went through his sister's belongings.

He started in her studio, a small space she'd carved out in the sunroom to do her art. It also contained resources for Ruby's teaching job, stored in boxes.

Stayer went through the boxes methodically. They included acrylic paints, examples of art projects to show students, clay, paintbrushes, paper, markers, paint pens, screen printing frames. He ran a new paintbrush down the inside of his palm, soft as a kitten's paw. Then while shifting one of the boxes, Stayer found a framed note written on the school letterhead leaning against the wall, as though waiting to be hung. It read:

RUBY STAYER
LETTER OF COMMENDATION

In recognition of over 90% of your students achieving BAND 6 in the Higher School Certificate.
And the selection of four students' work for display in the ARTEXPRESS exhibition at the Art Gallery of NSW.

Stayer knew little about the state curriculum or grading system, but he did know that achieving a Band 6 was some sort of Holy Grail, achieved by only the strongest and most well-prepared students, so for 90 per cent of Ruby's students to manage this feat was nothing short of remarkable.

Apart from this little light shining into Ruby's work life, the sunroom revealed nothing.

Next, Stayer went to his sister's closet, where she stored photographs and documents on the high shelf above the clothes rails. He sifted through the photos greedily, scouring them for any glimpse of her adolescence, perhaps of Phoebe Glasson, Mikaela Sorgensen, Jessie Phan. Or even Stanley Lacey. There were no photos from Ruby's teenage years at all. Most were of pictures of Ruby as a child, blonde haired, rosy-cheeked and chubby-legged. And, to his distress, many of them featured Stayer. He recognised his own brown curls and skinny legs, standing next to Ruby, carrying her, playing in a crappy garden with patchy grass, laughing together, hurtling down a slip and slide, holding Ruby's hand. She had kept these photos and seemed to treasure them. But she'd never found the strength to hang them up, to put them in a frame.

And then one photo tore at him. A photo of Ruby in Brazil. She was standing in front of *Christ the Redeemer*, the huge concrete statue in Rio. She looked about nineteen or twenty. Hundreds of people milled about in the forecourt around her, but she posed alone. She must have asked someone to take the photo. She had come to Brazil to watch Stayer swim in the Olympics. He had been so distracted in the days leading up to his race that he hadn't been able to see her. Then afterwards, once he'd won the gold medal, he'd felt bad and determined to make it up to her. He'd gone to her hotel, in a limousine, to take them both to an athlete's party. The concierge told him she'd checked out the day before.

She'd flown home without telling him. A whole year passed before they spoke again.

Stayer continued his search and found three boxes tucked under Ruby's bed. They contained items from her adolescent bedroom. She would stay with Carol during the school holidays, preferring to be there than go home. Stayer never visited her, preferring to stay at the Australian Institute of Sport than to either go to Carol's or go back to their dad's.

The boxes looked like they'd been long forgotten. Stayer opened the first one now and counted forty-two individual trophies for academic and sporting achievements. An award for representing the state in junior tennis, two for skiing. Five for academic excellence. A medallion for a perfect score in the state English competition. A national cross-country running prize. A medal for being dux of year seven, then eight, then nine. Nothing for year ten, he noted. He spread the trophies and medals out on the carpet and arranged them in order of date. This spectacular run of high achievement stopped abruptly the year Ruby had turned fifteen. He opened the other boxes and found trinkets, postcards and old textbooks, but no more trophies or medals.

He turned to Ruby's nightstand next. Books were piled on top: two detective novels and a trendy cookbook, all containing inscriptions from Carol. Inside the drawer lay an old watch, a packet of tissues and some lip balm. The bathroom cabinet contained the Valium he had been sampling, a toothbrush and almost empty tube of toothpaste, tampons, deodorant, bandaids. Everything decanted into little glass jars, everything neatly arranged. Ruby's drawer in the vanity contained a compact of foundation, a tube of congealed mascara, a wooden hairbrush, hair ties. Stayer sat on the edge of the bathtub and resisted the urge to smash the cabinet mirror.

He left the bathroom and sifted through letters on the kitchen bench. He opened the envelopes addressed to Ruby; one was a reminder to have her teeth cleaned, another was a water bill. He moved to the pantry and began looking through the jars and sauces in desperation. Then he went into ransack mode, pulling pillows from the fraying couches and upending the vintage coffee table. Finally, Stayer felt in his pocket and found Ruby's phone, which he'd kept there like a talisman ever since he realised she was missing.

The phone had died. He went into her bedroom and plugged it into the charger on her bedside table. The battery was so flat it would take time to turn on. He stared out the window, which looked into a neighbour's backyard. The hot wind was still blowing. Towels whipped on the Hills hoist. The phone finally booted up, Vermeer's *View of Delft* blooming on the home screen.

Stayer had assumed the phone would be password-protected, but when he slid his thumb across the screen the phone unlocked. He felt shocked at how easy it had been to get inside his sister's phone, then dismay. No password meant there was nothing Ruby had wanted to hide. He went through the text messages first. Hundreds of messages between Ruby and Carol: requests to meet up, to go to the movies, to go shopping. Ruby replied most of the time, usually making excuses, but accepting just enough invitations to maintain a surface relationship. The rest of Ruby's messages were polite exchanges with her old work colleagues, organising school events or requesting teaching resources; a welcome from her new boss at Thoorgala Grammar; unanswered texts from old friends from uni; spam from clothes shops, art supply stores, food delivery services.

A health app which tracked her running announced that she had run 4890 kilometres in the previous year, an average of ninety-four kilometres per week. An app for the state art gallery promoted upcoming events and 'paintings of the day'. Various food delivery and ride-share apps seemed unused and forgotten. She was not on social media. A music app revealed several playlists containing combinations of folksy rock music, classical music, and sugary pop songs. A playlist called 'sad favourites' included maudlin songs from the seventies, rock ballads from the eighties, and soft R'n'B laments from the nineties. Her internet browser revealed frequent visits to several broadsheet news sites, many art galleries, online bookshops, a few clothing stores. She may have looked at illicit material using a private search setting, but he would never know. In any case, there were no gaps in her official browsing history to suggest that.

He closed the phone. His eyes hurt and his back ached from slouching; he must have been sitting for hours in the one position. But he felt awake and wired. Stayer found her laptop next. It was the one issued by Thoorgala Grammar; a sticker with the school logo lay at the bottom edge of the keyboard. The laptop was password-protected but his despair was brief; when he went back into Ruby's phone, he found a page in the notes app titled *Passwords*. Once logged in, he saw that the desktop contained about a dozen folders. He went through each folder and every document. Assessment tasks, rubrics, professional development plans; yearly planners, weekly planners, unit planners. Lots of planning. Photography worksheets, scans from art history textbooks, stencils for vinyl cutting. It took him almost two hours but still he didn't tire. By the end of the search, he'd found not a single personal document.

Stayer's chest began hurting, so he lay on the timber floor.

He stared at the ceiling. Dead bugs and little piles of dust made black shadows in the bottom of the ceiling light above him. He turned his head and took in the pillaged house. The only thing left undisturbed was the old wooden bookshelf. Something caught his eye, between two cookbooks. He sprang to his feet. He tugged at a slender apricot spine and pulled out a school exercise book.

Stayer was delighted. He had so far in his search uncovered nothing at all from Ruby's youth, no photos, documents, and certainly nothing written in her own hand. The notebook had been wedged between the cookbooks, seemingly forgotten through numerous moves, when it should have ended up in a rubbish pile long ago. Or perhaps it had been secreted there all along. He leafed through it, and even though it was pedestrian stuff—study notes for a history test, an old timetable—it was like touching a live cable, connecting him to a Ruby he'd never known.

He turned a page and found something different. He paused. In the bottom corner of a page, beneath a doodle of a tunnel, swirling circles of pen, Ruby had composed something; he wasn't sure what exactly, but it seemed like a little poem or statement.

The beauty and intensity of the words floored him.

He read the words again, and then for a third time. He loved what she'd written—the fire in it. But it tore at him also, to know he'd had to rifle through her belongings to find this, had to sneak and steal to read something from his little sister's heart.

To be a painter is to challenge God. To say, no God, you're wrong. God shows the painter the ocean and says this is what a wave LOOKS like. But the painter says to God, sure, that is what a wave looks like, but this is what a wave FEELS like.

3 PM

It was mid-afternoon when Stayer arrived at the police station, where he had been expected at eight. On his phone were four missed calls from Walsh, eight from Joan, and two from Sister Catherine. However, when he entered the squad room, no one noticed. Joan, Walsh, and Sister Catherine all had their backs to him. They were gathered around Walsh's desk, staring at his computer.

'What's going on?' Stayer said. Still no one turned. He walked over.

They were looking at //Thoorgala, the internet forum. The computer screen glowed. Everyone was silent.

'Someone's posted a video,' Joan said to him at last. 'Play it from the start, Robbie.'

Constable Walsh dragged the play head back to the beginning.

An image appeared on screen. Five girls, all around fifteen or sixteen. The video was shot in portrait mode and had a graininess, like it had been filmed on an older-model smartphone. The girls looked dressed up: some were wearing long gloves; all were in heels. They stood on the lawn of a place Stayer knew. The manicured green blades of Carol's back garden.

An unidentified person behind the camera spoke. 'Names, please?' Stayer tensed as he recognised the voice. It was Carol's.

'I'm Phoebe,' said the girl on the left-hand side.

'I'm Miki,' said the one next to her.

'That's Phoebe Glasson and Mikaela Sorgensen,' said Joan, voice hushed.

'I'm Jessie,' said the third girl, flicking her hair off her shoulder.

'Jenny,' said the fourth girl.

'And I'm Ruby,' said the fifth.

Walsh hit pause. The video froze. The room was so quiet that Stayer could hear the wheeze of Joan's breathing. He could also feel Sister Catherine's eyes on him.

'That's your sister, detective,' Joan said.

'Is that Sergeant Nichols?' Walsh asked.

'Yes, that's Jenny,' Joan said. 'I'd know her anywhere. My god.'

Stayer gazed at the youthful faces of the three women found murdered on the sandhills. It was disorientating to see them reanimated in younger form, legs and arms moving, mouths talking, when all he'd known of them was rictus limbs and mottled flesh. In the video they burst with giddiness and light.

Phoebe Glasson was dressed in black and had gothic eye make-up, evoking a sort of teenage Morticia Addams. Mikaela Sorgensen wore a white dress with absurd ruffles and frills, like a bordello madam from the Wild West. She had a sly smile, like she found the whole thing ironic. The teenaged Sergeant Nichols looked smart and tidy in a tasteful black cocktail dress. Jessie Phan looked tough and beautiful in a green strapless gown. And Ruby looked nervous and slightly embarrassed in tight pink silk. His heart tore. He studied the other girls, but his eyes returned hopelessly to his sister. The video had paused on her face as she glanced away from the camera, wearing the saddest expression Stayer had ever seen. 'Press play, constable,' Stayer said in a soft voice.

Walsh clicked his mouse, and the video sprang to life.

The girls waved to someone, probably Carol behind the camera, announcing they were off to the formal; the pre-formal drinks on Aunt Carol's green lawn had apparently ended. The screen flicked to black.

Sister Catherine had glanced at Stayer several times, but he continued to avoid her eye.

'Who posted this video?' he asked.

'Tall Harry,' Constable Walsh replied, turning to look at Stayer. 'That is, the guy who calls himself that online.'

'That's Stanley Lacey!' Joan exclaimed, pointing at the screen. It had lit up again, playing a new video file which must have been tacked on to the first. The group of girls now stood in a darkened ballroom, with disco lights and a dancefloor, and circular tables arranged in rows. Ruby glanced at the camera briefly before looking away.

Stanley Lacey stood next to her, dressed in a tuxedo, with gel-spiked hair, a fifty-year-old boy band wannabe. Stayer recalled the autopsy photo of Stanley Lacey's head, with the right side of his skull opened, the spinal fluid leaking out.

The video cut and continued to another clip, this time showing the students dancing. Stanley Lacey was now behind the dancefloor, leaning in tightly, talking to Ruby. Her face was hard, and she was looking down. From the strained gestures and short words, they appeared to be quarrelling like lovers, their gestures and movements familiar, intimate, damning.

The sights and sounds of a high school formal spun around them: faux parquet dancefloor, DJ booth and lights, circular tables with white tablecloths, floral centrepieces. Everything looked slightly more upmarket than your usual high school event; the fact this was a private school made apparent in the expensive-looking suits and gowns, the hotel ballroom, steak on the dinner plates. But it still had the feel of a teenage function, of kids playing dress-up:

the girls wearing too much make-up and the boys fidgeting in their suits, regarding each other nervously, awkwardly, sweetly.

Stanley Lacey was not speaking with this young student in the professional, distanced way of a teacher or chaperone. He grabbed Ruby's arm like he had done it before, like it was nothing new to him. The way he leaned into her personal space made the older brother, the police officer, the adult in Stayer furious.

This went on for about thirty seconds, then the screen cut abruptly to black once more. Constable Walsh dragged the play head a few more times, but that was it; they had reached the end of the video file.

It was like a hurricane had been blowing outside, but now someone had shut the door, and everything had gone quiet.

•

//Thoorgala. A sandy corner of the internet to discuss all things God's country

TallHarry • 3.30 pm
Watch video file: https//watch?v=nfa3wXXYFo5hZk

HaroldBishop • 3.33 pm
Fucking bitches. Not so innocent now, r they

TallHarry • 3.34 pm
Indeed not.

MaryCronin • 3.40 pm
That doesn't prove anything. They were friends in high school and went to the formal together. So what?

JamesTileman • 3.45 pm
You must admit Mary Cronin. It doesn't look good.

•

Stayer led Sister Catherine into his office and closed the door behind her.

Then he told her everything: about his conversation with Nadia Traurig, in which she'd told him about Ruby's hospitalisation; about finding the *Sea Bitch* painting; about Carol's regret that she hadn't 'protected' Ruby and her refusal to elaborate on what she meant. He showed Sister Catherine the photo he'd taken in Stanley Lacey's old studio. He winced as he watched her take in the obscene painting of his sister's teenage body floating in the waves.

'It was dark in the studio; it might be hard to see properly,' he said.

'I can see it,' she said, nodding softly. 'I understand.' She studied the image quietly.

'I don't know what to do now,' Stayer said.

'There is only one thing to do,' Sister Catherine replied. 'Find your sister. Find Sergeant Nichols.'

5 PM

Stayer stood outside Mick's Camera House & Theatrical Hire on the main road and pounded on the door until it was opened by a middle-aged man carrying a clipboard. He wore a navy-blue shirt in heavy cotton drill, and trousers of the same material. A name tag on his shirt read: *Mick*.

'I'm glad you're open,' Stayer said. He stuck his head inside the shop. The blacks and silvers of machines and devices glinted in the showroom downlights: cameras, hard drives, laptops, USB sticks. A large white machine for self-printing photos sat in one corner, its lights off.

'We're not—I'm stocktaking,' Mick replied, holding up his clipboard.

'You know who I am?' Stayer asked.

Mick scanned his face, as though trying to place him. 'Matthias Stayer. Olympian.'

'Not anymore. I'm a detective now.'

'That's one hell of a career change,' Mick said.

'You rent out lights?'

'Yes?'

'Big ones?'

Mick nodded and snapped his pen under the metal bar of

the clipboard. He remained squarely in the doorway, not asking Stayer to leave, but not stepping aside to let him in, either.

'How many do you have?'

Mick checked his sheet. 'Two Day-Makers. Four Briseis. Eleven Blondies. Eight Redheads.'

'Lucky you have your clipboard.'

'It's come in handy for this situation.' Mick had the sort of pleasant drollness Stayer had observed in certain Australian men in their fifties. Probably nothing bothered him; probably nothing excited him either. Or maybe some things excited him, but they were buried very deeply somewhere, unlikely to ever appear in the daylight, in front of friends, bosses, families.

'Are the Day-Makers bright?' Stayer asked.

Mick's expression didn't change. 'They're called Day-Makers. There's a hint in the name.'

Stayer pulled out his wallet and handed over a credit card. 'I'll take them. A week's hire.'

'Sure. Which do you want?'

'All of them. The blondes, the gingers . . .'

'Redheads.'

'Yep, those. The Day-Makers, too.'

'You really want the lot? What are you lighting?'

'A great big patch of sand.'

Mick's expression finally gained some animation: he raised an eyebrow. 'Whatever blows your hair back, I guess. But one of the Day-Makers is booked, sorry,' he said, peering at his clipboard. 'A student short film.'

'Cancel it,' Stayer said. 'This is for a police operation.'

'Really?' Mick raised the other eyebrow. 'I could have been a cop, you know. But Dad wanted me to take over the camera shop.'

'Dads can be funny like that.'

He made a note on his clipboard. 'The students can shoot next week. You can have all the lights.'

•

After Stayer left Camera House & Theatrical Hire, he drove to three more construction hire centres across the Cundra Valley. He rented out every available outdoor light he could find. The grounds manager at the field where the local professional rugby league team played was a swimming fan; he gave Stayer the Day-Makers they rigged on the hill for night games. These lights were so big they came with their own trailer, and when fully extended, the stands stretched fifty metres above the ground.

Constable Walsh, Sister Catherine, Joan, Mick from the camera house, and the footy ground manager joined Stayer in the sandhills. They placed the lights every thirty metres or so along the perimeter of the dunes, plus smaller lights in between, powering them with generators on wheels.

After several hours of rolling, pushing, sweating, swearing, and repositioning, they stood back, armpits damp, arms and legs aching, and switched the lights on to admire their handiwork. They had lit up the sandhills so brightly, they could have hosted a football game.

'Try and bring another one here, you son of a bitch,' Stayer said.

Dr Dixon arrived, still wearing his green scrubs, as the footy ground manager left. Stayer nodded to him gratefully.

Stayer outlined the plan. 'We're going to stake out the sandhills until dawn, to see if the killer will still try to lead another victim out here. We've lit up as much of the sand as we can.'

'What if he tries to take Sergeant Nichols or your sister somewhere we haven't lit up?' Joan asked. She smoked a cigarette. Her hand was shaking.

'We'll just hope he doesn't,' Stayer said. 'Okay, let's get into position. You take the western corner, Joan, with Constable Walsh.

Sister Catherine and I will watch the eastern side. Dr Dixon and Mick will watch the northern side.'

•

Stayer watched the sandhills from the driver's seat of the squad car. Sister Catherine sat in the passenger seat. The sun dipped below the horizon in front of them, a little half-moon of fire that shrunk down to nothing. The giant lights from the camera house and football grounds shone onto the sand, turning it orange. Silence, apart from the hums of the generators.

Stayer propped his foot on the side of the car door. 'Ruby is my sister, but I don't really know her at all. My fault, entirely. But me and Ruby have nothing to do with each other. Nothing to say to each other.'

They sat that way for a while, him staring straight ahead, the nun looking at him. A fast wind blew across the sand, stirring it up in parts, sending flecks across the dunes in whorls and spins.

The radio sparked. 'Come in, Stayer, it's Joan.'

They both sat upright.

Joan spoke quickly. 'Detective, I'm sorry, I've made a mistake . . .' She was puffing, out of breath.

'What is it, Joan?' Stayer said into the radio. 'What's happened?'

'Constable Walsh went to relieve himself, and I got out of the car to have a smoke. The wind picked up—you know that disgusting hot southerly. Anyway I turned my back, just for a minute or two, and I missed it.'

'Missed what?' Stayer said.

'Someone must have gone onto the sandhills while I wasn't looking, because over at the southern corner, almost to the edge of the big dune, there's . . . there's . . .'

'There's what, Joan?' Stayer could hear the panic in his voice.

'A body. I'm sorry, detective.'

Sister Catherine gripped the dashboard.

'A body?' Stayer paused. 'Just one?'

'Just one.'

'Can you see who it is? Joan?'

Silence over the radio. They waited.

'Joan? Can you see who it is?'

'I can't, sorry.'

'Stay there,' Stayer said.

He jumped from the car and ran.

'Wait for me, detective,' Sister Catherine called after him.

But there was no time. He moved across the sand towards the southern end of the dunes. Joan came into view on the far side of the sandhills. She waved to attract his attention then pointed across the dunes. Stayer's eyes went to where she was pointing.

He saw it. A female body. Seaweed covering the face. But whose face? He couldn't really be sure what his sister's skin looked like, he realised sadly, and he didn't particularly know the shape of her elbows, her feet, the curve of her knees. Stayer had spent only days in her company since she was ten, he thirteen. He had no idea if the body lying there was Ruby.

Stayer kept running, though every breath now hurt, and his chest was so tight he feared he might have a heart attack. He kept going and finally drew close enough to see the body.

He slowed. His sprint became a jog, then a walk. Finally, he stopped a few metres away. Panting, he clasped his hands behind his head and tried to suck more air into his lungs.

Sister Catherine arrived beside him, breathless.

Stayer approached the body and crouched down. He used a pen to flick the seaweed away.

A plastic face stared up at them with a sultry expression.

'It's a mannequin,' Sister Catherine said.

Joan joined them, puffing like she was making fire from kindling. Constable Walsh arrived straight after, black hair matted to his forehead.

'Crikey,' Joan said, taking in the mannequin. 'Sorry, Stayer. My bad. It looked like a human being from where I was standing.'

'That's okay, Joan. Someone is playing a prank on us.'

The mannequin's plastic blue eyes stared at the night sky; its waxen face turned orange by the big lights they'd hoisted up.

2.11 AM

Jenny ran to the top of the stairs and peered through the wire gate leading into the house. It was dark. He was gone. After she'd torn off his mask, she'd tripped over one of the cats and he'd managed to knock her to the ground. He'd struggled to his feet and stormed upstairs, bleeding from where she'd beaten him with the wrench. She rattled the gate, hoping he might have neglected to lock it, but it held fast. She peered into the blackness, seeing nothing.

Then she heard it behind her, a voice so soft and hoarse it could have been the wind. 'Help.'

She had been hearing little cries ever since she had been locked down there in the basement, but she'd presumed these noises came from the cats, or that she'd imagined them, in her own delirium and disorientation. Now, as she stood in the stillness, she realised they had not been feline sounds, but human ones. Another woman lay somewhere in the room with her.

Jenny hurried back down the stairs.

'Where are you?' she whispered, not wanting to draw attention just in case he was still prowling around up above. 'Say something.'

She waited, and waited, and decided maybe she'd imagined it after all, hallucinated a companion for herself after countless hours in the fetid darkness.

Then: 'Here,' the voice said hoarsely.

Jenny moved towards the sound, peering into the gloom.

She found her: bound to a chair like she had been, her eyes closed, barely conscious.

It was Ruby Stayer.

'Ruby!' Jenny gasped. 'How long have you been down here?'

'I don't know,' the other woman said, her voice weak. But still the same as Jenny remembered from when they were kids. A grown woman's body now sat in the chair, a grown woman's face looked up at her, but the voice, still shockingly, happily, the same. In that moment, fifteen years melted away, and she was a teenager again.

'I'm going to untie you,' Jenny said. She started tugging at Ruby's bindings, then remembered how impossible it had been to loosen them with her hands alone. She needed something with a cutting edge.

She moved back into the basement, scanning wildly, feeling her way around the semi-darkness. She found the disgusting cat jungle, and after rummaging around frantically she located a thin strip of metal along its base. She ripped it off and headed back towards Ruby, only to find that *he* was coming back: leaping down the stairs towards her, agitated but smiling.

Jenny swung the metal strip. 'Get back, arsehole. I'll kill you—you know I will.'

'You won't,' he said. 'You will do everything I say. You're going to sit back down and I'm going to tie you up and then you're going to drink what I tell you to drink.'

She scoffed and swung the metal strip again. It wobbled in the air, slim and flimsy, and she knew as well as he did that it wasn't much of a weapon. Still, she had almost beaten him unconscious before with a small wrench, and she knew she could take him again, even with just her bare hands. She stepped back, gathering herself, ready to attack.

'Number seven, York Way, Lismore,' he said.

She froze.

'Nice-looking house, your father's. I like the flowers out the front. Are they azaleas? Always wanted to grow them myself, but I don't have the patience for gardening.' His sickly sweet voice turned sinister. 'Do what I say, or your father will have his throat slit in his sleep.' He motioned for her to sit back down in the battered chair, like he was a waiter at a silver service restaurant and she a guest.

Jenny felt a whimper escape from her. She walked back over to the chair.

'Why are you doing this?' she said.

'Because you ruined all my plans. You wrecked everything.' He worked the silver duct tape back around her wrists and ankles, adding twice the length this time. He bound her wrists so tightly her hands felt like they'd explode. Once he was done, he offered her the water bottle again. 'Drink.'

She opened her mouth, and he tipped the clear liquid in carefully, taking pains not to spill. She drank it in, surrendering to her horrendous thirst. It was water, but with something dissolved into it, some sort of powder, terribly bitter. The granules caught on her tongue, rough and nasty.

Once she'd swallowed all of it, he walked over to Ruby. He held the bottle to her lips. 'Drink,' he ordered.

'No,' Ruby said. Her voice was frail but defiant.

'You didn't hear me before? Do what I say, or I'm going to kill Jenny's dad.'

'Ruby, no!' Jenny screamed.

But it was too late. Ruby had opened her mouth and was swallowing the poison that Jenny was now certain would kill them both.

29 DECEMBER

10 AM

The hours ticked by, but no bodies were found, not on the sand dunes nor anywhere else. Stayer had issued alerts to all emergency services. Everyone was looking for Sergeant Jenny Nichols and Ruby Stayer.

They were back at the station. Mick from Mick's Camera House & Theatrical Hire had erected cameras over the sand dunes, to film anyone coming or going.

Stayer's phone rang. It was Dr Dixon.

'No fingerprints found on the mannequin, detective,' he said down the line. 'Sorry.'

'Worth a try,' Stayer said.

He was about to hang up when the doctor spoke again. 'Was it common knowledge that Phoebe Glasson was found with seaweed on her face?'

Stayer frowned. 'Not that I know of.'

'Whoever played this prank had to know about the seaweed.'

Stayer hung up and relayed the information to Sister Catherine. 'If they knew about the seaweed, I'd say it wasn't a prank,' Sister Catherine said.

Stayer looked at her.

'What I mean is, I think the killer wants to toy with us. So they put the mannequin there themselves.'

Stayer sat up.

'The killer was on the sandhills with us that night. He was right there.'

•

Stayer called Sergeant Nichols' father to update him.

He heard the dejection in Warren Nichols' voice as he answered. 'Hello, detective.'

'We mightn't have found your daughter yet,' he said, 'but I think that gives us reason to hope. I think she's still alive, and she's giving this dickhead a run for his money. Don't give up hope.'

'I won't,' Warren said, his voice brightening. He added, 'While I've got you, you asked me earlier to let you know if I thought of anything. About Jenny, from when she was a teenager. I do remember something. The girls were really into those games.'

Stayer gripped the phone. 'Games? What kind of games?'

'Letters on a board. Everyone moves an object over the letters to spell out a message . . .'

'A Ouija board?'

'That's it. They were really into witchcraft and that kind of thing. I thought it was just a phase all teenage girls went through, but Jenny and the others were really into it. That's why I remember. I didn't think it was relevant, or I would have said something earlier. It just seemed so silly at the time. I remember one day, I came home from work, and the girls were in our backyard chanting.' He cleared his throat.

Stayer felt confused. 'What were they chanting?'

'I didn't hear the words, but I must admit, it spooked me a bit. It was different from when they played with the Ouija board, which usually involved a lot of laughter. It almost sounded like they were growling. I made a noise in the kitchen—banging a saucepan, loud enough that they would hear. They stopped their chanting instantly, as though I'd surprised them, or caught them doing something they shouldn't. You asked me if I remembered anything from back then, so I'm telling you.'

Stayer stared at a crack in the plaster in the wall of his office. 'Warren, all teenagers were into witchcraft—'

'I know. But you asked me to tell you if I remembered anything. I know it's ridiculous, but Jenny is missing, and I'm going out of my mind.'

Stayer felt pained. 'Thank you, Warren. That's very helpful.'

'Something else. Jenny and I weren't on the greatest terms. That's why it took so long for me to contact you about her being missing. I didn't even know if she was coming to Lismore for Christmas. We'd made some faint plans, then we'd sort of stopped speaking.'

'Had something happened?'

'I didn't agree with her going back to Thoorgala. We'd lived in Thoorgala when Jenny was a kid, she grew up there.'

'Yes. She mentioned that.'

'We moved up to Lismore when she was sixteen or so. I've never been back to Thoorgala. Earlier this year, Jenny announced she would be taking a cop job there. I was surprised. I couldn't believe she would want to go back.'

'Why?'

Silence rang out on the line. A dog barked somewhere in the background; the hot wind howled. Stayer looked out the window. An empty chip packet spun down the road outside.

'Thoorgala isn't a nice place,' Warren Nichols said at last. 'Beautiful. But not nice.'

2 PM

The funeral for the second victim, Mikaela Sorgensen, was held that afternoon. The service took place in an old-school Catholic church: stone, wooden rafters, stained-glass windows of flayed saints. A space used to hosting thirty worshippers on a Sunday was now standing room only. The pews held three hundred comfortably, double that uncomfortably, and even more people stood at the back of the church and along the side walls. A gallery above seemed to bow with the weight of another hundred or so human beings. They peered down onto the congregation below, like press in a courthouse.

Stayer and Sister Catherine found a space to stand behind the stairs that led up to the choir. Stayer could see Mikaela's mother and father in the front row. Bill Sorgensen's back was ramrod straight, as though it was his duty to stay upright. Sabina had gone the other way; her back was crumpled, like her bones had collapsed.

The priest spoke to them briefly before returning to the altar. As he turned his back to them, the holy man fluffed his crimson tunic upwards at the waist, as though it had caught on something, and Stayer was afforded a glimpse of the dove grey collared shirt with short sleeves, and charcoal-coloured shorts he was wearing underneath. His knees below the shorts were marble-white and hairy.

The coffin lay in the middle of the aisle, in front of the altar. It was a dark brown wood with brass handles. A mound of purple flowers tumbled over the lid in an almost wild fashion, as if they had escaped from the arrangement. '*Campanula rotundifolia*,' Sister Catherine whispered, motioning to them. 'Bluebells. The national flower of Sweden.' Her face looked flushed and her cheeks pink; the air in the church was close and stifling, like someone had left on the ducted heating.

The service passed uneventfully, in a procession of tasteful music, solemn and seemingly endless prayers, and standing up and sitting down at regular intervals. The most interesting moment occurred when an altar boy tripped while carrying a glass pitcher of sacramental wine. The crowd let out a collective gasp, but to their disappointment, the boy righted himself without spilling a drop. There was a polite eulogy, read by the victim's aunt, who wore a yellow dress and put on a pair of tortoiseshell-framed glasses to read from her notes. She had flown in from Sweden for the funeral. Everyone seemed to crane their necks when she began, as though hoping for some mention of the other women, or the death of Stanley Lacey, or maybe even Tall Harry. But her speech comprised only sweet anecdotes of Mikaela Sorgensen's childhood, and a summary of Mikaela's achievements at school and university.

'Miki was a remarkable woman,' the aunt told the congregation. 'Generous and kind.' She mentioned several times Mikaela's love of reading but made no mention of how her bookshop was mostly alternative, selling banned and controversial books, and texts on the occult. She didn't speak of Mikaela's run-ins with the law, of her link to an anti-whaling group that had been implicated in eco-terrorism, including sinking a whaling ship in the Pacific Ocean, which caused one of the crew to drown. The mirror of her life had been scrubbed clean.

The mass ended as abruptly as it had begun. The priest told everyone to go in peace. A sallow-cheeked man, inexplicably wearing a red woollen jumper in the forty-degree heat, pulled a seat up to the organ and began playing a dirge, the melody generic and faintly familiar. The funeral home women wearing red Akubra hats took their places beside the coffin, then they wheeled it back down the aisle, their soft steps moving approximately in time to the hymn.

Stayer felt bereft. They'd discovered nothing. The funeral had been a whitewash, run by strangers, administered by a random priest, observed by rubberneckers. He scanned the room furiously, looking for anyone suspicious, anything untoward, as the coffin was wheeled outside. But no one looked out of place, and he grew depressed with the confirmation that most of the people in that crowd stood there for the same reason he did. They had nothing to do with Mikaela's death, or Ruby's disappearance; they were just hoping for drama.

Once outside, however, Stayer finally got what he'd been hoping for, though it wasn't what he expected. The father of Mikaela Sorgensen walked up to Sister Catherine with a tear-stained face.

'Where is your God now, sister?' Bill Sorgensen demanded angrily, his face reddish and damp.

The exiting congregation all stopped and looked at each other in shock and excitement. The carefully engineered reverence of the mass, the hymns, stained-glass windows and incense, had vanished, to be replaced by wild grief and unmanaged spectacle. The dead woman's father gripped Sister Catherine by both arms and shook her angrily. Stayer moved to stop the man, but Sister Catherine shook her head gently to warn him off.

'What do you want from me, Mr Sorgensen?' she asked him in a soft but steely tone.

'How do I go on, now?' he said in a cracked voice.

His wife and the aunt in the yellow dress rushed over to pull him away from Sister Catherine, but he waved them off, his attention still on the nun. 'How do I get through each day with this much pain? How do I go on with this broken heart? Your God can't help me now. He can't bring her back. He can't relieve my suffering. And don't tell me to pray, sister—don't you dare tell me to do that.'

'I wasn't planning to, Mr Sorgensen,' she replied in a dry voice.

'Then what *should* I do? Tell me!' He flung his head back, shouting his appeal to the sky.

The crowd was hushed, waiting, the only sound Sabina Sorgensen's sobbing.

'Give some of your pain to me, Mr Sorgensen,' Sister Catherine said to the grieving father. Her eyes were wet and earnest, her expression devoid of irony. 'That's right. Let me take on some. That is what I am here for. You say your heart is broken? Take mine. Take my heart. It is yours. Give me your pain. I am here and I'm not going anywhere. I am going to phone you every day until you tell me to stop. You will tell me about your daughter and tell me your pain. And I will take it on. I will bear some of this burden, so you don't have to bear it all on your own. But don't ever fear your pain. It won't end you. The pain you feel now gives your daughter's life meaning. The greater the pain, the greater the love.'

Bill Sorgensen had a stunned expression. The rest of the congregation waited.

Suddenly, the father seemed to catapult himself forward, collapsing onto Sister Catherine's shoulder and sobbing. The nun did not buckle under the weight of him, despite being half his size. Instead, she remained straight-backed, immoveable. She wrapped her small arms around the bear of man and held him as he cried.

3.25 PM

Stayer stopped at the petrol station on the way back into Thoorgala. He was alone. Sister Catherine had asked to accompany the Sorgensens to the burial. Stayer had agreed and watched her walking away next to Bill Sorgensen, her small, black-veiled head cocked gently towards him.

Stayer filled the squad car, listening to the tick of the bowser. Ruby had told him once that she loved petrol stations. They had been in their late teens and Stayer was driving Ruby to the train station after their father's funeral. He'd offered to drive her the whole way back to Thoorgala, but she had declined quietly. When they stopped at a BP to fill up the car, Ruby had got out and stood next to him as he put the petrol in, saying nothing. Stayer recalled flashes of the funeral and wake, dirt being thrown on the coffin, the eulogy read by one of his father's mates, neither Stayer nor Ruby speaking at the service. A lavish wake had followed, aggressively catered by Aunt Carol: there had been a croquembouche, sachertorte, an espresso machine with an operator. Stayer had hardly spoken to anyone. Ruby had followed Stayer inside the station and insisted on paying for half the petrol, even though she only rode in the car for this one small stretch from cemetery to train station, pressing a crumpled fifty dollar note into his hand. As they walked back to the car, she'd mentioned her love of petrol stations. Stayer had laughed curiously and called her weird. He regretted the weird comment instantly, they didn't have a joking relationship, and he wondered if he'd offended her. But then she smiled cheekily, and for a moment he glimpsed a different brother–sister relationship they could have had, one that shared jokes, and gently but affectionately teased each other. He asked her why she loved petrol stations, and she didn't immediately answer. Then, as they were pulling back out onto the highway, and he flicked his indicator and waited for a break in traffic, she finally gave her answer. 'You could be going anywhere,' she said.

The bowser clicked as it finished, and Stayer was brought back from his memory of one petrol station to the one he stood at now. He went inside to pay. As he tapped his card, he glanced at the attendant's name badge. It gave him pause.

'Angel?' he said, reading her name aloud.

'Yeah?' She offered a friendly smile.

'Angel who attends Thoorgala Grammar as a student?'

'Yeah?' she said, slightly wary.

'Were you the student who said the rhyme about Tall Harry at the end of year assembly?'

She froze. She met Stayer's eye, then ran out through a door marked 'Staff Only' to the back of the petrol station.

'Hey!' Stayer said. He grabbed the door before it locked shut and followed her through it.

Stayer found himself in some sort of break room, with a microwave, fridge, plastic table and chairs. The microwave whirred, food span gently inside. A woman sat at the plastic table, staring at Stayer, looking shocked. 'Which way did she go?' Stayer asked, showing his badge.

The woman pointed down a corridor. Boxes containing stock—potato chips, soft drinks, lollies—lined one wall. Stayer dashed past them, knocking his arm on the boxes. The end of the corridor hosted staff toilets. Stayer burst into the ladies', peering gingerly into cubicles. Then he saw, high up, by the sinks: the sole of a black boot slipping out of the toilet window. He raced back out of the toilets and pushed open the fire exit at the end of the corridor and ran into the daylight. The sun beat into his eyes. He saw Angelica 'Angel' O'Brien sprinting out of the petrol station towards an open field. He chased after her. Unlucky for her, a barbed wire-topped fence separated the petrol station from the field's overgrown grass. She was climbing it when he reached her. He grabbed her leg.

'Stop, police,' he said.

'Bugger off,' she replied, wiggling her leg.

'That's barbed wire up there. You'll rip your nice sneakers to shreds.'

She sighed and stopped climbing. Stayer helped her down. 'Do I need to arrest you?' he said.

'No,' she said with a sneer, puffing. A hot breeze blew. Fumes of petroleum wafted, fragrant, green.

'You said the Tall Harry rhyme at the school assembly,' he said. 'Why?'

'I didn't know it would cause all this. I didn't know it would work!' Angel's dyed-black hair stuck to her forehead, matted with sweat.

'Why did you do it? Did you read the rhyme somewhere, or did someone tell you to say it?'

'Nah. I just hate the school. Wanted to shake things up.'

Stayer felt confused. 'Why did you say those particular words? Did you know about Tall Harry, the urban legend?'

She looked at him blankly. 'Knew nothing about Tall Harry. Just something dumb to say.' The automatic glass doors of the petrol station slid open. A man walked out, eating a dim sim.

'Please. There's still women missing. If you know anything at all, you could help find them alive. Or maybe we go down to the station and speak there.'

Angel's cool and indifferent facade fell away. 'I was paid to say it.' She met his eye.

Stayer paused. 'What?'

'I got fifteen hundred bucks to say it. He came up to me that morning and offered me the money.'

'He? Who?'

'I thought why not. I hate that school anyway. Happy to fuck up a stupid assembly.'

'A man paid you. What was his name?'

'Don't know.'

'What did he look like? Where did this happen?'

'On my way to school that morning. A guy stopped me out of the train station. Dunno.'

'How tall was he? Skin colour? Eye colour? Hair colour?'

'I dunno! He had a hoodie on, covering his face. It was dark, we were in the tunnel. He might have been tall. I couldn't tell you. Dude. I'm sorry. That's all I know. Can I go back inside now? I don't want to get fired.'

Stayer watched her walk back inside the petrol station.

4 PM

The superintendent called as Stayer arrived back at the station. He flinched when he saw his superior's number on the screen, worried that he was calling with news of Ruby or Sergeant Nichols.

'The firebug has been found,' he said. 'Little shit was hiding out in an abandoned boatshed. This frees up the detectives you need. The first one arrives tomorrow, and three more the next day . . . Are you there, Stayer?'

Stayer had been wanting to hear these words for so long, he almost didn't believe them. 'Thank god,' he said.

The chief continued, 'I've also got you a dog unit, a mounted unit, and a dedicated homicide squad.'

'Wow. That's fantastic, chief, thank you.'

'I've heard you've had a nun helping you. You must have been desperate. Sorry about that.'

'Sister Catherine's been quite helpful actually.'

Stayer peeked through the blinds; the sun hit the window like a laser.

'I know Catherine Kelley,' the chief said. 'Known her since she was a kid. A strange one.'

Stayer's ears pricked up. 'Strange? How do you mean?'

'I can't say. Welfare stuff. I just don't want to breach her confidentiality.'

'I'll keep it to myself. Would love to know what you know.'

'She used to live in Rexley before she became a nun,' the chief said. 'Welfare kid, orphan. I attended callouts to her house for domestics. Then her parents died in an MVA. The father drove his station wagon into a tree one night. Maybe on purpose. Catherine was in the back with her little sister. Mum and Dad died; the two girls survived.'

'Jesus,' Stayer said. 'I didn't know that.'

'Wait until you hear the rest,' the chief said. 'Community Services, DOCS as it was then known, moved the girls around from home to home. Never lasted more than a few months in one place. Every season, they'd get a new mother, a new father. Then Catherine turned sixteen, and the foster parents needed the bed for the next kid, so she had to leave. She was put up in a halfway house, for the homeless and adults with special needs. It happens sometimes, with teenagers. There's nowhere else to put them. You still there, Detective Stayer?'

'I'm here.'

'Bernadette, the little sister, had cystic fibrosis. Her lungs never developed properly. Like a little bird she was. All papery skin, powdery, with a gaunt face and very pretty eyes. Looked like Wednesday Addams. Two weeks after Catherine was shipped out to the halfway house, Bernadette died. She stopped breathing in the night. Turns out, Catherine had been sneaking back into the house every night and sleeping on the floor in the little girl's room. The foster parents would pass out from drugs, they didn't take care of the girl properly.' Stayer sat back in his chair, feeling shell shocked.

'The day after the little girl died, I was there, doing the recovery. Catherine was howling beside the gurney as they wheeled her sister out of the house. Later that day, she turned up at the station and demanded I arrest her—for murder. I asked her how she'd done it.

She hadn't done anything; she just hadn't been by her sister's side the night before. She'd been caught sneaking out of her new accommodation and they'd put a lock on her window and door. I told her, "That's not murder," and she told me I was wrong, because Bernadette would still be alive if she'd been there to unkink the child's breathing tube when she rolled over on it. Next thing I hear, Catherine Kelley joined the nuns.

'The woman has endured a few events in her life, safe to say,' the chief said solemnly. 'Like I said, you'll have four detectives at your disposal tomorrow. More still in the coming days. A dog unit, homicide squad. I don't want her helping you anymore. To keep her around now would be reckless. There's WHS issues, for one thing. What if she got hurt?'

When Stayer hung up the call, it took him several minutes of staring into space before he could move. He imagined breaking this news to Sister Catherine and it made him ill.

•

//Thoorgala. A sandy corner of the internet to discuss all things God's country

Snookus52 • 3.11 pm
Has anyone heard from HaroldBishop lately?

JeepRinger • 4.26 pm
I think he's AWOL. Not on the other chats either.

Snookus52 • 4.29 pm
Who is he on other chats? Still called HaroldBishop?

JeepRinger • 4.29 pm
Nup. Tonka2 over there. I think?

4.20 PM

A soft knock rang out on the door to Stayer's office. Sister Catherine poked her head around and entered.

'I may have found something,' she said to him. 'It's likely nothing, but I'll show you anyway.' She opened her laptop on his desk. 'On the Thoorgala forum, there's a person who posts using the profile name HaroldBishop. They've blocked their IP address, as many of those on such sites do.'

Her veil fell across her shoulder as she leaned down, covering her arm like the edge of a blanket. Stayer wondered when the right moment would be to tell her she was no longer able to work on the case.

'HaroldBishop is the one who posts intimate details of the case online,' she explained, pointing to the screen with a small, thin finger. 'He was the first to post about the symbol carved into the bodies. We have no idea of his real identity. But our friends Snookus52 and JeepRinger may have inadvertently pointed us in his direction. JeepRinger states that HaroldBishop is known by the name Tonka2 in another chatroom. He posts on several other sites about Thoorgala news, sports, and surf conditions. But see here—he wrote, *I live like Madeleine. In a house covered with vines.*'

'We know that house,' Stayer said. 'It's the one on Peninsula Way. We knocked on the door but there was no one home. Sister, this is what's known as a breakthrough.'

Pride and excitement filled the nun's face. 'Let's go now,' she said, moving to the door.

'I'll go alone, sister.'

She turned and looked back at him with a puzzled expression.

'More detectives arrive soon,' he said. 'Freed up from the bushfires case.'

'That's wonderful. They must have found the firebug, then.' She cocked her head.

'The superintendent feels it's best if you cease your involvement in the case now. He doesn't want you getting hurt.' He waited.

She folded her small hands together and said nothing.

'You've been very helpful. You should feel proud of the work you've done.'

Her face darkened. 'I don't care about feeling proud, detective; I'm worried that if I'm not allowed to help with the case anymore, something will be missed. Ruby and Sergeant Nichols are still out there. I believe they are still alive; I don't know for how much longer.'

Stayer watched her. She suddenly seemed very small. 'Catherine, I heard about Bernadette. I'm so sorry.'

Sister Catherine snapped her head to look at him. Her expression was cold.

'I'll still try to get those scriptures for you.'

'I beg your pardon?'

'The ones written by Magda van Aachen. I understand why you want them now. You believe they will help you see your sister again.'

'How dare you.'

Several dreadful moments passed, with her staring at him icily. Stayer wished he could go back in time and start this conversation over.

'You must be keen to get to the house,' she said at last. 'I'll get out of your way.' She collected her laptop and left the room.

Stayer called after her to come back, but she didn't.

There was no time to waste. Stayer drove to Peninsula Way, fuming and regretful. He called Constable Walsh on the way and explained the situation with HaroldBishop.

'That sounds promising,' Walsh said. 'I'll come over when I'm done here.' He'd been doorknocking the houses on the other side of the peninsula. 'A few more houses are occupied now. People have returned from holidays.'

'Thank you for doing that, constable. I'm grateful.'

'I'll meet you at Peninsula Way now.'

He drove on, trying to put Sister Catherine's face out of his mind, but found he couldn't.

•

He was the first to arrive at 14 Peninsula Way. After five minutes, he had a text from Walsh to say he'd been held up but was on his way now. Too impatient to wait, Stayer got out of the car.

He moved down the concrete pathway running to the house. The house covered in vines rose from the earth, the building decrepit, the vines wet-looking. It was mid-century architecture, the walls made of sandstone. As he got closer, he saw where the vines originated: they came from a giant, overgrown monstera deliciosa, what people often called a Swiss cheese or fruit salad plant, and they weren't vines at all, but rather the plant's branches. It was a single plant, overgrown, and Stayer couldn't understand how something which usually sat in a pot in people's living rooms had managed to grow so enormous. The branches, green, smooth, bendy, stretched from the ground to the front wall of the house, climbing upwards, spreading then engulfing the entire facade, covering windows. Branches had been hacked away to make space around the front door. He knocked on it. To his surprise it opened immediately.

He had been focusing on the building and its engulfment by the monstrous plant, so when the door opened and the face appeared before him, a face he recognised, it took him a minute for his thoughts to form any sort of coherence. The face belonged to Dr Dixon.

4.50 PM

Dr Dixon wore a blue tracksuit and looked as unsurprised to see Stayer as the detective was surprised to see him.

'G'day,' Stayer said. 'I didn't know you lived here.'

The forensic pathologist shrugged. 'Gotta live somewhere.'

Stayer couldn't read his expression. The doctor seemed genuine. He met Stayer's eye easily, seeming cool and composed.

'I knocked on this door a few nights back. You didn't answer.'

'Was probably out. There's a big case on. You might have heard of it.'

They stood there for a few seconds.

'I'm glad you're in now, Dr Dixon,' Stayer said. 'Could I come in and look around? Specifically, I'd love to see your basement.'

'Call me Dane when I'm at home,' the doctor said. 'We don't have a basement anymore. There was a landslide risk, so we had it filled in.' He shifted his weight from one foot to the other. His tracksuit top was a touch too small. A mound of hairy stomach poked out. 'You're welcome to look around though. Come in.'

Their eyes met again, briefly. Dane stepped to the side and opened the door wider, as if coaxing Stayer inside. Stayer entered without speaking.

An open-plan interior stretched out before him, with a living area, dining area, and kitchen divided by backless shelves. With its minimalist furniture, geometric shapes, and bold colours, it could have earned a place in an architectural magazine, were it not for the paint peeling from the walls, dust covering every shelf and benchtop, and a dank, mildewy smell hanging in the air like a curse. He quietly moved his eyes over the windows and doors and ceiling fixtures, locating the exits, just in case he needed them.

'You'll have to excuse the dust,' Dane said. 'Don't bother much with cleaning once Hannah and the kids left. Would you like a soda water?' He held up an old, vintage-looking soda water syphon. Gold mesh covered the bottle.

'Er, sure,' Stayer said.

He watched as Dane walked to the sink and poured the water into the syphon. He screwed the little black tap on top of the bottle and pulled the lever. He moved carefully and deliberately, seeming to take great pleasure in dispensing the liquid from the ancient-looking thing.

'Don't you just love these old syphons,' he said, pouring himself a glass too. 'Dad used to have one when we were little. We were never allowed to touch it. I bought this on eBay.'

He handed Stayer a glass.

Stayer thanked him and walked over to a bookcase. 'Quite the house, Dane. Singular, even for Thoorgala.'

The doctor gave a generous laugh. 'Eccentric, you mean. It was like this when we bought it. The previous owners had gone bankrupt during the financial crisis in '08. They let it fall into disrepair. My wife repaired some shelves and had the floorboards repolished, but once she left I didn't bother with any more "restorations" or "maintenance". I decided that if nature wanted to reclaim this house, so be it.'

A multitude of orange Penguin Classics covers filled the shelves of an entire wall. Stayer ran his eyes over the spines of *Mrs Dalloway*, *Catcher in the Rye* and *Nineteen Eighty-Four*. He pinched the spine of *Mrs Dalloway*—a book he'd seen on Ruby's kitchen table—but found he couldn't loosen it from the shelf. Closer inspection revealed the book to be fake, existing of spine only. Someone had chopped up hundreds of books, retaining only the spines of each, and glued them to the wall.

Dane bellowed with laughter, doubling over. 'Gotcha!'

Stayer moved further through the room and found that, from a certain angle, he could see through the window and across a courtyard into what he figured was a bedroom upstairs.

Crime scene photos from the murders he was currently investigating covered the wall. Stayer did a double take when he realised what he was looking at. He inched closer to the window, continuing to laugh along with the forensic pathologist, hoping Dane hadn't noticed that Stayer's attention had shifted.

Jessica Phan was laid out on the sandhill, the red of the Jupiter symbol stark on her bluish skin. Next to that was a photo of Ruby, a portrait shot in a studio, downloaded from the website of Thoorgala Grammar.

The forensic pathologist walked over to see what Stayer was looking at. Stayer turned to him, and their eyes met.

'You've noticed my evidence room,' Dane said. 'What do you think?'

'I don't know, Dane. What am I supposed to think about it?'

Stayer thought of the gun in his shoulder holster, trying to remember whether he'd clipped it or unclipped it as he left the car. 'I know you've been posting details of the case online. You call yourself HaroldBishop.'

'Yes,' said the pathologist smoothly. 'Are you a *Neighbours* fan?'

'More of a *Home and Away* man, myself,' Stayer said.

Dane shook his head with a look of disgust. 'Dreadful show. Would you like to check it out? My evidence room?'

'Okay,' Stayer said brightly, trying to sound unalarmed.

'This way,' Dane said at last, and led Stayer towards the stairs.

Stayer had not unclipped his handgun holster, he was sure of it now. They reached a landing, and Stayer followed the doctor down a hallway, past bathrooms and bedrooms. At the end of the hall, the doctor unlocked the door with a key and showed Stayer inside the master bedroom.

5.25 PM

The bedroom looked like the operations room of a police station when they were working a big case. Crime scene photos covered the whole wall that Stayer had glimpsed from the living room. Jessica Phan with her limbs and black hair splayed, Mikaela Sorgensen with sand across her button nose, Phoebe Glasson with the seaweed covering her face, the sandhills undulating. The carved symbols on each woman featured in close-ups, clearly pointing to moles. Beside these macabre images hung pictures of Ruby and Sergeant Nichols: the one of Ruby from her schoolteacher's portrait, and Nichols' official police portrait, the sergeant posing in her dress uniform and hat. Against the other wall was the workstation of a computer hacker or professional gamer. The office chair had speakers in the headrest; three computer towers sat on the floor under the desk; and at least a hundred external hard drives were stacked against the desk's side, leaning precariously.

'This is what I wanted to show you,' Dane said.

He gathered a series of manila folders from his desk and spread them out on a trestle table. He removed sheets of paper from the various folders and arranged them precisely.

But the documents he handled had nothing to do with the current murders; rather, they related to the death of Stanley Lacey.

'Jessie Phan, she was the one who drugged him,' the pathologist said, tapping the autopsy report. 'What did she go on to become? A pharmacist. Her family are descended from the Rục people in Vietnam. Known for their practice of witchcraft.' He said this as though he'd made some damning discovery. 'There's no evidence of poison, of course; Jessie was too clever for that. No way would she have drugged him with something that would show up in an autopsy. And Ruby Stayer, she was the ringleader, the head of the coven.'

Stayer's ears pricked as he heard his sister's name.

'Ruby had been rejected by Stanley Lacey; that's why they killed him.'

Stayer felt his mind whir and ping. 'Sorry, I'm not following. I thought you were investigating the murders of the women on the sandhills?'

'Those? No, Tall Harry's responsible for them,' he replied as though it were obvious. 'I'm showing you what I found: proof that those women committed murder.'

'What proof?' Stayer asked. He wondered again about the service revolver in its holster. Had he loaded it?

'They were clever and cunning—they made his death look like an accident. Like I said, Jessie Phan drugged him, with an unknown substance, so that he wasn't in his right mind, and then they lured him to the blowhole. There they used a spell to curse his soul. With his soul damned, he felt a despair so black and terrible that he threw himself off the cliff. They're witches, see.' He pointed at the wall with the photos of the bodies laid out on the sand at Cundra. 'The moles are proof they cavort with Satan.'

Stayer felt like he was on one of those theme park rides that sent you up a pole, paused for a second, then dropped you from the sky.

'How could you buy into any of this? Witches, urban legends. These are fairytales, pieces of folklore. You are a man of science.'

'That's what makes this so intriguing!' He beamed.

He handed Stayer a book. 'Here. Read this.' It was Sister Catherine's text about myths and legends, the one he'd read several times now. The doctor flipped to the passage about the Black Heart Rite and showed it to Stayer. The one that had ended up on the internet.

'Did you post this online as Tall Harry?' Stayer asked.

Dane shook his head. 'Not me. The real Tall Harry is the poster. You'll never find him. I've tried to find him myself. He conceals his IP address. He's black mist. The killer has been putting out the information himself. You've been very slow on the uptake. I can't believe how slow you've been.' He chuckled ruefully. 'But since you're here, I can just show you everything.'

'What are you showing me exactly?'

'That those women were witches. *Are* witches. They're witches still. But justice has been served. You can close the case.' He patted Stayer's shoulder reassuringly.

Stayer flinched. 'Do you know where the missing women are? Ruby and Sergeant Nichols?'

'No.' The pathologist looked away, as though something had distracted him.

'But you don't feel bad about them dying?'

'It's for the best. I'm sure you'd agree.'

'You're aware that Ruby is my sister?'

Dane shrugged. 'I'm aware. Which is why I find it strange that it's taken so long for you to grasp all this. Wouldn't you rather know who your sister really is? *What* she is?'

Stayer resisted the urge to grab him. Instead he said, 'So this whole time, you were pretending to help with this case, but each night you came home and performed your own investigation, trying to prove my sister and Sergeant Nichols and the three dead women were involved in witchcraft?'

'Not trying to prove—*have* proved,' Dane said proudly.

'How can you have been taken in by this rubbish, Dane? I've been to the blowhole. I've read the coroner's report, as I'm sure you have. Stanley Lacey died by accident. He was drunk, he tripped and fell. Injuries consistent with a stupid, tragic accident. The German backpackers witnessed it.' He softened his voice. 'Your divorce has traumatised you, Dane. Spending Christmas Day apart from your young children must have been heartbreaking. You look exhausted. You're not yourself.'

He waited for the doctor to respond. Dane sipped his soda water, looking thoughtful. For a moment, Stayer thought his pleadings had gotten through, that his kind words had reached him.

'On the contrary. My divorce has just solidified my position,' Dane said at last. 'That all women are cunning, secretive, witches.'

'Tell me where the women are,' Stayer said. 'Is there a basement in this house?'

'No! I already told you.'

'Don't lie to me, Dane. All the split-level houses along the peninsula have spaces under them or behind them. The builders cut them into the hill slope.'

'I promise you, I have no basement,' the pathologist said. His voice was growing frantic. 'Yes, houses in this street have basements. Most of them, in fact. And this one used to. But there was fear of a landslide a few years ago, and it was filled in. I already told you this.' The forensic pathologist looked at Stayer imploringly. 'I could show you?'

Stayer nodded. 'Let's go.'

Dane led him back downstairs then along a hallway to the back of the house. A glass wall on one side looked out onto a tangle of monstera branches and tree roots, slick, rectangular and green.

Dane turned a corner and paused. 'See?' He pointed to a wall of polished concrete. 'We had a basement, but it was filled in.' He knocked on the wall with his fist. It made a dull and solid sound.

Stayer needed to regain control. 'You could be hiding them somewhere else. Let's go—I'm taking you to the station. You know something.' He reached out and grabbed Dane.

'No! Let me go,' he said, wrestling with Stayer, his body a walrus, a solid mass without angles, hard to get a grip on. Stayer finally managed to loop his hands around his meaty wrists and wrenched them together in front of his body. He prodded Dane in the back with his own hands until the man began to walk.

Outside, Stayer scanned the street for Constable Walsh, expecting to see the other squad car parked somewhere and his giant frame hurrying towards him. Stayer checked his phone, but he'd heard nothing more since the text from Walsh saying he was on his way. Stayer called him again as he lead Dane across the road. He left a voicemail, asking Walsh where he was. At the car, Stayer paused before urging Dane into the back seat. 'Please, Dane,' Stayer said quietly, finding the man's eyes. 'Tell me where my sister is. *Please.*'

A triumphant look flashed across the doctor's face. 'You're too late,' he said. 'She's already dead. Harry's got the witch, and he's made her pay for what she did.'

5.45 PM

Catherine remained at the station. She knew she wasn't supposed to be there, but she couldn't bring herself to leave. She had hidden in the toilets, sitting on the plastic lid, feeling idiotic. She had only emerged once she was sure Detective Stayer had left.

Joan found her sitting outside his office and, taking in her expression, told her not to worry. 'Stayer has made an arrest,' the receptionist said.

'He has?' Catherine sat up in her chair.

Joan told her how the detective had gone to the vine-covered house on Peninsula Way and found Dr Dixon, the pathologist, and a room full of crime scene photos, along with pictures of Sergeant Nichols and Ruby Stayer. 'Cheer up, sister. You did a great job. He's caught the killer because of you.'

'Dr Dixon? I'm shocked,' Sister Catherine said.

'Always the quiet ones,' Joan said. 'Hasn't been the same since his wife left him.'

Catherine exhaled. It was over, then. She gathered her things, keen to leave before Stayer returned. As she checked Stayer's office, she glanced over the files spread out on the desk. Her eyes fell on a document she'd not seen before. 'Where did this come from?' she called out to Joan.

Joan popped her head in the office. 'The animal hospital in Rexley sent it over just now. It's the post-mortem report for Mrs Lacey's cat. She came in a few days ago, saying her cat was murdered. She paid for a private autopsy.' A photo was attached to the report of a middle-aged woman holding a cat. She looked like an ageing groupie for a 1960s rock band: velvet scarves, macrame shawl, a mood ring. Eyes lined with black.

'Is this Mrs Lacey?' Catherine asked.

Joan nodded. 'And that's Pericles,' she said, pointing. An overweight tabby cat snoozed proprietarily in the woman's lap in the photo.

Catherine read the report. As well as recording the measurements of the brain and spleen, and the contents of the cat's stomach, it also listed a substance present in the cat's bloodstream: oleander.

'Did Mrs Lacey say that the cat ate some flowers? Leaves, perhaps?'

Joan shrugged. 'She just said the cat was murdered.'

Catherine felt light-headed and spacey. She had been too hot for too long, and the air in the police station was stifling. She wanted to go home to bed. 'Do you have an address for her?'

'She's on Peninsula Way—number one twenty-eight. Along the headland, out by the fisheries. Do you know it?'

Catherine nodded, thinking. A headache was beginning, she could feel it. She had no paracetamol in her handbag and felt silly asking Joan, even though she was sure the receptionist would have found her some.

'Are you going to go out there?' Joan asked. 'If so, watch out for the cats.'

'No.' She took her phone and dialled Stayer's number, breathing heavily, holding her forehead in her hand. The phone rang twice, three times, then went to voicemail. She left a message, long and detailed, then hung up.

She looked down wearily, rubbing her eyes. She felt exhausted.

'Has the detective found his sister?' she asked Joan. 'Or Sergeant Nichols?'

The receptionist shook her head. 'No, they're still missing. Detective Stayer is bringing the suspect back to the station now to question him, though, so hopefully they'll be found soon.'

'Does that usually happen? Suspects confessing everything once they're brought back to the station?'

'Not really, no,' said Joan. 'They tend not to volunteer information that could get them into trouble.'

Catherine adjusted her veil. Sweat trickled past her ear. Her hair would be drenched underneath when she removed the black fabric tonight.

The detective had said that Catherine was to have nothing more to do with the investigation. But surely there was nothing wrong with a nun going to comfort a woman whose cat had died?

6.18 PM

Catherine arrived at 128 Peninsula Way and looked upon Eveleigh, the current residence of Mrs Lacey and the former residence of her cat, Pericles. A once-grand mansion, now in a state of disrepair. Many cats—perhaps ten or fifteen—prowled the property. A black cat watched Catherine from a window as she approached the house. A grey one with fur missing in patches wound itself around her leg as she paused on the front porch. They seemed to emerge from everywhere to watch her, like a chorus. Cats in the shed, by the overgrown garden, in the trees.

Then she saw them, a huge row of oleander trees. They lined one entire side of the property, like a wall. The pointed green leaves stabbed the air, the delicate pink flowers ruffled in the hot breeze. These plants took pride of place in many Australian gardens: they grew easily and looked great. Few people knew how poisonous they were, how death could come from ingesting just a few leaves.

She approached a large oak door, painted mint green. She knocked and waited. No one came.

She looked for signs of life other than the cats. A car sat in the red gravel driveway. The engine was ticking, like it had only recently been switched off.

She knocked again and this time heard floorboards creaking inside. She peered through a window, which looked into a rustic French-style kitchen, with an old, AGA-style stove and worn wooden floorboards. She felt like a stickybeak, and very un-Christian. People deserved their privacy, especially victims of cat murder. But peer in the window she did, and someone was indeed walking around inside, making those floorboards creak. But the person was not Mrs Lacey; it was Constable Robert Walsh.

Catherine knocked on the window. Constable Walsh turned.

She waved, and he looked a little startled, then waved back. He opened the door to let Catherine in.

'This is a surprise,' he said to her genially. 'Come in.'

Catherine stepped inside the house. A putrid smell hit her nose, almost throwing her backward. A hot and meaty odour, with hints of ammonia. She choked. 'What is that smell?' she asked Constable Walsh.

'Pretty awful, isn't it,' he said, standing in the kitchen, smiling. 'Probably the cats.'

Cobwebs swayed from the corniced ceiling in long strands, like hair. Paisley wallpaper peeled from the walls. Dust caked an oak side table, upon which stood tarnished brass candlesticks with no candles. It looked as if someone had been preparing for a party a hundred years ago then left abruptly.

'What brings you here, sister?' the constable asked. He wore a friendly expression.

'I came to visit Mrs Lacey. To discuss the autopsy she had ordered for her cat. Is she here?'

'Stayer sent you over here by yourself?' Walsh asked, looking concerned. 'That's not cool.'

'No, he's out arresting Dr Dixon, the forensic pathologist. Detective Stayer doesn't know I'm here. I came of my own accord.' Australian animals were rendered in leadlight on the kitchen windows: a koala curled around a eucalyptus branch; a kangaroo drinking at a stream, their thick silver outlines looking dull and blackened. The koala stared at Catherine with beaded eyes. She held a hand to her nose. The horrendous smell continued to hang in the air, like a living thing. She feared she might pass out.

'Well, I'm here as part of the search of properties on Peninsula Way.' He paced the room. The smell didn't seem to be affecting him at all.

'Do you know where Mrs Lacey is?'

'Doesn't seem to be home,' he said. 'I've had a look around. No sign of her.' His eyes seemed to keep darting towards the kitchen window. Every time he spoke, they flashed there.

'I suppose I'm not needed now, since you're here. I might head off,' Sister Catherine said.

'Oh yes, very well. Back to the convent with you,' Walsh said cheerfully.

Catherine turned to the front door, and in doing so was afforded a glimpse of what Constable Walsh's eyes had been drawn to. Time passed in a funny way then, it went both fast and slow, as Catherine's brain processed what she was looking at and grappled with the decision she now had to make. The first part came to her quickly, the second required more time. She finally made her choice.

'I might use the bathroom before I leave.'

'Sure, sister,' the constable said casually. 'It's just down the hall.'

Catherine thanked him and walked past.

Walsh had not been looking through the window, as it turned out, but rather at the oak shelf by the front door, which held a picture frame. A photo within that picture frame featured two people. The first was Mrs Lacey, whom Catherine recognised from the photo stapled to the autopsy report for Pericles. The second was Constable Robert Walsh.

6.35 PM

Catherine entered the bathroom and locked the door. Little hexagonal tiles in varying shades of green lay unevenly underfoot. A claw-foot bathtub stood by a window. Water dripped from somewhere. A creeping plant lay dying in the corner. She stared at her face in the vanity mirror. Her cheeks were red and sweaty. Beneath her veil, her eyes were wide; she looked like a startled animal. She ordered herself to stay calm. She flushed the heavy white toilet with the wooden seat, turned the gold taps on and off again, and exited the bathroom.

She found Constable Walsh standing in the hallway, blocking her path.

The temperature in his gaze had lowered; all politeness had gone.

'Go on, sister, tell me what you are thinking.'

He was so close she could feel his breath on her cheek. Its sourness made her recoil.

'I think it's you,' she said. 'I think you killed those women, and you are holding Sergeant Nichols and Ruby Stayer hostage. I think you're Tall Harry.'

The bulk of him loomed over her. He seemed as heavy as a tree. He raised his hand slightly and she flinched, thinking he would hit her.

He laughed. 'Well done, sister. Are you scared? You should be.'

She realised how easily he could kill her. He would slam her head into the wall or strangle her and she would be dead.

'What did you think, sister, when you saw the symbol?'

A skinny black cat slunk past her leg. She could feel its ribs as they brushed her shin. 'Excuse me?'

'When you saw the Jupiter symbol, the symbol of Tall Harry, exactly as it appears in your book, how did that make you feel? Were you excited? Scared? Aroused?'

Catherine froze.

'I've never traced anything before. I never did those normal kid things, tracing over drawings of horses, trucks, cartoon characters.'

'You copied the Jupiter symbol from my book,' Catherine said faintly.

'And everything else, yes. The Tall Harry rhyme, the symbol pointing to moles, the messages, the costume. I stole everything from your book. Gave it a certain something, didn't it? And it sucked you in, sister, and everyone else. Boy, how it sucked you in!'

Horror gripped her. She could hardly comprehend his words. The last few days swarmed around her in awful flashes: seeing the carvings on the bodies, meeting the detective, the excitement she felt to be on the case, investigating the exact symbol she had written about. She felt foolish, and used, and terrified. 'You really stole everything—the symbol, the costume—from my book?'

He nodded cheerfully. 'Wait, no. Almost everything. The one thing I didn't get from you was using the oleander. That was entirely me. You don't say in your book how Tall Harry kills his victims, because in the legend, he sucks their souls out, using black magic. I needed a little more help than that. Stroke of genius on my part—not even you had thought of it! I spooked Dr Dixon well and good. Better yet, I spooked the people of this town. How easily everyone was taken in! How quickly they turned on the women. All thanks to your book, sister. And for that I shall forever be proud.'

The more he talked, the larger he seemed to grow. She felt small and stupid in return. The only emotion she could process was fear, the only question she could ask herself was how she'd been so gullible. 'Why?' she asked. 'Why did you pretend to be Tall Harry?'

'I knew the truth, and I needed to make others see.'

'The truth about what?'

He grinned tightly. Didn't answer.

'Are Sergeant Nichols and Detective Stayer's sister still alive?' she asked. 'Please, if you know where they are, tell me.'

His face softened. 'Forget about them. They deserve to die. Everyone will thank me. They're already doing it. Seen the internet? I'm famous now. I'm a hero.'

'A hero on the internet is not the same as a real hero.'

He smirked. 'Oh, sister. It's real.'

'Please tell me where they are, Robbie,' she said, hoping that a more personal appeal might touch him. 'You can still do the right thing.'

'I've already done the right thing. The world is better off without those bitches.'

Catherine was desperate. 'Please tell me where they are,' she begged.

He grabbed her elbow and propelled her down the hallway. 'No need to tell you—I'll show you.'

He dragged her all the way through the house to a wire door that led down to a basement. A hairless cat with blue eyes watched them from a bookshelf.

Walsh undid a padlock, pulled the door open, and gave Catherine a little push. She stumbled down a set of wooden stairs into a dark basement. The constable disappeared back up into the house. She heard the door swing shut and the click of the padlock behind her.

She looked around frantically in the darkness.

The wire door allowed a small amount of light to shine through from the house. Catherine's eyes adjusted to the gloom.

She made out two bodies. Slumped in chairs.

Grey duct tape bound their wrists and ankles, and their eyes were closed, like they were sleeping. Catherine fell to her knees beside the first body. It was Ruby Stayer. The other body belonged to Sergeant Nichols.

6.45 PM

Ruby Stayer seemed unconscious, eyes closed, head slumped on her chest. Catherine shook the woman's shoulder, trying to rouse her. 'Ruby, can you hear me?'

Ruby stirred and muttered angrily.

'Ruby, please listen to me. My name is Sister Catherine Kelley.'

She reached up to touch her face. Detective Stayer's sister, looking as beautiful and pained as she had seemed in her photograph, knocked Catherine's hand away aggressively with her chin.

'Ruby, listen to me,' Catherine urged. 'You have been poisoned by the oleander plant. It disrupts the rhythm of your heart. You feel agitated because of this. Soon you will go into cardiac arrest. We need to get you to a hospital where they can administer an antidote.'

'I don't think she wants to get better,' rasped a voice next to Ruby. It was Sergeant Nichols. 'I don't care about myself,' she said. 'But Ruby—I let her down. Again.'

'We need to get you both out of here. Tell me what I can do.'

'Get this tape off us.'

Catherine ripped at the tape around Sergeant Nichols' wrists. Sweat covered the silver fabric. It was wound around the skin so tightly it had cut off the circulation to Sergeant Nichols' hands.

The layers of tape felt plastered together. 'I can't loosen it,' Catherine said frantically.

'Find something to cut it with. In the shelves.'

Catherine moved to a set of steel shelves against the wall. She felt around for something she could use to cut. 'How long do we have? Before he comes back down?'

'About fifteen minutes,' Sergeant Nichols said. 'He always takes about twenty minutes to gather his thoughts, to re-evaluate his plan,' she said. 'And he's already been gone about five. So we've got fifteen minutes before we have the pleasure of his company again.'

Sister Catherine rifled through old clothes, broken kettles and yellowing documents with corners nibbled by rats. She found nothing with a sharp edge. Nothing she could use to cut through the tape.

'What are we doing down here?' Ruby Stayer spoke into the darkness. Her voice was feeble.

Catherine momentarily stopped searching. She put down the pile of stinking old clothes she had been sifting through and turned to the women.

'Five days ago, a woman's body was found on the Cundra sandhills,' Catherine said. She spoke into the darkness. She could hear both women breathing. 'It was Phoebe Glasson. She had a symbol carved into her hand and was found with a note which read, *They shall confess, or four more.*'

Neither woman said anything. Catherine could make out the outline of Ruby Stayer's face. She seemed to be watching intently. Listening.

'I saw Phoebe's body,' Sergeant Nichols said quietly. 'I helped bring her down off the sandhills. I dropped her.' She hung her head.

'The next day,' Catherine continued, the body of Mikaela Sorgensen was found on the sandhills also. The same symbol was carved into her, and another note was found, reading, *She refused to confess. She had to die. Make the others confess or they die too.* The following day, Jessie Phan was found on the sandhills. The same symbol carved into her. No note this time.' Catherine recounted the details of the symbol, and the Tall Harry legend. The women both listened quietly, nodding, saying nothing.

'Why did he kill Phoebe, Miki and Jessie?' Ruby said at last, in a quiet voice.

'Constable Walsh is convinced that those women killed Stanley Lacey while they were students at Thoorgala Grammar. He plans to kill you too.'

A cat meowed roughly in the corner; it sounded hungry. 'Stanley Lacey was an alcoholic; he was drunk and stumbling along the rocks and fell into the blowhole. His death was ruled an accident,' Ruby said.

Catherine was startled to hear Ruby speaking of these events so casually, naming Stanley and the three women who had been found dead on the sandhills. It put the events in technicolour, it made everything real.

'I know that. But Constable Walsh claims that you lured Stanley Lacey to the blowhole and made him fall to his death using witchcraft. Specifically, the Black Heart Rite.'

Sergeant Nichols bellowed with laughter in the corner. Ruby Stayer made no sound.

'Okay. And what has this guy got to do with it?' Ruby said.

'Constable Walsh?' Catherine said.

'Yeah. The guy prowling around up there. What's his connection to this whole thing? Why does he care so much about a guy who died fifteen years ago?'

'I don't know,' Catherine replied. 'But it seems personal.'

Something moved in the corner of the basement near the stairs, and the three women tensed. But it was only a cat with patchy orange fur, walking around the staircase, purring. Catherine followed it to the stairs. Something had caught her eye. A pile of cat food tins, opened, licked clean, save for a few brown dabs of food rotting on the insides of the tins and lids. The smell was horrendous. She zeroed in on the lid of one tin. Its jagged edge glinted dimly.

'So you're a nun, huh?' Ruby Stayer said as Catherine hunted around the stairs.

'Yes. My name is Sister Catherine Kelley. I'm a folklore expert; I've been helping your brother with the investigation. We've been trying to find you for several days now.'

'You know Matt?' A new lightness had entered her voice.

'Yes,' Catherine replied. 'I've been working with him since Christmas Eve.'

Ruby sounded pained. 'Is he angry with me?'

'I see no anger in him,' she said. 'Only a terribly worried man who is desperate to find his sister.'

Catherine returned from the stairs. She drew close enough to see Ruby's face. Ruby blinked, several times. Tears had formed in the rim of her eyes. Catherine touched the back of her head gingerly. An egg had formed where it had slammed into the wall.

Ruby gazed at the concrete floor. 'I didn't want to tell Matt about any of this,' she said. 'He came to Thoorgala without knowing any of this story.'

Someone—Walsh, presumably—turned a light on upstairs, which threw a soft glow into the basement. The women all straightened. Catherine looked around, trying to orientate herself. Bottles of wine were stacked haphazardly along one wall, signalling the space's original use as a cellar. Cat baskets, kitty litter, and a giant carpet-lined cat jungle sat around the room's perimeter. Three or four cats prowled the space, staring accusingly at the women.

A mangy black-and-white cat walked up to the top of the staircase and meowed at the door. Catherine held her breath, waiting, watching. But nothing happened. No sounds could be heard inside the house.

The cat walked back down the wooden stairs and began prowling the cellar again, its shoulder blades rolling under its patchy fur.

As Catherine exhaled, the door opened, and Constable Robert Walsh came bounding down the wooden stairs.

'Everyone is praising me,' he crowed. 'I've been checking online, and everyone has finally accepted the truth: you bitches murdered Stan.'

'Please, constable. Set these women free and they can get to a hospital. They may survive if you release them now.'

He laughed cruelly. 'No thanks.'

'What do you want with us?' Ruby asked.

'I want to make you pay for what you did! You cast a spell to lure Stan to the blowhole and then you made him walk off the edge. You made it look like an accident. But Stan would never have got himself killed like that.'

Ruby went quiet. Her eyes were fixed in a squint. She remained in this state for several moments, scanning him, studying. 'I know you from somewhere,' she said at last, not dropping her gaze.

'What is it, Rubes?' Sergeant Nichols said.

'Holy shit,' Ruby said to Constable Walsh. 'You're Stanley Lacey's nephew.'

7.15 PM

Catherine watched the small, skinny form of Ruby Stayer. A switch seemed to have flicked in her. The detective's sister was staring at Walsh, studying him eagerly. 'You went to Thoorgala Grammar,' Ruby said. 'You were in our year. You lived with Stanley in the creepy old mansion that's above us right now. You used to hang around Stanley's studio. You would stare at me. It made my skin crawl. You've changed. You look completely different now.'

'Changed for the better,' Walsh said. A dab of spit escaped his mouth. 'No more "puny ranga". That's what you used to call me.'

Ruby looked incensed. 'I never called you that.'

He shrugged angrily. 'All the kids did!'

'I knew it!' Sergeant Nichols said, straightening in her chair. 'There was something off about you, but I couldn't put my finger on it. You were called Robert Lacey back in high school.'

'Back to Robert Walsh now,' he snapped.

'Been on the roids diet, have you?' Nichols said. 'You look like a gorilla.'

'Shut up, Nichols,' Walsh said. 'You always were a bitch.'

Walsh took out a smartphone. He pointed the lens at Ruby.

'Living with Barbie and Stan was the best thing that ever happened to me. Then Stan died and I was sent back to live with my shit of a father. Now I'm getting justice for Stan. Something I should have done years ago. I gave Phoebe, Mikaela and Jessie the opportunity to admit they killed him. I'll extend you the same courtesy.' He thumbed at the phone. 'I've hit record—confess to what you did and I'll set you free.'

Ruby was frantic. 'This is ludicrous! I'm not going to admit to something I didn't do!'

'Please, Ruby, just tell him what he wants to hear,' Catherine said.

'You killed Stan. Admit it.'

'Robert,' Catherine said. 'Just think how grateful Detective Stayer will be if you return his sister to him.'

'That fuckwit? Why would I care what he thinks?' He turned to Ruby, still strapped to the chair with duct tape. 'This is your last chance,' he told her. 'Admit to what you did.'

Catherine turned to Ruby and held her breath. Sergeant Nichols had moved her head too and was watching her friend closely. All the air seemed to have been sucked from the room.

Ruby met Robert Walsh's eyes. 'Not until the oceans run dry will I ever admit anything to you, you piece of shit.'

He backed away, then disappeared behind the steel shelves beside the cat jungle.

'Robert! Where are you going?' Catherine called, desperate.

She soon had her answer. He returned carrying a large hessian sack and a box of matches.

Sergeant Nichols seemed to be squinting, trying to focus. 'What the fuck, Walsh?' she said. 'Don't you dare.'

'I'm sorry,' Walsh announced to the room, 'but she had her chance.'

He hauled the bag towards them. The weight of it bumped against his leg as he walked. 'My aunt uses this biodegradable kitty litter. It reeks. Made of wood shavings and other hippie crap.

Highly flammable. You know you can make a bomb out of kitty litter? You put the kitty litter into an enclosed space, like a drum or a water tank. It's basically a glorified pipe bomb, with a detonator, sparkler for a fuse, kitty litter for the explosive. I've been tinkering with one upstairs for a while now. When it goes off, the exothermic reaction would be enough to blow this place into the sky. I'm quite the pyromaniac.' He opened the bag and poured the contents over Ruby. Pellets and wood shavings tumbled over her head and shoulders and pooled in her lap. It smelled like the lining of a rat's cage. Ruby screamed.

Walsh pulled a match from the box.

'No, Robert!' Catherine cried.

He struck the match, and it ignited. He held it over Ruby's head. The little flame flickered, yellow and warm. The kitty litter looked dusty and dry in Ruby's lap. The flames from its ignition would devour her. He prepared to drop the match onto her, grinning. Tension filled the room so completely that Catherine wondered how Ruby was still breathing. Walsh flicked the match to throw it, but before it released from his hand, something hit him on the side of the head. The little flame fell to the floor and went out. He crumpled to the ground. Sergeant Nichols stood above him, gripping a metal pole from the carpeted cat jungle.

The duct tape clung to her wrists and ankles in strips. Catherine quietly thanked God that she had stumbled upon that cat food tin with its jagged lid, and that she had been quick enough to cut the tape free.

Walsh leaped to his feet. Snarling, he sprang towards Sergeant Nichols. She hit him with the bar again, in the neck this time, his flesh making a soft, meaty sound as it connected with the metal.

Ruby sat straighter, as though arriving at the good bit in the movie.

Walsh yelped at a third hit and dived towards Nichols.

They grappled on the floor. Sergeant Nichols landed another blow, and Walsh rolled away, stunned. He staggered to his feet. Nichols swung back the bar to hit him again. She charged him. He caught her this time, and used her momentum to slam her against the wall.

'You crazy bitch!' he yelled. She slid to the floor.

Sergeant Nichols grabbed her head and tried to stand. Walsh gathered the hessian bag of kitty litter and ran to the stairs. Blood spurted from his head where Sergeant Nichols had hit him.

'Get back here, you fucker,' Sergeant Nichols called after him, her words slurring.

He reached the stairs and tipped the kitty litter onto the floor. He lit another match, this time not hesitating before he threw it. The pile erupted into flames as Walsh ran up the stairs.

The fire spread to a pile of rubbish: balled up papers, broken chairs, weathered cat toys with the stuffing ripped open. The mound ignited, forming a ring of fire around the base of the stairs. The crackle of flames grew to a roar.

Sergeant Nichols ran back to them and used the sharp edge of the cat food tin to saw at the tape around Ruby's ankles. The tape came free. Catherine helped her to stand.

'We have to get out of here,' Sergeant Nichols shouted.

The women moved towards the stairs, hoping to reach the door, but the flames pushed them back. The fire evaporated the moisture from their eyes and chewed their skin. The smoke strangled them.

'Move to the back wall, away from the flames,' Catherine said. She hurried to the metal shelves. From a pile of what looked like old clothes, she pulled a blanket stinking of cat urine and covered in fur. Returning to the other women, huddled on the floor now, she threw the blanket over them. The blanket wasn't big enough to cover her as well, so she sat beside them, trying to take shallow breaths, and murmuring a prayer. The fire grew larger. The smoke engulfed everything. The room felt so hot that it might explode. Unless a miracle occurred, they were all going to die.

7.20 PM

Stayer waited while Joan processed Dane at reception, entering his details into the computer and logging his personal items. He looked dishevelled and desolate: lank hair, jittery hands, filthy tracksuit. He muttered something under his breath, which Stayer didn't hear and had to ask him to repeat.

'I said I want my lawyer,' Dane said, turning to Stayer, almost sneering. 'I know my rights. You're about to get a whole bunch of trouble. What are you charging me with? You don't even know yourself.'

At Joan's command, Dane emptied his pockets, dumping his keys and phone onto the tray she was holding.

Joan opened the door which separated the reception area from the rest of the police station and guided the forensic pathologist inside.

She smiled at Stayer in the hallway. 'Give me a minute to get the interview room ready and you can question Dr Dixon.'

Stayer tried to gather his thoughts. He felt nauseous. The pathologist was right, Stayer wasn't even sure what he could charge him with. There was no direct evidence linking him to the murders on the sandhills. Worst of all, Dane appeared completely genuine when he said he didn't know where Ruby was. Dread filled Stayer, that he was pursuing the wrong man, and that Ruby was still out there, somewhere, being held by someone else, and that he was wasting time questioning Dane. He pulled out his phone to check the time and saw he had a voicemail from Sister Catherine. He hadn't expected to hear from her again, considering how they'd parted. He clicked to listen. The nun's gentle, clear voice flowed into his ear.

'Detective Stayer, perhaps you saw my number and rejected the call. I'm looking at the autopsy report for Pericles Lacey. Mrs Lacey's cat. The report concludes that the cause of death was poisoning, by oleander.' A plastic chair stood next to Stayer in the corridor. He sat down. 'Oleander is not tested for in regular toxicology screenings, because people rarely ingest it voluntarily. This lab only tested for it because Mrs Lacey asked them to—she has oleander trees in her garden and must have wondered if Pericles had eaten some. Symptoms of oleander poisoning include nausea, vomiting, confusion, cramps, and diarrhoea, but this isn't what kills the person. Oleander contains cardiac glycosides which disrupt the heart's rhythm. It's a slow death, the person eventually dying from heart failure. In many ways, oleander is the perfect poison. Slowly moving, largely clearing the body long before it has killed the person, making it extremely difficult to trace. I was wondering if maybe the killer used oleander to poison his victims. It would have given them enough time to walk out onto the sand before they died.' The voicemail ended. Stayer tried calling her back, but got no answer. He checked his phone. Sister Catherine had left the message over an hour ago.

Joan emerged from the interview room and called to Stayer in the corridor. 'Room's ready, detective.'

'Where did Sister Catherine go, Joan?'

'I think she was going to talk to Mrs Lacey about her cat on the way home.' She was studying his face now. 'Are you okay, detective?' she asked. Then, as Stayer turned on his heel, 'Where are you going? What about Dane Dixon?'

But Stayer had already walked out the door.

7.30 PM

Returning to Eveleigh, the Lacey house, for the second time, Stayer found it in flames. He radioed for the fire brigade. Smoke billowed from the windows. He jumped from the car and ran towards the house.

Finding the front door locked, he smashed a window and pulled himself through. He landed in a deep white kitchen sink, and a haze of smoke engulfed him.

Drawing his handgun, Stayer crept through the house, clearing rooms. Smoke hit his throat like a scouring cloth. He worked his way around the walls and the staircase, pawing at the wallpaper. He screamed Sister Catherine's name.

Then he heard it. Faint at first, then growing louder. A clanging, like someone was banging on metal.

'Sister!' he shouted again, his throat burning, voice hoarse.

Another clang. He stopped, listened. Someone was hitting a pipe underneath him.

He rushed to the back of the house, following the sound. He reached a cage door leading down to a crawl space or basement.

Stayer stuck his head through the doorway. A wall of smoke greeted him. He coughed and reared back. Whatever had created those fumes must surely have already killed anyone in the basement below.

Pulling his shirt up over his nose and mouth, he unlocked the cage door and stepped tentatively onto the top step. It creaked ominously but held his weight, so he descended another step, and then another. As he passed the middle, the stair collapsed under him. He leaped, hitting the ground. His knees slammed into concrete. The remainder of the staircase collapsed behind him. A cloud of smoke and flame rose up.

Peering into the smoke, he called for Sister Catherine.

'Here,' he heard faintly.

He looked in the direction of the voice and flicked on his torch. The beam of light shone into the smoke. It parted and revealed a scene both welcome and terrible.

They looked like a mound of rags. Two figures covered in a soot-stained blanket. He hurried forward, then hesitated—did he really want to see what lay beneath?—then lifted the covering.

'Matt?'

It was his sister, though her voice was so charred and faint he barely recognised it.

'Ruby!'

And next to her was Sergeant Nichols.

Then he heard a groan from the sergeant's other side and realised there was a third figure. It was Sister Catherine. She saw him and smiled.

'Fire brigade's coming,' he said.

Stayer tried not to show his fear as he calculated the odds of getting them all out. The only way in or out was the door leading back into the house through which he'd come. The staircase leading up to that door had collapsed. Flames burned all around him. Smoke inhalation could kill in ten minutes. He didn't know how long they had already been down there, but he guessed it would be close to that.

As if reading his mind, Sister Catherine spoke. 'Get them out. Forget me.'

'No,' Stayer replied.

He helped his sister and Sergeant Nichols to their feet and led them, stumbling, to the stairs.

The lower half of the staircase had vanished, so that only the top three steps remained, as if someone had lowered a ladder, but only the last rungs.

Stayer put his hands together to make a basket. Nichols placed her foot in it, and he lifted her. She reached up but missed the stairs.

'I'm sorry,' she rasped. He shook his head; there was no time for apologies. Something exploded in the corner of the basement behind them. A cat screeched. Fire now engulfed the entire basement. The clear path to the stairs was growing narrower. Soon it would vanish altogether.

They tried again, and this time Sergeant Nichols grasped the lower stair and hung on. She hauled herself up. She turned and crouched. 'Now Ruby.'

Stayer made a basket of his hands once more, and his sister placed her foot in it. He lifted her upwards. The smallness of her body shocked him, he hadn't remembered her being so skinny. She reached for Sergeant Nichols' outstretched hands. Nichols caught her arms and wrenched upwards with a groan. Stayer threw his sister's leg upwards, and she swung into the house.

Stayer looked around for Sister Catherine. Nothing but black smoke and flames greeted him. 'Where is she?' he said.

'She didn't come with us,' Ruby shouted down to him. 'She's still in the corner. She couldn't walk.'

'I'm going back to get her,' he told his sister. 'I'll be right behind you.'

They shared a look. He knew the insanity of what he was saying.

'Matt,' said Ruby, 'You'll die if you breathe in any more of that smoke.'

Stayer paused. He took the deepest breath of the clearest air he could find, the air flooding from the doorway above. He opened his chest as far as he could, until he felt he might burst. Then he jumped back down into the basement.

The flames nipped his body as he waded around the burning piles of rubbish, the broken appliances, a collapsed shelving unit. He reached Sister Catherine. Her eyes were closed. She lay like a rag doll, floppy and white.

He picked her up, cradling her in his arms, and carried her towards the stairs. Each step made his chest and legs ache. His head felt like it might burst from holding his breath so long. But he shut his eyes and went back to what he always knew. He wasn't going to breathe in; he would pass out first.

Not many people in the world could hold their breath for that long—but Stayer, an Olympic gold medallist, who could swim the length of a fifty-metre pool without breathing, was one of them. He reached the stairs and felt the air clearing. He allowed himself a small breath.

His sister and colleague waited at the top of the stairs. Stayer raised Sister Catherine high in his arms, and Ruby and Sergeant Nichols reached for her, groaning as they grasped her under the armpits and heaved. Sister Catherine's head slumped forward, touching her chest, as she was wrenched to safety.

Then Stayer took a few steps back and made a running leap, catching the lowest stair and pulling himself upwards, ungraceful, ungainly, out of the basement and back into the house.

Walking through the living room towards the kitchen, Stayer noticed something on the floor. A body. 'Who's that?'

'Walsh,' Sergeant Nichols replied. 'Must've collapsed from the head wound I gave him.'

Stayer watched as the flames approached a ten-gallon drum near the kitchen door. A pile of empty hessian bags lay next to it. The words BIODEGRADABLE KITTY LITTER: HIGHLY FLAMMABLE were stamped across them. A sparkler was lit at the top of the drum, emitting brightly coloured sparks as it burned down. He turned to his sister and the sergeant.

'Run!'

As Ruby and Sergeant Nichols clambered one by one through the kitchen window, Stayer gathered Catherine in his arms. The nun made no sound as the two other women pulled her carefully over the broken glass.

Stayer heaved himself through the window. 'Get behind the car,' he order, pointing up the gravel drive. How many seconds did they have left before the whole place blew?

He had his answer almost immediately, as Walsh's homemade bomb must have gone off and the house behind them exploded. The force of it threw him forward. His hands crashed into the gravel. Sister Catherine tumbled from his arms. She did not wake.

Stayer picked the nun back up and carried her the last metres back to the car. His sister and the sergeant cowered behind it, holding each other.

'Are you alright?' he said to Ruby as she flung her arms around his neck.

'Yes,' she whispered into his shoulder.

Sergeant Nichols looked shaken. Stayer turned to her, but she answered before he could even ask. 'I'm fine, sir. Thank you.'

They all turned to Sister Catherine, motionless on the ground beside them.

Stayer put his ear to the nun's mouth. Even when someone is unconscious, in the deepest, quietest sleep, there is still a sense of life. There was no such sense here. Stayer looked at her limp form and waxy face and realised she was gone.

Ruby began to cry.

Stayer knelt by Sister Catherine and placed his mouth on hers. She smelled of smoke. He puffed two breaths into her mouth, then began pumping her chest.

'Please,' he said softly. 'Please, sister.'

He knew he couldn't bring her back; he knew CPR wouldn't work in this situation. He knew she'd been deprived of oxygen too long, that he was battering her for no reason, and that he should just leave her, let her go, but still he continued, knowing it was pointless, yet unable to stop himself, for what felt like hours.

And then he looked up and saw the lights and sirens of the emergency services vehicles coming towards them, and when he next looked down, in an image that would stay with him for the rest of his days, he found her staring at him, her eyes wide open and very much alive. She opened her mouth to speak and uttered words too soft to hear.

He leaned down and put his ear to her mouth and she whispered them again.

'Thank you.'

AFTER

TWO WEEKS LATER

Police recovered one body from the burned-out house on Peninsula Way. Mrs Lacey—the wild woman who had lived in the property for thirty years and turned a place once famous for obscene parties and art into a cat sanctuary after the death of her husband—had been found in an upstairs bedroom.

Hers was not the body police had been looking for. They had been hoping to find Robert Walsh, Mrs Lacey's nephew. He had been last seen in the downstairs living area, face down, with a fire burning around him. But when police searched the house, they found no sign of the man wanted in connection with the Tall Harry murders. They issued alerts and set up roadblocks. Warnings and reported sightings of the rogue policeman flooded social media. In online forums and encrypted group chats, people spoke of a caped figure behind a petrol station off the Hume Highway, a masked man creeping in the bushes at Cundra Beach. They hadn't seen it themselves, but they knew someone who had. Uniformed police pulled motorists over at designated points, checking licences and shining mirrors under cars. They found no trace of the man who had murdered three women and carved symbols into their skin, and had also murdered his aunt, and attempted to murder three others. The story made the front page of the tabloid newspapers for six days in a row and the broadsheets for four, before a federal cabinet minister's post–sex scandal resignation, the finals of the Australian Open, and a celebrity divorce replaced it.

•

Detective Stayer arrived home from work and met Carol on the doorstep as she was leaving Ruby's house. Her face was drawn and tear-stained.

'Everything okay?' he said.

'Of course,' she said, forcing a smile. She donned a large pair of sunglasses, Jackie Onassis style, and walked to her sleek European car.

The scene had grown familiar. Carol had visited every day since Ruby had come home from hospital. She had not left her bedside in the intensive care unit either, sleeping in a vinyl-covered armchair next to Ruby's IV stand. Ruby had refused to talk to her, keeping her back turned once she'd awoken from her induced coma, and had repeated this routine daily at home. Carol had shown up each day bearing gourmet meals from local restaurants and self-help books. Ruby had accepted the offerings wordlessly, maintaining a wall of silence, for reasons she kept to herself. Stayer walked inside and found Ruby on the couch, staring out the window.

'What did Carol bring this time?' Stayer said, glancing at the kitchen counter. She had delivered a box of class one Tasmanian cherries, an osso bucco and tiramisu from a local overpriced Italian restaurant, and a mindfulness colouring book for adults.

'Are you ever going to speak to Carol again?' Stayer said, tossing a cherry in his mouth. It hit his teeth, dark and sweet. 'She means well.'

Ruby emitted a loud scoff and didn't look up.

Things had seemed okay between Stayer and Ruby for a few days. They hung out, sharing food, even watching movies together. It felt strange but nice. Then three days ago, Ruby had started going on long runs again. Stayer began staying late at work when he didn't need to, in order to avoid spending time with her. It's not that they didn't like each other. They just couldn't seem to find the words to say.

The afternoon sunlight streamed in through the net curtains of the living room, dust motes floating. The waves crashed softly outside the window, the relentless soundtrack to that house.

Stayer offered his sister a kind smile. 'I'm going to find my own place. I'll be out of your hair as soon as I can.'

'Stanley Lacey raped me,' Ruby said abruptly. She pulled at a loose thread on the couch arm. 'When I was fifteen.'

She turned her face to him. Her eyes were wet and filled with panic. A bent wicker chair rested by the door to the kitchen. Stayer sat on it.

'I was the weird kid at Thoorgala Grammar. Dirt poor. Not into clothes or cars or getting tanned. I put European movies on in the common room and caught the train to Sydney on weekends to visit the art gallery. It felt like no one understood me—until Stanley Lacey arrived.' The thread on the couch arm came loose, she wrapped it around her finger. 'I was obsessed with waves,' she continued. 'I would sit on the sand at Cundra Beach and watch them for hours: the way the light hit them, how they moved. That's the thing about waves—they're always moving. Even on the calmest day, they never stop. How can you paint something that never stops moving? That's what I wondered. My dream was to paint a wave that felt more like a wave than the real thing. I wanted a person to look at the waves I had painted and see God.'

She glanced at him to see that he was listening, and he nodded, casual, as though these were things she shared with him often, though he had never heard her speak like this before, about art, about anything.

'That's why, when I found out Stanley Lacey was coming to our school, a part of me hummed. He was everything I wanted to be. I felt like he was trying to show God in his paintings. He wasn't there yet, but at least he was trying. That sounds arrogant, I know—who was I, a teenage girl, to pass judgement on a world-famous painter?

'Stanley hosted seminars after school and on weekends. I signed up for every class. For the first few weeks, it seemed like he didn't even know I existed. If I put up my hand to answer a question, he never called on me; he always went to the prettier girls, the sexy ones. It was like he looked straight through me. I had seen pictures of the women who had hung around Picasso, Matisse. These women were so confident, so comfortable. They had windswept hair, floaty clothes, low-cut blouses. They were at ease with their bodies. I wasn't bohemian. I wasn't sexy. I dressed in an oversized shirt to protect my clothes from paint spatter. I hated my body. But I was desperate for his attention. So I went to an op shop and found a slip made of crushed velvet . . .'

Ruby began weeping softly. Stayer rose and moved towards her, not sure what to do. He sat down next to her, at the other end of the couch. She didn't stop him.

'I turned up at the seminar that Saturday wearing my "muse" outfit. He held me back after class and asked to see my paintings. I was so excited. I offered to bring them to the next class. He said I should bring them to his studio.

'I chose three to show him, all my waves. I couldn't believe that Stanley Lacey, winner of the Doug Moran prize, would look at my work.' She laughed bitterly. 'What a fucking idiot I was.

'I put my velvet slip on again, and Aunt Carol drove me from the boarding school to his house—I was still too young to drive. He took me to his studio at the back of the property. When he had closed the door, he turned to me, and I saw his eyes go to my breasts. I wasn't prepared for it. But I wanted to show him my paintings.'

She paused. 'Would you like a drink? I think I'm going to have one.'

'Sure,' Stayer said. 'If you're having one.'

She stood from the couch and moved to the kitchen. She returned with a bottle of wine and two glasses. 'White okay?'

'Fine with me.'

She poured two glasses. 'Cheers,' she said. She took a gulp, then another, then put the glass on the coffee table.

'I showed him my paintings of the waves. I watched his eyes as they flipped back and forth over the three canvases. He was quiet for a long time. So quiet, I thought something was wrong.'

'He didn't like them?'

'I think he was jealous. That sounds ridiculous, I know. How could a famous artist be jealous of a teenager?'

'That doesn't sound ridiculous, Ruby,' Stayer said. 'Several people now have relayed to me your genius. That man would have had every reason to be jealous of you.'

'I knew the paintings were good,' she said. 'I don't know how to describe it. Like when you touch the wall in a swimming race, knowing you've broken the world record before you've even checked the clock. Does that make sense?'

'It does,' Stayer said. 'So what did he say about them?'

She took another sip from her glass. 'My paintings were problematic. He said they weren't awful, just ordinary, and immature. I was crushed. Mortified. He told me I had a lot to learn, but that he was prepared to teach me. He said I needed more exposure to art and artists, that I needed to have my mind expanded, to move beyond the conventional world I'd grown up in. He said a good start would be to sit for him, to let him paint me. I said I wasn't sure, but he said if I was serious about improving, I would have to become freer and more open . . .' Her voice trailed off.

'Ruby?' Stayer said softly. 'If you want to stop, please let me know.'

'I will,' she said. She wiped her eyes on her sleeve. 'There was a bathtub in the studio, which he filled with water. He told me to get in. He'd given me a dress to change into—a much lighter fabric than what I'd been wearing. When the water soaked it, it basically became transparent. It clung to my body and you could see everything. I was mortified. He told me I was too stiff, I looked wrong. Nervous. I told him I *was* nervous. He put on some music, then he poured me a drink; he said it would help me to relax. It was alcoholic, of course—vodka, maybe—and it was vile. It tasted like medicine and burned my throat.

'He said that I was too constricted. He was probably right. Artists need huge egos, and I didn't have that vanity. I was too sensible, too worried about giving pieces of myself away, whereas a true artist believes every piece of themselves is interesting and a gift to the world. I never want to reveal too much, and my art probably suffers. I pay a price for that. So it turns out he was right. Thank you, Stanley.' She raised her glass to the ceiling.

'The studio had seemed so cool and grown up at first; I felt like I was touching a line going back through history, to every artist who had put brush to canvas. Da Vinci, van Gogh, Rembrandt. They'd all stood in places like that, trying to show God in a door, in an apple, in a face. But that day, when he asked me to pose in the bath, everything felt wrong. The music he'd put on was teenybopper R'n'B or some dorky boy band. A pair of orthotics, cracked and smelly, lay beside the tub. When I had gone to the toilet earlier, I'd seen a packet of hair dye. I remembered that he was forty-eight—older than our father! I was fifteen.

'Lying there in the bath, I started to feel strange. The water was only lukewarm, but I was sweating. Then my head started to spin.'

Her voice grew softer. 'I woke up on the couch, on a sheet spattered with paint. My dress had been pushed up. My underpants were on the armrest. I will always remember thinking how funny they looked, placed there.

'He was on top of me and inside me. I didn't know what to do. I was too stunned to speak, couldn't find the words to tell him to stop, that he was hurting me.

'When he was finished, he rolled over and told me it was time to leave. I was too frightened and ashamed to ask to use the phone to call Aunt Carol to pick me up, so I used my school pass to ride the bus back to the boarding school.'

•

Stayer watched his sister as she downed the last gulp of wine from her glass and brushed hair from her face with a shaky hand. A fan blew, cooling the sweat on his neck. She walked over to the window. Stayer found the wine and poured her another glass.

'About two months later, Stanley won the Archibald Prize. The painting was of me. He'd changed it so I wasn't in the bath anymore. I was in the ocean now, like in a tidal pool, with the water around me moving out to sea in little waves. The canvas he had used was mine. He'd painted a portrait of me over one of my own paintings. They were my waves. Not a copy. Not an approximation. They were *mine*. He'd painted me into my own waves. I had no way to prove it because I'd left the paintings at his house.

'It's always one thing, a small thing, that makes a painting a masterpiece. The way the light hits the pitcher in Vermeer's *Milkmaid*. The way van Gogh made the wheat swirl. The shine on Rembrandt's nose in his self-portrait. Well, Stanley Lacey won the Archibald for those waves. He raped me, then he stole my waves.'

The words echoed through the room.

'The following week, I broke down in the science labs. I was summoned to the principal's office. I told her everything. She listened in silence, then told me to leave it with her, and that I would hear from her soon. I waited for two weeks and then I went back to her office and asked what was happening. She told me to come back that afternoon.

'When I did, Stanley Lacey was there. He denied everything and said I was infatuated with him. He said that we had never had sex, and that he was outraged by the accusation, saying he had a wife and child at home. He said I was clearly a compulsive liar. By the end, the principal was accusing *me* of causing trouble.'

'You never went to the police?'

'No.' She brushed this away quickly, angrily. 'Who would believe me? The principal hadn't. Aunt Carol did, though. She knew something was wrong and kept harping at me until eventually I told her.'

'Did Carol try to convince you to go to the police?'

Ruby breathed deeply. 'I had expected she would. I had secretly hoped for it. I imagined her going ape shit, ringing up the school, turning up at Stanley Lacey's house with a pitchfork. This was Carol, the closest thing I had to a mother.'

'What did she do?'

Ruby looked broken. 'She took me out to lunch, then for a pedicure. A girls' day out, she called it. As we sat side by side in those massage chairs, a woman squatting below each of us, clipping our toenails, she leaned in and whispered, smiling, like she was sharing some juicy secret. She told me to never tell another soul about the rape. It would be like walking through life with a stain on my clothes that never came out. "There will be a mark against your name," she said. "People will always think less of you, even if they knew that was wrong." I would be thought of as less capable, less likely to handle responsibility. This stung almost more than the rape. The woman kept cleaning my feet in that spa place.

I've never felt lonelier in my life. "Don't let this become a part of you," Carol said as she paid for our pedicures. But it became a part of me anyway. I could never paint as well again after that. My direct line to God was gone. My little patch of yellow wall had been taken from me.'

'Your what?'

'In his book, *The Captive*, Proust wrote of a character who goes to see Vermeer's *View of Delft*. The character becomes fixated on a piece of the painting which he thinks is particularly beautiful. He calls it a little patch of yellow wall. It's a roof, not a wall, but that's not important. What's important is that the character, who is a writer, sees the little patch of yellow and finds it so perfect he re-evaluates his life. He decides his writing should have contained more flair and colour in it, that he should not have written so dryly. That little patch of yellow is what the best art is, a soundless hymn to the world. Those waves were *my* little patch of yellow. Then they were taken from me.'

'*View of Delft* is the home screen image on your phone,' Stayer said dumbly.

Ruby nodded.

'The painting you looked at for hours in that gallery in the Hague.'

'Did I? Yes, I suppose I did.'

Stayer remembered her little shaking body, her sobs in the night in the blackness of the hostel.

'Why did you never tell me any of this?'

She sipped from her glass. 'I tried. Several times.'

'When?' Stayer said, a feeling of disbelief gripping him.

'At the Olympics.'

'In *Rio*? Ruby that was a crazy time—'

'I know, I know,' she said quickly, hands raised. 'As soon as I showed up there, I knew I'd made a terrible mistake. The crowds, the hoopla. It was not the time to tell you, not by a long stretch. But I tried again. When we were backpacking in Europe.'

He shook his head, feeling baffled. 'When?'

'In Madrid. In that Cathedral.'

These scenes came to him. He tried to object, to explain, but he knew it was futile. He knew she was right. Something was up that day in that church in Spain. He knew and he'd avoided her. He'd turned away from her. He dropped his head.

'I knew something was wrong. But I didn't say anything.'

'Why?' She spoke in a whisper, almost breathless. She looked forlorn.

'I didn't want to hear it.' He felt awful. 'I knew it was bad, and I knew you had something to tell me. But I didn't want to know. Because I knew whatever it was, I wouldn't be able to help.'

She raised her eyes to him. He observed how much she resembled a glass vase that had smashed and been repaired inexpertly, with cheap glue and unsteady hands; how she seemed ready to break again at any moment. Shame gripped him, he felt desperately sad. He spoke in a whisper. 'You are my little sister, Ruby. My only family in this world. And if I couldn't help you, what would that have made me?'

She raised her hands in exasperation. 'I didn't need your help, Matt. I've never needed it. That's not your job.' She smiled, her voice earnest.

'What do you need, then?'

'Just say, *That really sucks. I'm here.*'

'That's enough?'

Ruby shook her head as though he still didn't get it. 'That's everything.'

Watching Ruby as she talked, her face more animated and alive than he'd ever seen it, Stayer felt like he'd been in a foreign country for years, one where he didn't speak the language, but now he had finally come home.

They drank in silence for a time. The clock with the exposed gears ticked on the wall in the kitchen. The sunlight went from orange to bluish-grey. Ruby looked down at her glass. 'This wine has a certain something, doesn't it? A colleague gave it to me as a Christmas gift. She's a cheapskate.' She took a large sip. 'It tastes like fermented apple juice.'

Stayer took a swig from his own glass. 'I think it is.'

She laughed. Stayer felt warm.

'Ruby. I'm so sorry he took your little patch of yellow.'

'Thank you,' she said, and Stayer could tell that she meant it.

TWO DAYS AFTER THAT

Detective Stayer rang Sister Catherine to tell her that Robert Walsh had disappeared. 'We'll keep looking until we find him.'

'A shame,' she replied. Her voice still sounded hoarse and rough, like it pained her to speak. The trauma surgeon had called it the worst case of smoke inhalation he'd seen in someone who'd survived.

He paused.

'What is it, Detective Stayer?'

'I don't want to be a cop anymore,' Stayer said finally, uttering aloud the words he'd been carrying in his heart for years. This was as good a time to stop as any.

'Why not?' she said.

'I became a police officer because my father wanted me to. At least, I thought he did. He told me I'd never make the Australian swimming team. I think I did it just to prove him wrong. I woke every morning at five for a decade. Swam up and down a black line, thinking up ways to make him proud of me. Then, when I made the Olympic team, he didn't even come to watch my race. Told me I'd just got lucky; that it was an easy year to make the team. He always spoke about a friend of his who was a detective: how that was an honest, decent living, not like the flashy life of swimming. So what did I do? Hung up my goggles and enrolled in the academy. I became a cop to make my dad happy. How sad is that? Didn't work, either. Now I'm stuck being a cop and there's no pleasing him because he's dead.'

Sister Catherine replied, 'So you joined the police to impress your father. Worse things have happened. Why do you wish to leave now?'

'For each body we find, there's ten we never do. For every family I help, there's ten I can't. For every rapist I catch, there's fifty I don't. This is a game I'll never win. Sometimes I feel like I can't even be bothered to get out of bed in the morning.'

'You do get out of bed, though, don't you?' Sister Catherine said. 'Why do you do that?'

'Because if I don't, who will?' His shoulders slumped. He already knew what she was going to say and he did not want to hear it.

'That's why you do it,' Sister Catherine said. 'For the one person you can help. For the one rapist you can put away. For the one family you can help.'

He stared at his hands; his burns from the fire had blistered, and some had burst, revealing fresh pink skin underneath, like ham.

'I promised to show you God, Detective Stayer, do you remember?'

'I do,' he said wearily.

'Well, let me do that for you now. You are at the station, yes? Walk over to the hat rack by those big double doors that let all the heat in . . . Are you doing it? You're not, are you? I'm offering to show you God, and you're sitting down, looking at your hands.'

'I'm not,' he said, folding away the hand not holding the phone sheepishly.

'You are. It's what you do when you feel lost.'

He groaned, but got up from his chair. 'Okay, I'm doing it.' He walked over to the hat stand. A mirror stood beside it.

'You asked to see God—well, there he is.'

Stayer focused on his own reflection. He laughed. 'Are you saying that I'm God, sister?'

'I am. God is not a bearded man in the sky. He is anyone fighting for those who can't fight for themselves. He is you turning up to work every day, bearing that sorrow. You have been given this burden because God knows you can handle it. You say God is gone; that God does not exist. But you getting out of bed every morning, saving as many as you can? If that's not God, I don't know what is.'

'That might be the cheesiest thing I've ever heard, sister.'

He could feel the hot shameful sting of a tear. He pretended to cough and begged for the moment to pass and, at last, thankfully, it did.

'My sister and Sergeant Nichols owe their lives to you,' he said. 'I wish I could repay you.'

'Their lives are payment, thousandfold.'

They spoke about Thoorgala and the weather and then ran out of things to say. Sister Catherine excused herself, saying she had to see her neighbour, and Stayer reluctantly let her go.

'I don't think we shall be seeing much of each other anymore,' the nun said.

The words caught Stayer off guard. 'Oh?'

'You said it yourself: Tall Harry will never be found. And you have more important things to do than humour a nun.'

'I was never humouring you, Catherine.'

She said nothing. He nodded silently. He opened his mouth to say something more, and he could tell that she was waiting for him to speak again. But then she beat him to it, jumping in with words of her own.

'Goodbye, Detective Stayer,' she said.

'Goodbye,' he replied, and hung up the phone and stared out the window.

EPILOGUE

A knock sounded on her front door, and Catherine rose reluctantly from her chair to answer it. The sister who had moved in next door had turned out to be less than a soulmate. She'd knock on Catherine's door when Catherine was in the middle of reading and invite her around for tea. Catherine had initially accepted these invitations eagerly, hoping for a conversation partner. She didn't mind what they talked about, so long as her companion had an opinion. But Sister Maxine was not like that; she conducted their interactions like she was taking minutes, running through a list of grievances like agenda items: all the people who had wronged her that day, the children with no respect, the dirty town, the rude man who ran the milk bar—didn't he know she was a nun? Now Catherine had tea with Maxine dutifully, out of obligation.

These were small, not strenuous aggravations, and Catherine could bear them. But every now and then, she'd recall how she had never felt more alive than during those few days over Christmas last year, and now they were gone. They were memories she could revisit, but this came with pain, because to remember them was also to acknowledge that the time had passed and she could not go back to it, like a beloved holiday destination she could no longer return to.

She reached the door and braced herself for Sister Maxine, wondering how long she'd need to remain in her company—two hours, three?—before she could concoct an excuse to escape.

She peered through the peephole, expecting to see the black dome of Maxine's veil, yet the little fisheye view revealed no person at all. Catherine opened the door and looked left and right, and when she stepped out to investigate further, her foot hit a parcel that had been left on her doorstep.

Barry the postie had a habit of dropping parcels there silently and departing, even when a signature was required, a grown-up version of knock and run. She brought the box inside, its weight surprising her.

Catherine placed the box on the kitchen counter and cut its tape open with a knife. She was a woman rarely surprised, and she prided herself on that. Her moods remained steady always; she was not one to shout or exclaim with delight. But in that moment, she startled herself with the broadness of her smile and the joyful laugh that emanated from her, a sound she didn't think herself capable of making.

Beneath a layer of bubble wrap was a leather binder that cracked as she opened it and looked upon the lost scriptures of Magda van Aachen.

News of the loss of a document from the state police evidentiary processing vault made no headlines. They didn't like to advertise that a celebrated policeman and Olympic gold medallist could slip in there one day, into what was basically a glorified storeroom, and remove some junk that was part of a long forgotten and convoluted dispute between two customs agencies.

Catherine rushed to the sink and donned kitchen gloves to pick up the scriptures. She looked at the box and stopped. It contained no postmark, so it mustn't have been delivered through the post.

She returned to the front door and opened it. Looking out across the car park, she saw a figure walking away across the road. As if sensing her gaze, Detective Stayer turned around. She waved. He waved back. He looked at her in a way he'd looked at her before, sometimes, glancing over his desk or at her side of the car when driving. It was a look that promised a different life to the one she lived now. She drank this look in, this other life, for a moment, for longer than she probably should have. Then she turned away, and when she turned back, he had resumed walking, and Catherine returned to her scriptures with a smile.

•

It was almost seven months later when Catherine returned to Thoorgala to attend a spring fair, organised by the local council. Children performed a maypole dance on an outdoor stage in the middle of the shopping plaza, watched by a large crowd. The children, dressed in white, danced in circles, winding coloured ribbons around the pole, to the drums and flutes of a folk song. With a wry smile, she applauded as they danced a pagan ritual which had existed for thousands of years, honouring the female god of the earth, Eostre, who represented spring and the new beginnings. From the corner of her eye, she caught sight of a woman with soft blonde hair. The woman turned and revealed herself as Ruby Stayer. She watched the crowd too, with a gentle smile. A few moments passed in this way, and then Ruby was joined by Detective Stayer, who handed her a drink purchased from one of the food stalls. They watched the performance together, and Catherine watched them. As if he could feel her watching, the detective's eyes drifted over to where Catherine was standing.

They met up at the side of the mall a little away from the crowd.

'Hello, sister,' Detective Stayer said, smiling.

'Hello, detective. Hello, Ruby,' she replied.

She hoped her smile didn't look forced. She wasn't sure why things felt so strained between them, as she had perfectly warm and respectful feelings for both. But she suspected that they felt the awkwardness too. They had come so close to death, the three of them, but now they had become strangers again, as if the intimacy they'd felt in those terrible moments had never existed.

'Are you enjoying the fair?' Ruby said.

'Tremendously,' Catherine replied.

A moment passed. The children continued circling the pole with their ribbons, wearing looks of concentration.

'And the maypole? What do you think of it?' Ruby asked.

'It's wonderful,' Catherine said. 'The children are doing very well. Interesting choice, the maypole. Originally a fertility rite. Women and girls dance in such a way that they weave a pattern. The dance brings fertility to the people, and to the seeds being sown.' Catherine took in Ruby's blank expression. 'Sorry,' she said, 'I'm rambling.'

'Not at all,' Detective Stayer said. 'I love a good pagan ritual.'

Ruby nodded silently and seemed to be studying Catherine. Catherine felt herself scowling; she couldn't work Ruby out. She'd spent almost an hour with the woman trapped in a basement, with a person trying to kill them both. She thought she might learn some things about a person at a time like that, but Ruby still seemed as opaque and blank to her as a stone.

'How have you been?' Detective Stayer asked Catherine.

'Very well, thank you. Will you be staying for the swimming races later? Down in the baths?'

'Oh.' Detective Stayer said. 'Maybe.'

'I doubt I'll stay,' Ruby replied, without looking at her brother.

The children finished their dance, and the crowd applauded. Detective Stayer and Ruby said goodbye and disappeared into the crowd, leaving Catherine alone once more.

Catherine spent some time wandering through the spring fair, and then through the rest of the shopping plaza, which was now filled with market stalls selling jams, surfboards, wetsuits, pastries, hot sauces and jewellery fashioned from coral. She strolled a little aimlessly, in no hurry, for she had nowhere to be. She had no pressing appointments and no one waiting for her at home, not even a good book. It was at times like this that the path she had chosen stung; when she found herself at events made for families. She almost wished for some crisis, so that her help would be needed.

She walked around a little more. She shared a joke with an older man who tried to sell her a long board. 'I sold a board to a woman last year, sister, who surfs in a burkini! You could do that!' They laughed, then ran out of jokes, so she moved on.

She tried the hot sauce at a jerk chicken stall and some schoolboys applauded; she had done better than them, sampling the hottest recipe without sweating.

She kept smiling and shared laughs with people, who enjoyed the novelty of a nun checking out a surfboard or eating hot sauce, but after a time she grew tired of this, the fun had gone out of her, and she found herself aching for her home and her bed. She was making her way back to the car park behind the mall when she ran into Ruby Stayer again.

'Ruby,' she said, surprised.

Ruby was staring at her with an odd expression. 'I've been waiting for you,' she said.

'Where is Detective Stayer?' Catherine said. 'Can I give you a lift home?'

Ruby gave a chuckle and flicked her head, as though dismissing Catherine's concerns as stupid and banal. 'It's all very nice and tame and regional, isn't it, but something's missing. There's no need to be polite with me, sister; just because I moved back here doesn't mean I have a blind love for this place. It's run by men. They're not particularly cruel or nasty men, just boring, bland, incurious men. Men who like to accost pretty girls at parties with their stories of travel and business. I saw the man try to sell you the surfboard. You stood there for twenty minutes listening to him speak of his travels in Bali.'

Catherine shifted her feet, feeling uneasy. This was a side of Ruby she'd never seen.

'How are you coming along with your scriptures?' Ruby asked her.

'I'm sorry?'

'The ones my brother gave you. Written by Magda van Aachen.'

'Oh,' Catherine replied, caught off guard, 'they are wonderful. Intriguing. They're not scriptures, technically. Van Aachen was branded a heretic.'

'You can't make them work, can you? But you'd like to? So you can see your sister again.'

Catherine went still. Ruby seemed to be searching her face.

'I had avoided speaking with you like this before. After all, you are a nun. But then I heard you wanted those scriptures, and today you were talking about the maypole, and I thought you must be a friend.'

'Of course I am your friend, Ruby. We endured something terrible together.'

Then Ruby proceeded to utter the words which would make Catherine's hair stand on end and keep it there for days afterwards.

'*Non exerceas maleficia*,' Ruby said.

Catherine felt like someone had dropped an ice cube down her back. 'What did you say?'

Ruby offered a crooked smile. '*Non exerceas maleficia*. It's from the Old Testament: Leviticus. It means—'

'I know what it means,' Catherine said. She found the wall behind them and placed a hand on it, as though needing it to stay upright. 'Quoting Leviticus 19:26 is how witches identify themselves,' she said cautiously.

'It is.' Ruby said, continuing to smile in that crooked way. 'That man took my waves. I took his soul.'

Catherine felt her eyes widen.

'When you're ready for my help, come seek me out,' Ruby said. 'You know where I live.' She turned and walked away.

And as Catherine watched her go, her mouth moved into a crooked smile of its own.

ACKNOWLEDGEMENTS

Thank you to Sister Marie O'Shea for your helpful advice on nuns and their habits, pun very much intended.

Thank you to Dharug and Dharawal Resources for their excellent background information on Dharawal peoples and culture.

Thank you to Dave, Jane and Elle, for reading the manuscript and providing invaluable suggestions.

To Ali Lavau, thank you for expertly shaping and trimming. And to Rebecca Hamilton, thank you for your terrific proofreading.

To Robert, Alisa, and the magnificent team at Ultimo, I have felt very much at home. In particular, thank you for your editorial suggestions which added pace and moved the story forward.

To Sarah McKenzie, thank you for your enthusiasm for this manuscript, your professional advice and your terrific spreadsheet, which really is the star of this show.

Thank you to D, F and T, for our lovely life.

Finally and most importantly, thank you to Dave, for making all of this, and I mean all of it, possible.

Rachel Givney is an internationally bestselling author and filmmaker. She has worked for many of Australia's most beloved and critically acclaimed shows, including *Offspring*, *McLeod's Daughters*, *All Saints*, *The Warriors*, and many more. Her short films have been official selections at Tropfest, Flickerfest and the Sydney Film Festival. Her debut novel, *Jane in Love*, received a starred review from Booklist and was shortlisted for the Virginia Prize. It has been published in fourteen countries and translated into eight languages so far. Film rights were optioned by Di Novi Pictures, the producers of *Little Women*, and Amazon Studios. Her second novel, *Secrets My Father Kept*, was released to critical acclaim. *Don't Say His Name* is her third novel.